I
AM FROM
BROWNSVILLE

Arthur Granit

Illustrated by Gerald Hahn

Philosophical Library
New York

The Author's stories have appeared also in periodicals and anthologies as indicated:
"Usher."*Commentary*, Feb. 1956.
"The Penny Is for God!" *The Chicago Jewish Forum*, Sept. 1965.
"Tessie, Don't Give Away the Raisin; without It, You're Lost!" *Brooklyn Literary Review*, No. 5, 1984.
"Free the Canaries from Their Cages!" *Commentary*, Sept. 1955; *The Best American Short Stories of 1956*, edited by Martha Foley (Boston: Houghton Mifflin Company, 1956); *Prize Stories of 1957* (The O'Henry Memorial Awards), edited by Paul Engle and Constance Urdang (Garden City, N.Y.: Doubleday and Company, Inc., 1957).
"No Golden Tombstones for Me!" *Commentary*, Nov. 1956.
"They're Killing Jews on Sackman Street!" *Midstream*, Autumn 1956; *The Chosen*, edited by Harold U. Ribalow (London, New York: Abelard-Schuman, Ltd., 1959); *The Midstream Anthology*, edited by Shlomo Katz, (New York, London: Thomas Yoseloff, 1960).
"Fire Is Burning on Our Street!" *Midstream*, Sept. 1964.
"Come into the Hallway, for Five Cents!" *Commentary*, July 1960; *My Name Aloud*, edited by Harold U. Ribalow (New York, London, 1969).
"Hello, Lenin! Hello, Stalin! How's the Revolution Today?" *The National Jewish Monthly*, March 1974.
"Songs My Mother Taught Me That Are Not in *Hamlet*; or, 'Come into My House, Horatio! There Are More Things under the Mattress than Are Dreamt of in Your Philosophy!" *Brooklyn Literary Review*, No. 4, 1983.
"I Went to the Market Place to See the World! Oy, Mama, Oy!" *The Mizrachi Woman*, May 1969.
"With a Herring in One Hand and a Bottle of Schnapps in the Other; Oh! How He Did Dance!" *Brooklyn Literary Review*, No. 6, 1984.

Library of Congress Cataloging in Publication Data

Granit, Arthur.
    I am from Brownsville.

    I. Title.
PS3557.R256812   1984   813'.54   84-1789
ISBN 0-8022-2456-3

Published, 1985, by Philosophical Library, Inc.
200 West 57th Street, New York, N.Y. 10019.

Manufactured in the United States of America.

To Rachel

In you, there are three women:
the woman one first falls in love with,
the woman one marries,
and the woman one loves forever.

Table of Contents

Usher

THEIR HOUSE PEEKED ANONYMOUSLY FROM ITS ROW with nothing to show it was a cross they were bearing up to their Golgotha. In days gone by, someone had built this row and for a two-thousand-dollar down payment, whether the pipes froze or the roof caved in, they were "landlords."

Around them seethed Brownsville, decaying even in those days, and while the old women sat on their stoops chewing sunflower seeds it was nothing unusual to have a body shot up and thrown into some side alleyway.

Together with the gang wars, there grew up a host of hothouse radicalisms and splinter movements in this period, so that on our dark and alien, suffering street it was said that the capitalist "landlords" had moved in, the rich bloodsuckers. That Usher's "capitalist" father worked and gave every cent he made to the upkeep of this house, or that his "capitalist" mother was required to take in a boarder to make ends meet, went disregarded among our neighbors; for, as I see it now, all the world had come upon evil and unhappy times, even unto our street.

First there was my friend Bibi. Bibi's father died when Bibi was an infant, and Bibi himself was to die in Canarsie, our open graveyard for gangsters, with three bullet holes in his chest. Then there was Robby. His mother sat at her window day after day until she was taken away to sit at a window in a madhouse. Robby ended up in jail as a third-time offender. Pickles, so named because he once robbed a truck of a barrel of useless pickles, was compelled to marry a girl of our street whom he had "knocked up." He ended up with a family of four at the age of twenty-three. And Usher, my good and faithful friend Usher, who came from the "landlords," the people of substance, set apart from our unhappy street, ended up as a dentist.

Bang! Crash! Bibi had overturned an ash can and the cover rattled raucously down the lonely street. Bang! Crash! Untold numbers of cans, countless covers, rolled endlessly along the pavement. This was happiness.

Bang! Crash! A shattering of glass. There went a street lamp as Usher lifted a rock and scored a direct hit. Bang! Crash!

For a fraction of a second they were caught in blindness as the last light went out, and since darkness meant forbidden things, Pickles, destroyer of ash cans and knight-royal of the street lamps, screamed hysterically: "Girls! Let's get girls!"

"Chicks!" shouted the young Robby.

"Tomatoes!" came the hoarse cry from Usher.

"Dames!" I meekly annotated.

And so with this clatter they proclaimed their call to arms, and stalking near the railroad tracks they came upon a street, so dark, so lonely, there was none to compare with it in Brownsville. A long line of freight cars, forty-five in fact, so they counted, hammered the steel tracks as our stalwarts pelted the monstrous moving mechanism with assorted rocks, bottles, shoes, and even the fender of an abandoned automobile. Then retiring into the niches provided by garage doors and factory entrances, they laid their plan. Bibi, the brave one, stood first. Robby, the fat one, stood forty feet away on the other side of the street. Pickles, the tall one, held the redoubt at another remove, followed by myself and the landlord Usher.

They waited. They counted another line of freight cars. They waited. They heard the muted tones of Brownsville in the distance. Backfiring of cars. A fire engine in the distance. They waited. I prayed to myself that God would turn away anyone who thought of appearing on that street. They had all but given up hope when she appeared.

She came with heels clicking. She came innocent and oblivious of the huge, monstrous demon lover (really, it was only Bibi) who reared out of the darkness of his niche and grabbed at her. She screamed in fright, and pursued by her demon lover ran across the street, only to be confronted by an even more hideous apparition (really Robby), and now pursued by two lovers she screamed frantically into the night, only to run into me, who, quaking with terror, merely raised his arms and shooed her toward the oncoming Usher, debonair and gallant, who queried: "Hey! What's going on there?" Breathing heavily on her savior, she cried, "They're trying to get at me! Save me! Save me!" "Hey, youse kids," said the gallant Usher, shaking his fist as she hid behind him, "let this dame alone or I'll let you have it!" For a moment the others stood in their tracks, for a moment the frightened girl was permitted to stop, for one solid moment she believed that her knight-errant had come, when Usher himself, turning on her, put out his hand and screaming in uncontrollable laughter breasted her. With one full sweep she brought her pocketbook down on the head of our landlord, who shook one great big shake, paled, and fell quietly on the ground. And now, taking on the whole crew, she scratched at their fallen faces as they retreated down the empty street with her in full pursuit.

Sunday morning had its ritual. The Usher family, those rich "landlords," kept a boarder, a short, rotund, puffy-faced baker called Mr. Katz. Dignified as he was by his Anglo-Saxon name, he gave added dignity to the household by depositing every week on the kitchen table a round enormous bread which we would immediately seize, butter, and swallow down.

And to top it all, our cup running over, this white-skinned, pallid baker would send down to the corner restaurant for hot steaming coffee in which we would dunk the bread. It all went well until we would remind ourselves of the baker's bald head, and then it was impossible to have any respect for him—coffee, bread, and all. Benign as was his round and chubby face, there on top of his head always was that source of derisive speculation which for Usher and myself held such a mysterious fascination. In later years Usher himself was to get bald, but that was later; now Mr. Katz's bald pate made him a man apart.

One morning, while rummaging through the baker's room, we came upon an old World War I helmet. Then and there it was established that while in the service of his country Mr. Katz's pate had been shot off. Thus it was that we endowed the boarder with a needed dignity, but not for long.

I bounded up the stairs to Usher's house in anticipation of the black bread and coffee—I grant you, too, there were other considerations, such as a ten-cent tip, but as I was properly brought up I had made up my mind not to accept it—when I saw that something was amiss in the household.

There was a frantic look on the face of Usher's mother as she nervously trod the kitchen floor. Usher's father was laughing, while the would-be dentist sat mouth agog taking it all in.

"It's not right," cried his mother. "Katz is a good man. Never did he do this before."

I thought at first she was referring to the bread, which was missing from the table, but I soon realized it was something much more exciting.

"This is a respectable house. In front of the children? What will Goldberg think?" she went on.

And as it slowly dawned on me that it was about something forbidden, something unmentionable, the door of Katz's room opened, and he, bald pate and all, came out and said:

"Hey, kids! Here's a buck! Bring back a dollar's worth of pastrami!"

A revolution or war could not have caused greater havoc than this order from Katz, as we, Usher and myself, frantically sped down the stairs to buy the delicatessen. It was as if God himself had come out of the door and handed us His holy writ and commandment.

A dollar's worth of pastrami! This was going to be no little sandwich with two or three miserable slices of the stuff between two chunks of bread; this was going to be tons. And oh! with what tender hands did Usher and myself carry it, he holding one end of the precious package and I the other. How carefully we crossed the street! How wonderful it was to be alive! But as we came to the stairs we began to argue over who was to have the privilege of bringing it up and started fighting, and the package opened, the delicatessen leaped out and was scattered in the dirt of the street.

Disaster! The end of the world! We had no right to live! Ten thousand living deaths we died! No! Ten times ten thousand!

I bent down and wiped the dirty pastrami against my clothes. Usher, trembling in the knees, turned white and nearly fainted as he leaned against the wall. And as I tenderly cleaned and rewrapped the package, my heart pounded as if I had committed the original sin.

If anyone had chopped our heads off right then and there, he would have done us an act of kindness, for never did two people walk up a flight of stairs with more dread in their hearts than did Usher and myself. So stunned were we by our own guilt that it took us time to assess the new situation in Usher's house.

There was the black bread. Usher's mother was smiling and standing over coffee that perked deliciously on the stove. The table was set with jam and napkins.

"This is Ramona!" she said, as she introduced us to a tall, dark, handsome woman who how-de-doed us. She looked like a teacher.

Yes, she was a true Ramona! I watched my heart showing on Usher's face. It spoke for me. He stood with his mouth wide open and the pastrami forgotten.

To me, at that moment, she was the most beautiful woman I had ever seen. We gobbled down the pastrami and black bread, oblivious of the fact that only a minute before it had been on the pavement. We drank hot coffee.

Ramona sat down at the piano and sang. It was the mission bells themselves that we heard.

Somewhere in the back of my mind was the thought that she had slept that night with our baker. She was a "bad" woman. I noticed her stomach was a bit high, as if pregnant. All this, I imagined, had happened in one night in Mr. Katz's bedroom. I knew everything, but nothing mattered. What I saw was her long slender fingers, her black tearful eyes as she sang. Mission bells.

We escorted Mr. Katz and her to the stairs as he led her down. We opened doors for her. We watched her disappear down the hallway.

"You know," said Usher, "that guy Katz might not really have had a bald head if it hadn't been shot off in the war."

Our lumberyard was the place in which we all congregated when we wanted mystery, manufacturing it if need be. It was where we leaped from one four-story pile to another, where two or three times a week mysterious fires would break out bringing the fire engines with all their excitement, where we smoked, gambled, and had the watchman run after us.

Many months after Usher's encounter with the sad Ramona, he and I ventured into the lumberyard to join the boys. We dutifully executed a few standard leaps as the earth, four stories below, sped by. That only the previous week Bibi had made the selfsame leap and fallen screaming to the ground to be taken away in an ambulance did not faze us in the least. We performed a few leaps, embellishing them with a shaking of the head, or some humorous gesture like sticking out our tongues. And topping it all, we sat down on the tallest pile of all, drew out a cigarette apiece, the danger of fires notwithstanding, and fell to smoking and talking of things in general, when Usher, without so much as a previous hint, arose and dashed down the side of the pile in a frenzy.

"Da place is burnin'!" he cried, pointing in the direction of the railroad tracks. "Look!"

And sure enough, there near the edge of the railroad, black smoke spiraled upwards.

I clambered down after Usher, who said, "We're caught!"

"What do you mean?" I inquired.

"Our fingerprints and footprints are all over da place!" he explained in great excitement. "They got us cornered!"

Tears came to my eyes in my awe of this "they." My heart started to pump madly. Perhaps on our street we were all born guilty, and so I assumed guilt immediately, not stopping to consider who "they" were but imagining something impossibly awesome and terrible.

"What are we goin' to do, Ush?"

"We gotta put da fire out!"

We ran. We ran with blood beating madly through our veins. We ran pursued by "they" and by everything that ever frightened us. We ran pursued by demons within and without. We ran until we came to a clearing and were confronted by a ghastly sight. There before our very eyes stood Robby and Pickles (Bibi being in the hospital), roasting a dead dog in a fire.

My stomach retched. It was not Robby and Pickles that I saw any more. It was two ancient fanatics we had come upon, two priests conjured up from some prehistoric memory. They stood stock-still, poking the ashes of the dying fire with a slender stick, while in the center lay the dog, whose insides had burst open and glistened in the sun.

"You guys nuts?" screamed Usher.

"What's it to you?" demanded Robby.

"Nuts! Nuts! Nuts!" cried Usher, and without further ado he leaped on the mad Robby and began flailing away in a wild fury.

Their clothes turned brown with the dirt, their faces were streaked with perspiration and earth. When Robby's nose began to show blood, Pickles threw in the towel and Robby gave up.

"You don't have no right to hit me," whimpered Robby. "The dog was dead. Me and Pickles found it. Rather than let the worms take it, we decided to burn it. So, we burned it."

Ignoring him, the triumphant Usher arose, all battered and torn, and wobbling over to the now dying fire he threw sand on it and put it out.

"That's true," said Pickles. "Only we weren't burnin' it, we were crematin' it."

"It's a dog, ain't it?" said Usher. "Ain't a dog man's best friend?"

"He was no friend of mine," said Robby.

Then picking up some sticks, we four, Robby, Pickles, Usher, and I, began to scoop a hole in the ground for the dog.

We cried as we shoved the burnt carcass over into its grave.

We cried gobs of senseless tears. And I remember thinking how sad everything was, how sad I was, how sad my family was, how sad the dog must have been, and how sad it was to hurt this animal that had been hurt so much already.

"We need a cross for the grave," said Usher.

And tying two sticks together, we Jews set up a cross above our mound.

Then retreating to the lumberyard, we all climbed up to the topmost pile and proceeded to smoke under the now starry sky. We cried a little. We laughed a little. We wiped our eyes.

"You know," said Usher, smoking his cigarette, his body extended, his hands under his head, looking straight up into the sky, "that guy Katz might not have had a bald bean if it had not been shot off in the war."

Then there was the very dry summer the "landlords" were besieged. It all started with the clothes closet in Usher's bedroom while he lay asleep—something leaped from the top of the shelf right over our hero's head. Usher was to remember that night and the many nights that followed, for the rats now not only leaped but plunged, pirouetted, pas-de-deux'd and all but did lascivious dances in front of him, and knowing perhaps how white and agitated their poor victim lay under his blanket, they probably even stuck their tongues out at him. At least so Usher averred.

Usher was at a loss, even Usher. For before mice and rats Usher was an indecisive Hamlet, incapable of anything. They became not mere rodents, but points of view, objects of wonder and intrigue, main currents of speculative thought, even a way of life, everything but four-legged things.

Many a night when I came home late, I would look up to Usher's window and see his sad, wide-eyed face peering out.

"What's the matter, Ush?" I would call up.

And then the helpless Usher, with a burden so big that it

could not be mentioned for fear of calling forth the four-legged ones with long tails, would point to the rear of his room and whisper:

"I'm surrounded!"

And surrounded he was. Like in Hamelin of old they came, big rats, little rats, gray rats, all kinds of rats. When the "landlords" plugged up the holes in the closet, they came through the floor. When they plugged up the floor, they came through the ceiling. They came. At night our hero did not sleep for fear of being bitten. During the day he went about fearing the night. He feared rats even when they were not about. He was surrounded.

We were sitting in the kitchen one day in Usher's house having the usual, when I spied a small mouse looking out from under the stove. It looked at me and I looked at it. Usher, following my glance, saw the terrible monster and with a loud hysterical screech bounded up a chair to the top of the table and screamed:

"There's a mouse running around loose! Do somethin'. Take it away! Do somethin'!"

I stamped my foot on the floor, and the poor frightened animal scampered away.

"Did you see it?" he screamed. "Did you?"

"We're gonna do somethin' about it!" I said.

"What? What?" he cried, helplessly tearing at his hair.

That very night we began. I led him to a hardware store and made him buy a ten-cent trap. I showed him how to roll bread up into a small pellet (Mr. Katz's bread) and helped him bait the trap. I even placed the trap for him.

The next morning Usher was at my house rousing me from bed.

"We caught somethin'!" he cried. "Help me get rid of it!"

I showed him. I ran the water in his bathtub, held the trapped mouse under the faucet, and drowned it. Then I helped him slide the mouse from the trap into the garbage can.

"That's that!" said the greatly relieved Usher.

But that was not that. For the next night, we set another trap and caught another mouse. And the night after, another. And another and another and another. Twenty-nine anothers there were, in fact.

By this time my stalwart friend was in complete command of the situation. He would bait the trap, drown the mouse under the faucet, and even empty it into the garbage pail without my aid. But he crowned himself with glory in my eyes when he was able to take the dead mouse out of the trap by the tail and drop it into the garbage can. I did feel, however, when he began to swing and send them sailing through the air, that he was going a little too far. As for the rats, we only caught sixteen of them, but we gave all of them the treatment.

Now our street endured an epidemic of dead rats. People found dead rats on their stoops, on their window sills, would find them sailing through an open window into their houses. Suddenly a dead rat would appear on the counter of the candy store, or in a bag of potatoes, or in a plate of soup in a restaurant. As for bald men or pregnant women who appeared in our street, they were doomed. And if some poor girl was unfortunate enough to walk along our street, rats would be thrust under her nose, thrown under her feet, or pushed up her skirt. It was the way in which Usher told the world he had conquered his fear of rats.

But do you think that one ever really conquers, even rats? Do you? Let Usher pick up ever so many rats by the tail and send them spinning through the air, does he really conquer? For I am sure, even though Usher is now lost to me, and even if he can still trap rats, that often in the night the slithering, creeping, slimy things come crawling from the marrow of his bones to plague him, that even today they still jump, leap, dive, and pirouette in front of him. For this was our legacy from Brownsville.

Then there was the grandfather, a patriarch of the old school. Here was no mere grandfather, here was a shaker of floors, a breaker of chairs, a pounder of tables, a hard and merciless taskmaster who inspired everyone with fear and who held everyone to strict account.

When he first came to America, he had worn a long white beard. But as time Americanized him, his beard got shorter and shorter until it was a small insignificant Van Dyke. But he became Americanized in beard only, for all else about him remained the same.

When my friend Bibi saw him for the first time, his mouth opened wide and pointing helplessly he cried, "God!"

"Come again!" cried Usher.

"That old guy scares me. He looks like, like,—" began Bibi.

The hair on the nape of Usher's neck stood up. He caught Bibi in a vicious headlock and screamed:

"What's dat! What's dat again? What did he look like?"

"Like, like—God!" sputtered the choking Bibi.

"Dat's better!" cried Usher, pushing the culprit from him and wiping his hands. "I thought for a moment you said, 'God'! Dat's much better!"

"He don't look like no God to me," said Robby.

"If he were God, he wouldn't come to our street," said Pickles.

"And why not?" asked Bibi.

"It don't make sense. Would God ever think of coming to our street?" asked Pickles.

"He might! Don't see why not!"

"You nuts! God wouldn't think of ever coming to our street! He's God!"

"Maybe you're right," said Bibi.

"He's not God, you dopes! He's my grandfather!" said Usher.

This old man appeared at Usher's home only at catastrophes and the High Holidays. I remember one holiday when my unfortunate friend Usher was compelled to attend the synagogue with his grandfather. He had been seen by the old man on the street corner. That was all the old man needed. He ran up to Usher and without warning cracked him right across the face. Crack! Crack! Again and again. Then taking my friend Usher by the ear he led him through the streets.

"Street corners are for *goyim* and bums, not for Jewish boys," he thundered.

Crack! Right across the face.

"Jewish boys don't stand on street corners!"

Crack! Right across the mouth.

"Jewish boys know their prayers!"

Crack! Right across the ears.

"Jewish boys go to *shul!*"

Crack! Right across the head.

"And here is an extra one for good measure!"

Bang! Right across the posterior.

The edict was pronounced. Poor Usher was sentenced to pray. The next thing you knew, a humiliated Usher was miserably dragging himself after the patriarch with bowed head looking like a sick cat.

The synagogue was filled with stale, heavy air smelling of tobacco. The broken Usher sat down in his pew. The fearsome grandfather put a prayer book in front of Usher, turned to the right page, and lifting his hand as if to strike, thundered: "Read!"

"Can't read."

"What!"

"Can't read the prayer book," our lost and broken hero cried, preparing to receive even more terrible blows.

"Black years on your father, that apostate," cried his grandfather, but seeing Usher weeping bitter tears he softened and whispered, "Sh! Sh! Don't cry, little one! Here, turn to this page and keep the book open, pretend as if you're reading. When I turn the page in my book, you turn in yours. We don't want anyone to know you can't read a prayer book."

Then he bent down, patted Usher's head and kissed him.

"Remember, too," he added, "when I stand, you stand. When I sit, you sit. Don't worry, young one, we'll manage somehow."

And so Usher turned when his grandfather turned, stood when he stood, and even snuffed tobacco at the proper time. Up he went! Down he went! Turn the page! Keep his eye on the page! Up you stand! Take some snuff! Down you go! Turn the page! Amen! Amen!

Every street has its "beauty"; ours was no exception. On our street, it was Miriam. The tough ones, who hung out on the corner, whistled, shouted obscenities, and made indecent proposals to her as she walked by. She was the mother of five children.

"Hey, Miriam!" Tough Maxie the Pug would scream. "How about a little jazzin'?"

"Hey, Miriam!" Fat Moe the Dope would cry. "If I climbed up your fire escape, would you let me in?"

The women of our street said she was beautiful but stupid, and ignored her, but the men and children remembered her forever. And beautiful she was, with her long, dark chestnut hair, her skin with so high a coloring that it seemed as if there was a constant glow about her face, and her strong, tight body that had seen many births and countless miscarriages.

Yes, Miriam, I remember you! I remember you so well that even today I must often stop myself from thinking that only a woman who is sad can be beautiful. And even now that I am married, I remember and love you still.

I was a friend of Jakie the Snotnose, one of Miriam's sons, and remember very clearly Usher and myself coming to visit them, when who should be awkwardly pushing himself in, carrying a big round bread, but Katz the baker.

"I brought you a present," he grinned, showing his black teeth.

Usher and I took one look at Katz and began to laugh.

"Thank you, Katz," said Miriam. "It'll come in handy."

"Good! Good!" said the floundering Mr. Katz.

I could not stop laughing. It was all so funny. In return for Katz's kind consideration, Miriam asked, "Would you care for a glass of tea?"

"It can't hurt," said the ungainly Katz. And so Miriam began to brew the tea. I remember feeling that the whole thing was strange, and could see that Miriam herself had a furrow in her brow, but good and beautiful soul that she was she remained silent. I looked at Usher and Usher looked at me and then we were off again. Remembering what the street said about her, I decided she was stupid.

"I have heard—"began Katz.

Miriam ran to the tea kettle to put out the light.

"I have heard—" began Katz again.

"Here, Mr. Katz, suppose I cut off a slice of bread. You will start first. After all, it's your present."

"Miriam," he courageously began again, "things are not good with you."

"Would you like some butter on the bread, Mr. Katz?"

"I have heard," began the intrepid Mr. Katz again, "I have heard that things are not going well, that he's no good."

"Sh!" she whispered. "The children!"

"Oh, the children! What do they know?" he said.

"They know everything," she said.

Suddenly we stopped laughing. And before you knew it everyone, including myself, was crying and Katz was on his knees before Miriam, weeping, and he was saying:

"Miriam! I'll take you away from him! He's no good! He'll never be any good! You'll never have a happy day with him! We'll run away together, to Canada, to Chicago, to California! Anywhere! Come with me!"

"Are you crazy?" said Miriam. "I've got children!"

"We'll take them with us! Don't you understand! I love you. I love them, Miriam. Miriam! Miriam!" he cried, banging his fists against his temples. "I'd do anything for you. If you asked me to kill myself tomorrow, I'd kill myself for you! Anything!"

"That's foolish talk!" she said. "I don't want anyone to kill himself for me. I'm not worth it. Find yourself a nice young girl and get married."

"Miriam! Miriam!" he said, crying as if his heart would break. "I can't love anybody else! Don't you understand? I lie awake at night, thinking only of you. Miriam! Miriam! I think of him, and think of you. And I think of how happy I could make you. It's all so wrong, so unfair, when I love you so and see you suffering so because of him. It kills me!"

"Go with him, Miriam! Go with him!" I wanted to scream.

"Get up from the floor!" she said. "Somebody is liable to walk in! How would it look?"

And there was Katz on the floor, clutching at her knees as she struggled to get free of his grasp.

"Stop this nonsense!" she said. "Get up from the floor! You're a grown man! You're exciting the children!"

"The children! The children!" he said, mocking her.

And sure enough, there were we, all screaming and carrying on at the top of our lungs: Jakie the Snotnose, Miriam's other three children, an infant Miriam held in her arms, and Usher and myself.

She calmed Katz down and then calmed us down and taking her youngest to breast she moved up and down, rocking him to sleep. Then she put the infant in his carriage and rocked him, singing:

> *On the Pripet burns a fire,*
> *But in this house it's cold.*
> *There sits a rabbi with a group of children,*
> *Teaching them the A—B—C's.*
>
> *Say it, children, say it once again!*
> *Say your A—B—C's!*

Say it, children, say it again!
Say your A—B—C's!

"Have another glass of tea," said Miriam.
Finally the unhappy Mr. Katz rose to leave.
"Go in peace," she said.

But Katz did not go in peace. He went in agony, and was dead within two months. When Usher's grandfather appeared, and it was not a High Holiday, I knew that some catastrophe had occurred. But since it was Katz who died, it was only a "small" catastrophe.

Yes, poor Katz was dead within two months, dying of some dread disease which could not be mentioned in front of us for fear the very word would spread the contagion. It was Usher's grandfather who rose to the occasion. He was an expert on funerals, knowing what to do to the last detail, but although he handled the religious end of it like an artist, he had no control of the social.

Katz's waiting hearse. Robby's mother sat in her window chewing polly-seeds, her empty, vacuous face with its moving mandibles churned with a vengeance, showing no emotion. Pickles, smoking a cigarette, looked up curiously from the street corner and looked away. Bibi, deeply curious, walked brazenly up to the hearse, peered in, examined it very closely, and even fingered it.

"Make it quick! Make it quick!" called the chauffeur from the hearse. "What do you think I have, all day?"

"A Yankee Doodle funeral!" said Usher's grandfather.

White and contorted grew Usher's face, my hero Usher's face, as they brought the bloated body down. Screams. He screamed and threw himself about uncontrollably.

"Ah!" said Usher's grandfather approvingly. "He's giving the funeral dignity."

But at that moment the railroad train ran by, and all I

remember is Usher's face, all swollen and red, crying without a sound.

And on that miserable street, nobody except Miriam, beautiful stupid Miriam, and Usher and myself cried for the dead Katz. Nobody else. And this on a street that cried easily. I hate that street for this. I hate that street even to this day.

Make it quick! Make it quick, Katz! And it was as if Katz had never been.

That evening we met in the lumberyard. Usher was flaunting a wooden sword he had made.

"Katzie was a good guy!" he said.

"An ace! He was an ace!" chimed in Robby.

"Katzie was a great guy!" cried Usher.

"The greatest! There was none greater!"

"Katzie died for his country! He was a hero!" said Usher belligerently brandishing his sword in the air.

"For his country! A hero!"

"Whoever said Katzie had a bald bean!" said Usher.

"No! Nobody ever said Katzie had a bald bean!"
"Well! Did Katzie have a bald bean?"
"No! Katzie never had no bald bean!" came the answer.

Suddenly from down below, announcing the arrival of Bibi, came flying a dead rat that landed at Usher's feet, and soon after came Bibi, huffing and puffing up the pile of lumber.

"Hey!" he shouted, picking up the creature by its tail. "What do ya say we shove this up some skirt!"

And as if an alarm had been sounded, like one, they began jumping from the pile shouting:

> *Last one off will have bad luck!*
> *Last one off is a big shmuck!*
> *Last one off will never get fucked!*

And they tore down into the street screaming and shouting, thundering like a herd. And many were the girls who screamed that night.

The Penny Is for God!

ONE EVENING, WE WERE SITTING OUTSIDE USHER'S house, telling ghost stories.

"And then it came nearer and nearer," Pickles was saying. "And it put out its long, bony fingers. And it was covered with a white sheet. And the hot breath came out of its nose. 'Where is my broom?' it cried. 'Who dared steal dat broom?' "

"Stop!" said Usher.

"What's the matter?" cried the annoyed Bibi. "What're you interruptin' da story?"

"Listen!" said Usher.

And from the hallway came the sound as of stairs creaking and the faint patter of feet walking.

"Look!" said Usher.

"What is it?" sputtered the shaken Pickles.

"It's the witch!" said Usher. "Look!"

I stared in fascination at the hallway door, holding my breath and hoping against hope that a weird monster would emerge; and I was not disappointed, for at that moment, out came a withered old lady, wearing a brown wig in Orthodox style and carrying a small change purse in her hand. I could not believe my eyes. She was everything a witch was supposed to be and more, from her bent back to her black garments.

"Is she a real witch?" asked Bibi.

"Real!" exclaimed Usher. "She's better than real. At night, she turns into a cat. Sometimes, she decides to turn into a fly and buzzes all over the place; but if she don't like you, watch out, she'll turn into a mosquito and give it to you right on the neck. She can slip under doors, through windows; she opens locks."

"You're foolin'!" I ventured skeptically, half in belief and disbelief.

"Of course, I'm fooling," said Usher. "It's Hannah Sarah, the new boarder!"

"She's no boarder! She's a witch!" insisted Bibi.

"Jerk! I'm tellin' you who she is!"

"You're lyin'!" cried Pickles with tears in his eyes. "You're lyin' purposely because you know she's a witch, and you don't wanna tell us!"

And no amount of explanation was of any avail that night, for Pickles, Bibi, Robby, and I refused to accept the fact that this was only Hannah Sarah, the new boarder.

I remember when this hunchbacked old lady appeared from out of nowhere, carrying a cardboard suitcase in one hand and a carefully wrapped paper bag in the other. She set the objects down before the house as she took out a small sheet of paper and studied it, looking up at the number every so often.

"Hey, small one!" she said to Usher. "They told me that the house would have a garbage can outside. I see no garbage can."

"What number are you looking for?" asked Usher.

She gave him the slip of paper.

"Dat's the right number. You must be the one for the front room," said Usher.

And just as he said this, the large stupid Robby came bounding down the street, being chased by Pickles. Racing like a madman, he ran smack into the old lady's suitcase and ripped into the paper bag.

Somehow I got the feeling that she did not care an iota about the suitcase, but the moment the paper bag was touched, she began shaking her withered fists at them, screaming:

"Bums! I'll give you to tear my package! You dirty lousy bums!"

But the retreating Pickles and Robby continued to race heedlessly down the street, turning only for sufficient time to stick out their tongues at her and then to disappear.

"Your feet should fall off! Wait! Just wait! I'll get you yet, bums!" she cried after them as she began to tie the package, then turning to Usher, she said, "You carry the suitcase. I'll carry the bundle."

Then Usher, putting out his chest as far as it could go, flexed his muscles, did three or four turns at a bending exercise, and spitting into the palms of his hands, put them to the suitcase, and with great gusto carried it up the stairs.

"Murderers!" she muttered to herself as she mounted the stairs. "Murderers!"

She was soon ensconced in the front room, but unlike many of the other boarders of this house, she never became a permanent fixture. Amazingly enough for an old lady, she was rarely home, but made long and frequent excursions into the street, after which she would return with small packages of food at which she would nibble, sitting at the window.

Needless to say, Usher and I had to make our "investigations"; and so one day when the new boarder was out, we went through her room. There stood the suitcase, unopened, upon which Usher did his "detective" work while I attended to the package.

"Well?" I asked Usher.

"Junk!" he said.

"Nothin' here," I said in disgust trying to put the package together. "Only a white dress."

"Witches should wear black," said Usher, stating a law of life.

She was really beneath our contempt, that is, at first; because this old lady, who regarded children as a little less than vermin and just ignored their existence, was to dominate our lives just as her room dominated the street. Actually it was not we who were contemptuous of her, it was she who was, of us.

So disdainful was she, that even when the lone bulb in her room would signal her presence to our street, she would not even deign to lower her shades. And our entire street would be a spectator on her doings as she would put on her white dress and preen herself in front of her mirror. And this, she would do every night. Then tiring of that, she would extinguish her light and sit at the window while the whiteness of the dress shone out of the dark. And then spitting out of the window as if in judgment of our street, she would turn her back on us and leave us to our sins.

One Friday, I was in Usher's house having the usual cup of coffee and black bread, when Hannah Sarah came into the kitchen in her white garment. From somewhere in the shadows of her former life, the housewife in her emerged, and she had kneaded some dough in the quiet of her room and was now bringing it out in a baking pan.

"Dear, good housewife," she said obsequiously to Usher's mother. "It's Friday. The stove is burning anyway. I'll just take up a small corner of the stove. You won't even know that I have a baking pan in your oven."

Usher's mother gaped at Hannah Sarah.

"Dear God!" she exclaimed.

"You're a good Jewish woman," continued Hannah Sarah. "You are a golden diamond. You wouldn't deny me this pleasure."

"God protect us all!" cried Usher's mother.

"He will bless your house," said Hannah Sarah. "He will protect you. No evil eye will ever fall on you. Only grant me this wish, dear good one. Permit me to put my bread in the oven."

"What is that you're wearing?" Usher's mother finally managed to say.

"Why! What do you mean what am I wearing?"

"God in heaven! Hannah Sarah, tell me quick! I don't believe my own eyes! What are you wearing?" asked Usher's mother.

"Why, I'm only wearing my death sheet," said the old lady in a matter-of-fact tone.

"I'm dying!" said Usher's mother.

"No, my child not you! You have many good years ahead of you," said Hannah Sarah, and then with a twinkle in her eye, added, "That is, if you let me put my bread in the oven."

"Put the bread in the oven! Put a thousand breads in the oven!" said Usher's mother, and turning her head away, afraid to look, said, "Only, please, please, take off that dress or I'll die!"

Already the days were growing shorter, and people were beginning to put on their winter things; so that, on our street some were still wearing summer clothes and others, overcoats.

My friend Pickles had brought a pile of loose wood which he had gathered in the lumberyard, and we had started a small fire on the street in front of Usher's house. Usher sat bundled up in his heavy overcoat, cupping his hands over the flames and blowing with all his might and main. Every now and then Robby threw in a small stick, and it was not long before we had created a blaze that lit up all the houses and appeared to make the windows dance.

Picture that street! People sitting on their stoops. Automobiles racing by. Crowds of wage earners coming home from work. Hannah Sarah preening herself at her mirror in her white shroud. And there, right smack in the middle of everything, this little unholy group, sitting hunched around a roaring fire.

It was like a magnet. Small figures became arrested in play, heads appeared in windows, and from doorways and stoops came all varieties of children to inch their way slowly to our fire.

"Hey! Get away from dere!" coughed a choking Usher as the smoke drifted into his face.

"Go back where you came from!" said Bibi.

"You don't belong here!" said Robby to one child. "Get to your own block!"

A small, emaciated girl, dressed in a thin cotton dress, inched her way forward.

"We don't want no girls here!" said Usher.

"Especially if their name is No-Tit Gertie!" added Pickles.

In other circumstances, she would have probably scratched our eyes out. Instead, she said nothing but shyly pushed herself closer and closer. Then without a word, she left, and in a few moments appeared with three or four large potatoes, which she handed over to my hero Usher.

"Here," she said.

"O.K.! You can stay! Everybody else has got to leave!" commanded Usher as he distributed the potatoes to his cohorts and began to roast his at the end of a stick.

Picture our landlord! Choking and sputtering because of the

flames, the front of his face red-hot and the rear of his body, cold, twisting and turning a blackened potato on a stick while his jaw was set in fierce determination.

Suddenly Hannah Sarah was at her window, screaming. The next thing you knew, she was racing down into the street, carrying a blanket before her. And Gertie, with her cotton dress aflame, her head enveloped in smoke, her hair afire, was hysterically running down the street, a human torch.

The people of our street were thunderstruck. Some began to run in circles; others, for no apparent reason, in the opposite direction. Some put their hands to their ears as if not to hear; others moved their hands up and down in awkward positions, not knowing where to put them. Some of the children ran to hide behind stoops as if believing that being hidden from the horrible sight would mean, it did not exist. Parents came out and began to beat their children. I, myself, although frozen to the ground, felt my heart beating madly and heard my throat rasping weirdly as I began to pant.

"Good-for-nothings! Bums! Murderers! Who dared set fire to that child!" cried Hannah Sarah as she raced after Gertie.

Where the old lady found the energy to do what she did, I do not know. But she pursued the fleeing Gertie and finally catching up with her, threw the blanket over her, and held on for dear life until someone released her hold and rolled the girl on the ground.

"My dress!" cried the old lady as she pointed to her blackened shroud. "Look! I can't be buried in it now!"

"Don't cry, grandma," said one of our men. "Where you'll be going, you won't need a thing."

"First I'll bury you! Idiot!" she said as she spat three times on the ground. "I know you murderers! You all deliberately set fire to that child!"

And then she stormed off.

As for Gertie, her life became a succession of hospitals.

Now our Hannah Sarah became the wonder of our street. People came from neighboring blocks and pointed out her window. Then they pointed to the spot where the fire had occurred and then down the street to show the path Gertie had taken. Even the children developed a new game, called "catch the torch," weaving in and out of Gertie's trail. And when the old lady passed on the street, little children and grownups would stand aside in awe of this woman.

But, somehow, my friend Usher was not convinced.

"Do you see dat dead cat?" he asked. "Dat's the old lady!"

And if a fly appeared, he would say, "The witch is buzzin' tonight!" Or else, he would suddenly look up to the sky and keep looking in rapt attention while Pickles, Robby, Bibi, and I, dying of curiosity and not being able to contain ourselves any longer, would burst out, "What is it, Ush?" And then, he would, in apparent disgust, say, "She's done it again! Look! Up dere in the sky!" And sure enough, we would look up and invariably we would make out the shape of an arm, or nose, or even the body of the old lady herself in the shifting clouds.

One early morning while we, Pickles, Robby, Bibi, and I, were playing ball in the street, a sudden hush fell on our group. Somehow, I knew it was because the "witch" had made an appearance. And sure enough, there she was racing busily down the street and crossing at the corner, looking as old and mysterious in her black dress as ever.

"Come on," urged Usher, knowing how impossible it was to play ball now.

We charged down the street and crossed at the corner, but instead of seeing the new boarder, there at the corner was a little black dog.

"You see!" said Usher. "What did I tell you! She's changed herself into a mutt!"

Goosepimples formed on my arms.

We ran down the street as if someone were chasing us when

in the distance we could make out the figure of the wizened old lady.

"She jumped the gun on us when we weren't looking," said Usher. "She's Hannah Sarah again."

From the distance, we could see her holding out her purse while she kept stopping people in the street.

"She's casting spells!" said Usher.

Then we looked up again and she was gone.

We began searching the neighborhood for her until we came to our open-air market. Lined with open pushcarts, the street poured forth a multitude of odors and a vast horde of women bargaining for all kinds of articles while the peddlers hawked their wares, banging against cans or against their carts to attract attention.

"Ladies! Ladies! No rotten tomatoes here! Nothing but the best! Hey, no squeezing those tomatoes!"

"Garters to keep your stockings up! Red, white, and blue garters! We'll put them on! Let your husbands take them off!"

"Praised be Israel! Give a few pennies for the poor orphans in Jerusalem! Plant a tree in the Valley of the Kings!"

"Kids, there she is!" cried Usher. "She's Hannah Sarah again!"

We had been searching in this crowded market for her. One moment we saw her and the next, she had disappeared, but now we were right up on her. And there she stood weaving her way through a crowd of women in a butcher shop.

We followed her in, and suddenly found our nostrils assailed by the odor of chicken droppings and our ears, by the cackling of the stupid birds in their cages. Pushing through the heavily packed crowd of housewives, we came upon a back room.

"Da chamber of horrors!" said Usher.

And sure enough, we looked in and saw the walls of the back room splashed with blood, while in the center stood a bearded man, surrounded by women offering him live chickens while he slashed the necks open and let the blood run out.

There, in the middle of everything, stood Hannah Sarah with an outstretched hand and an open change purse, crying:

"Give to the children of Jerusalem! Give a few pennies to the children of God!"

"Hypocrite!" snorted a tall buxomish woman, covered with white feathers, whom I recognized as the troublemaker of our street. She was at work over a bin in her official capacity as the feather plucker of this market. It was not that I knew her so well as much as I knew her son, Chink, a big fat congenital "mongolian" and the idiot of our street.

"Give to the poor in Lodz! Give to the poor in Kiev! Don't forget them in Cincinnati!" cried Hannah Sarah.

"A thousand blessings! May your years be bright!" cried Hannah Sarah as one of the women dropped a penny into the purse.

"Look who's giving away blessings!" shouted the Feather Plucker.

"May you know of no unhappiness!" cried Hannah Sarah.

"Old witch! Tell them where all those hard-earned pennies go!" said the Feather Plucker.

"Your tongue should fall out!" cried the old lady.

"Better go to work, old lady. Pluck chickens like any decent woman!" said the Chink's mother.

"Pluck chickens to the end of your days!" said Hannah Sarah. "You deserve nothing better! May your only child fall and break his neck because he has such a heartless monster of a mother!"

And with this, the old lady picked up one of the chickens, hanging from a hook and with blood dripping from its neck, feathers and all, she sent it sailing into the face of our Feather Plucker and ran off.

Screams! Screams!

"The witch has cursed my baby!" cried the Feather Plucker.

Hordes of excited women began to mill around the screaming Feather Plucker.

"Baby!" exclaimed one of the housewives. "An ox!"

"Not a word against the child. He's been sufficiently cursed by God," said another, tapping her forehead.

Screams! Screams!

The Feather Plucker could not be contained. She wiped the blood from her face, tore off her apron, and hollering all the while, she ran out after Hannah Sarah, pursued by a horde of children and panic-stricken women.

"Idle women!" shouted the butcher. "Have you nothing better to do?"

Now people began streaming from houses. From nowhere appeared old graybeards and young ones. Mothers pushing baby carriages. Young infants toddling along. The street was black with people.

Picture the scene! The Feather Plucker screaming at the top of her voice. A vast unruly crowd pouring into our street. The cellar door of Usher's house open. An ambulance in front of the house. And the Chink being carried up in a stretcher into the street.

Prophecy of prophecies!

The Chink had fallen into Usher's open cellar.

From out of nowhere, a lawyer appeared and handed the Feather Plucker his card. In a second, he took out a paper, wrote a few words on it, and said:

"Sign!"

The Feather Plucker x'ed in a cross.

"Remember," said the man. "I'm your lawyer now."

"Rich bloodsuckers!" screamed the Feather Plucker shaking her fists at the house. "Capitalist landlords getting fat on the blood of the poor!"

I thought of Usher's mother and her boarders.

"Wait! Wait!" she screamed. "For this, I'll take you for everything you got! I, too, can be a fancy lady living in such a fine house!"

I thought of Usher's leaking roof.

"As God is my witness," shouted the Feather Plucker, "they'll put you out on the street. You'll go plucking feathers in the market yet!"

My hero Usher slunk away in shame.

How could you be so cruel, my unhappy, unfortunate street! How could you be so cruel!

From a heroine of our street, the unlucky Hannah Sarah now became the most despised and feared. If a child fell out of a baby carriage or did not eat his oatmeal, it was Hannah Sarah who had bewitched him. If the plaster of a ceiling fell down on someone's head, it was Hannah Sarah who was responsible. If the pipes in someone's toilet became clogged and the place flooded, it was Hannah Sarah who had done the plugging.

Poor woman! Every mishap on that street was attributed to her.

And even though the Chink was on his feet the very next day, it did nothing to assuage the madness of our unfortunate street.

As for the old lady, she took to sitting at her window in her blackened shroud, muttering to herself and spitting from her perch, as more and more our street grew frightened of her. And if something displeased her, she would let us know it in no uncertain terms by banging her window shut. Or if the children made too much noise playing ball, she would let loose a barrage of invectives mixed with saliva that would frighten us into insensibility. Or if a cat sat singing in the middle of the street late at night, she would pour forth a rain of garbage and tin cans at the unruly animal to deliberately awaken our street.

And as she sat there, she learned the secrets of our street as no one else. This, we found out later.

We were playing baseball in the middle of the street when my friend Bibi struck out.

"Dat's not an out!" cried Bibi as he threw the bat to the ground.

"What was it then?" asked Usher.

"It's a hit! No, it's a home run!"

"That's what you say!" said Usher.

"The old lady is givin' me the twisted eye. She curved da ball just when I was gonna hit it. She's takin' out my brains."

Usher smashed his glove to the sidewalk.

"I'm through with this bunch!" he said. "I'm not playin'!" Then he began to walk.

"What's the matter, Ush?" I asked.

"Ush, I didn't mean nothin'," said Bibi, not knowing what had brought on this storm.

"He's innocent!" said Robby.

But it was to no avail. There we ran pleading after Usher while he, with clenched lips and blood drained from them, walked down the street without a word, turned a corner, walked down another street, turned another corner, waited for a light, turned many more corners and walked down many more streets until we, now, found ourselves in an unknown neighborhood.

"Give me another chance," pleaded Bibi. "Can I help it if it ain't safe when the old lady is around?" he asked. "She gets on her broom, takes off, zooms to the ball, gives it a twist, and is back in her window before anyone can see. No wonder Usher thinks what he thinks. Who do you think was responsible for Gertie getting burned? The old lady! She stood in her window, looked to see if anyone was watching, gave one good puff with her lips, and the fire caught Gertie. Then the witch runs down and saves Gertie in order to fool everyone. First she burns them, then she saves them. Didn't she herself say she was going to push the Chink down the cellar stairs; and sure enough, the Chink falls down the stairs?"

Usher stopped walking.

"What else can happen?" asked Usher, now blissfully visualizing all kinds of happy horrors.

"She's going to murder us like she murdered all the chickens!" blurted out Robby.

I didn't need much to fall away from Brownsville, away from

Usher, and Robby, and Bibi, and Pickles, and Miriam and her
five children, and my mother and father; and I saw myself as
plucked and there was Hannah Sarah sweeping with a broom;
and she was sweeping me into my grave. And in that awful
darkness, I heard the earth being thrown over my coffin while
from the outside came the sound of the chickens in the butcher
shop, crying, "Cock-a-doodle-doo! Cock-a-doodle-doo!" And
I sensed that beyond the darkness and the earth in which I lay,
there was a blaze of light that I wanted oh! so desperately to
reach. Cock-a-doodle-doo! Cock-a-doodle-doo! And I cried,
"A penny quick, give me a penny quick, or terrible things will
happen! I want a penny for the witch so I can be free to go to
Coney Island!" Cock-a-doodle-doo! "A penny quick, give me a
penny quick! I must have a penny to give to the children of
Jerusalem, to the poor of Lodz, to the orphans in Cincinnati!"
Cock-a-doodle-doo! Cock-a-doodle-doo!

Suddenly Robby exclaimed, "Where did you take us, Ush?
To the police station?"

And there before us loomed the Liberty Avenue Police
Station.

So we sat down at the curbstone and looked.

The light! The light! Off I went again. What would I have not
given to have been able to pass under that astonishingly beautiful incandescence that hung from the Liberty Avenue Police
Station! I was not concerned about the crimes that I might
have committed, nor about being a witness for Hannah Sarah's
sins. What concerned me was that glow of glaucous green
which lit up the neighborhood, and for one fleeting moment,
transformed the decaying tenements into ships and sirens as
the windows reflected back the thousand eyes of my Tetra-
grammaton.

But, of course, in the world of Brownsville, I was not entitled
to even my own hysteria because the next thing I knew, Usher
interrupted, "I've had enough! I'm going home!"

For everyone, it was as if we had never left, but for me, it was as if I had returned from the grave. There were our neighbors out on their stoops. Some of our more enterprising ones had taken out chairs on the sidewalk. The toughs were on the street corner. Miriam and her brood were sitting quietly outside their house. And the old lady was up in her room before the mirror bemoaning her ruined shroud, while every so often she snipped off some of it with a shears or attempted to sew parts of it with a needle and thread, but gave up in despair.

We sat down tired on a bench beside Miriam.

"Hey, Miriam!" Fat Moe the Dope cried. "If I climbed up your fire escape, would you let me in?"

Suddenly I gripped Usher's arm and cried:

"Ush, look!"

And there was Miriam's husband tottering down the street, walking now this way and now that, singing at the top of his voice. Panic hit us. He was drunk!

Not to Miriam, I cried to myself! Let anything happen to anyone else! Let it even happen to me, but not to the beautiful, the sad, the good Miriam!

"Moishe," she said to him, putting her hand on his shoulder as he came up. "Would you not like to come upstairs? The food is waiting."

Food, I thought! Poison, she ought to give him!

He threw her hand off roughly and, balancing himself precariously on the bench, he clicked his fingers and, flapping his arms as if he was a chicken, began to dance.

Picture this man! With his eyes closed. Elevated on a bench. Clicking his fingers. Furiously gyrating his pelvis in the ecstasy of a mad Hasidic dance.

Picture our lousy street! A crowd assembling!

Picture Miriam!

"Moishe, the supper is getting cold," she said. "Tomorrow is a working day."

"Ta! Ta! Da! Da! Da!" he sang.

"Shake it, brother!" cried Willie September.

"Beat out those snake eyes!" cried Mary Contrary the Whore.

"Look at the old geezer's balls fly!" cried Jerk-Off Louie.

Suddenly I felt the pit of my stomach turn and my heart pumping so madly that my kidneys hurt. And I wanted to urinate. And all hope, all illusion, was gone; for there was the drunken Moishe beating his wife Miriam, right on our street.

"What's going on there?" cried the curious Feather Plucker, trying to edge her way into the crowd.

"Some broad is getting hers!" answered Willie September.

Laughter! Laughter!

"Give it to her!" cried Jerk-Off Louie.

"In the fanny! Where it's soft!" urged Mary Contrary.

And Miriam, my sweet, gentle Miriam, was standing there while that lousy bastard of a husband was beating her. No love! No hope! Animals lived on my street!

Usher attempted to push his way through, but Willie September banged him in the shins and said:

"Mind your own business, or I'll kick your teeth in!"

Even I tried pushing my way through, knowing only that I had to be at Miriam's side, when all of a sudden, an apparition appeared as if from another world, dressed in a burnt shroud, with a pair of shears held over its head in one hand and in the other, a long, white, gleaming needle.

"Bums! Hooligans!" shouted Hannah Sarah. "Give me that faithless provider!"

Then with fists, legs, arms, and body, she began to pummel the drunken husband. She even jabbed him with her needle.

"Stop it, Hannah Sarah! Have mercy!" cried Miriam.

But Hannah Sarah would not be appeased. She kicked. She spat. She threw him to the ground. She all but tore out his hair.

"Is this how a good Jewish husband treats his wife? Bum!" she said. "And such a wife! No better, no finer woman exists on this rotten street! Pig, I'll bash your brains in!"

The hushed crowd hung on her words and listened.

"Bums! Whores! Feather Pluckers!" she cried as she stood with her legs planted on either side of the fallen Moishe and addressed the street. "Have you nothing better to do than to stand by while a drunken bum of a husband beats his wife? Go back to your homes and clean out your toilets!

"I have sat and watched and cried that such a terrible thing should be!" she screamed as she now turned on the frightened Moishe. "Vermin! Bedbug! I know what is at the root of your trouble! I'll fix it so that you can be a good and faithful husband!

"Let me at him!" she shouted as she began stamping on him. "I'll crack his manhood in two!"

And the crowd, like one, gave forth with a frightened, "Oh!"

Then holding up her shears for the crowd to see, she screamed, "Watch me cut it off! I'll make a faithful husband of him yet!"

And with this, she fell upon the white and shaken Moishe, snapping her deadly shears while the street let out roar after roar. I think the men were even more afraid than the women.

How they subdued the mad Hannah Sarah I do not know, for it was with the utmost of effort that a group of our men grabbed her and held her off before she could do any damage.

"Let me up! Let me up!" she screamed. "Have you no respect for old age?"

Then turning about, her shroud all ripped to pieces, she tore it off her shoulders and flung it into the faces of the crowd, but not before she spat three times. And looking at the now-risen Moishe, she said with the utmost of contempt as if it were the lowest thing she could say:

"A Yid! A Yid and a *shicker!*"

"Hooray for Hannah Sarah! Three cheers for the witch! Hip! Hip! Hooray!" shouted the crowd.

"Bums!" she said. "May the devil take you all!"

And she stormed off.

From that time forward, our street avoided Hannah Sarah.
If they called her the "witch," they said it now quietly and with
dignity as if it were a badge of honor. But "witch" or no
"witch," she was now without a shroud and without the white
garment, it was as if she was without life.

The last I remember of her was her standing outside Usher's
house, unreconciled, with only her cardboard suitcase alongside her.

"Bums! Murderers! Who can live on this godless street! The
devil take you all!" she shouted, waving her fists at our street.

Then with her suitcase in one hand and her open change
purse in the other, she accosted some woman on our street.

"Give to the poor children in Jerusalem!" she said. "Give to
the children of God!"

Tessie, Don't Give Away the Raisin; without It, You're Lost!

THE FIRST QUESTION IS WHERE AND HOW WAS TES-sie ruined. The answer is it occurred in our back yard and Usher was responsible.

It all happened when we wouldn't let Hymie Goldberg into our "house" in the back yard.

"No snotnose is coming in this here hide-out!" said Usher, lying spread out on our mattress.

"Even if he did wipe his nose," said Pickles, "it won't do him no good. This place is bustin' at the seams, as it is. If one more person comes in, the walls'll fall apart."

"Besides," noted Robby, "Hymie's a rotten squealer. All you

gotta do is hit him one and he runs cryin' to his old man. I wouldn't trust him as far as I can spit."

"You is right," cried Bibi the Lookout, who was looking from the roof of our hut. "Comes the snotnose to our hut—out goes our secret code to our enemies."

"According to the Constitution," I said, "we gotta take a vote."

"What constitution?"

"Why," I said, "the Constitution of these United States of America!"

"Cut it out," said Usher, "we is against cops!"

"The trouble with you, Usher," I said getting angry, "is that it ain't your idea. If you had thought of it first, you'd a hollered your head off that we should take a vote."

"Take a vote," said Robby, "what've we got to lose?"

"We took a vote already," said Usher.

"We didn't took no vote," I said. "I didn't see nobody put a mark on a paper and drop it into a box."

"What d'you need a vote for?" retorted Usher in that slow, insidious manner of his. "Didn't Pickles say he's against Hymie? Didn't Robby say so? Didn't Bibi say so? Didn't I say so?"

"Go on," said Robby, "let's have a vote! It's fun!"

"O.K.," said the reluctant Usher, "go on and vote if you gotta have a vote."

In a second, scraps of paper appeared and each of us penciled his, taking severe pains to hide it from the others. Dropping them into a cap, we dug them out and counted.

"Five no's!" cried Robby in surprise.

"I told you we didn't have to vote," said Usher.

Suddenly there came a tap on the door as we all went rigid.

"Let me in!" came Hymie's voice. "Don't you hear me knocking at the door?"

"Don't answer him," ordered Usher, calmly.

"Let me in!" continued Hymie. "You think you're smart, eh!

You think you can fool me! I know you're in there!"

"Listen, Big Mouth," said Usher, "we don't let any squealers in here."

"No," echoed Robby, "we don't let any squealers in here."

"If you don't let me in," screamed Hymie, "I'll tell my father on you!"

"Go on," said Usher, "go on home to your father and tell him. What can that big crook do anyway?"

"What did you call my father?" shouted Hymie as if the world were falling apart.

"I called him a crook. And you can tell him for my money," added Usher, "that I didn't call him a little crook, either. Tell him I said he was a big crook."

"Wait," screamed Hymie, "wait until I tell my father what you said!"

"I'll be right over here—waiting," said Usher.

"Hey, Big Mouth Hymie," cried Bibi, "what's your father gonna do about it?"

"He'll take off his strap and kill you with it!" shouted Hymie.

"Yeh," said Usher, sadly, "you can't help it, poor kid, if you have a father, a crook; and you can't help it either if your father, the crook, is married to your mother, who is a whore."

Silence!

"What did you call my mother?" finally asked Hymie, very calmly.

"I called her a whore," repeated Usher.

"Say it again! I dare you to say it again!"

"Your mother is a whore, spelled w-h-o-e-r."

"Boy, am I glad you called my father a crook and my mother a whore! Just wait until I tell them. Will you get it!" said Big Mouth Hymie the Squealer as he began to race out of the back yard, screaming at the top of his lungs for all the world to hear. "Pa, Pa! Usher called you a crook! Ma, Ma! Usher said you is a whore! Am I glad! Am I glad!"

At this, we all breathed a sigh of relief and sat back.

"There ain't nothin' to do," said Bibi.

"Why don't you take your head and bang it against a stone wall," said Usher, echoing his father. But it was true! Now that Hymie was gone, there was nothing to do. So we sat puffing away at our cigarettes, breathing smoke into each other's face and just looking.

"Usher," said Pickles after a long period of silence, "how do you know that Big Mouth Hymie the Squealer's mother is a whore?"

My friend Usher the Landlord's son just sat there.

"Usher," said Pickles again, "I asked a question, didn't you hear me? I wanna know how you know Big Mouth Hymie the Squealer's mother is a whore. I'm not asking you about his old man being a crook—everybody knows that, but since when did his old lady turn into a whore?"

"I said she's a whore! And when I say she's a whore, she's a whore!"

Silence!

"Usher," I said, "that's no answer. How do you know Hymie's old lady is a whore?"

"She's Hymie's old lady, that's why! Only a whore could have Hymie for a son!"

Silence!

"Usher," I said, "I challenge you! I challenge you to tell me why she's what you said she is!"

"Yeh," said Bibi, "I challenge you!"

"I challenge you, too!" rang out the cries from the others.

Silence!

"She's a whore," said Usher slowly, drawing it out nice and long, "because she's knock-kneed."

Silence! Deep thought!

"Dat's no reason," said Robby slowly.

"He's right, dat's no reason. Whoever heard of dat for a reason," said Pickles.

"I said she's a whore because she's knock-kneed! And that's the way it's gonna be!" insisted Usher.

More silence!

"How do you know she's knock-kneed?" asked Bibi. "She always covers up."

"Yeh," said Robby, "she wears dresses down to the floor."

"So how do you know, Usher?" asked Robby. "That's what I want to know."

"I know," said Usher, "because I saw!"

Silence!

"Then that makes Mary Contrary a whore, too," said Robby, thoughtfully.

"Yep!"

"And No-Tit Gertie and Gussie the Beautician and Tessie the Slob," I said.

And that is how Usher was responsible for Tessie being "ruined" in our back yard.

Now Good-Time Charlie used to sit in front of our candy store, and he was called "Good-Time" because he never had a job. Hour after hour, day after day, he sat so, smoking endless cigarettes, with only grunts and groans as he shifted. An expert with cards, he never had any trouble getting someone in on a game with him; and right out in the open with the bench as a table, he would straddle the seat with both legs and slam cards down left and right as the coins went back and forth.

"Charlie is working," my friend Pickles would say to me. "Let's watch the game."

And we would stand around and watch Charlie slamming the cards on the wooden bench, I looking over Charlie's shoulder and Pickles looking over the shoulder of Charlie's opponent.

It happened one day that Tessie the Slob passed, and Charlie took time off from the game and looked.

"It's true," observed Pickles, "she is what Usher said she is, and her knees are like Usher said they were."

I could not bring my head up to look. To do so, first, would have meant that I showed concern over what Usher had said.

Second, it might lead to an admission that Usher was right and this, I could never do. But the truth of the matter was that I was more concerned than I dared let on.

Up to the time my friend Usher the Landlord's son had made his statement, I never knew Tessie existed. Tessie lived "around the corner" and as far as I was concerned, this meant a million miles away; thus, she came from "nowhere." And now that Usher had said what he said, I was compelled to sit it out on the bench of the candy store and watch Tessie's knees. Oh, how I prayed that her knees would not knock; not that I cared about Tessie and her lousy feet, but just to prove that Usher was wrong. But it was not to be!

And so she would come from out of nowhere to our street, walk by swinging a big black bag, and then come back from out of nowhere, this time laden with all kinds of packages, and then disappear into nowhere.

It was a problem. Her skirts were usually so arranged that they fell just below the knees. A problem, but also suspicious, because it meant that she was hiding something.

It got so that I made it my business to sit beside Good-Time and watch. Tessie would come down the street, her head full of curls dancing in the breeze. This, I didn't care about! Her rear-end would jut out beyond the plumb line because of the angle of her 45-degree walk. This, I didn't care about! It was only her legs! her legs! that held my eyes. This, I cared about! And it was that lousy Usher who had planted the poison in my mind.

Encased in sheer stockings, the muscles of those calves bunched out, giving the fine black lines of the seam a curve. From the heel of her foot there grew a black patch, stitched heavily in rectangular fashion. Her legs were in constant motion. But what was particularly annoying to me was that Tessie's legs were only the beginning because I found that I began to be fascinated by all legs. And I would sit next to Charlie as he played cards, with my eyes following first one set of legs, then another and another.

One fine morning I was standing outside the elevated station, just looking, when a voice said:

"Hey, kid, help me with the packages! They're breaking my back! They're killing my feet!"

Sure enough, it was Tessie the Slob carrying a host of assorted items.

"Sure, Tessie," I said, "I'll help you."

"Oh," said Tessie, "you know me?"

"Sure I know you, Tessie; everybody knows you," I said. "You live around the corner."

"That's a good kid," she said, handing me a number of packages and retaining a few for herself.

Tessie the Slob was real fast. Before I knew what was happening, she was off. The next thing I knew I had a good view of her legs as she went racing down the street.

Now Usher had decided that Tessie was you know what, and my friend Pickles had confirmed it; but walking behind Tessie's feet, I realized that I had not decided anything yet. First, her legs moved so rapidly you couldn't see. Second, she wore her skirts so that they reached just below her knees. And with the rapid movements of her walk as she thrust first one leg forward and then the other, now you saw it and now you didn't. And just as you thought you saw it, it was all gone.

Down the street, with their steady pace walked those legs. It had gotten so that it seemed as if Tessie's legs were even more important than Tessie herself. Over the pavement the heels of those legs struck, agitated, full of a life of their own. So important had her legs become that if it were possible for Tessie herself to be detached from them, her legs would go walking away by themselves.

Over the curb, across the street, up the curb walked those legs, when suddenly, outside the candy store, a new movement appeared as the ankles twisted, the feet arched, and the knees buckled in a strange sort of way. So slight, so infinitesimal was the change that only an expert could detect it; and by this time, I was an expert.

It was Good-Time Charlie, sitting on the bench outside the candy store, who was responsible; for something got into those legs as they passed the bench, and they reluctantly seemed to shift into slow speed. And as they left the bench behind, again reluctantly as if against their will, they returned to their original frenzy.

And so I chased after our Tessie until we rounded the corner and came to the stoop of her house which was nowhere. Up the stairs we mounted, and here I had a good view as I followed her, hypnotized by those agitated knees.

"Hey, kid," she said, "can you hold another package while I get the key into the door? Those damn packages are getting me down."

"What's the matter, Tessie?" I asked. "Don't you like packages?"

"Like them?" she exclaimed as she began to fumble for her key. "I hate them! If I never saw another package, I'd be happy!"

"You don't like packages," I said. "Then why do you do it?"

"A girl's gotta wear a dress," she observed.

"Dat's true," I said, "girls gotta wear dresses."

"You buy a dress," she continued, "you gotta have a pocketbook. You buy a pocketbook, you gotta have a hat. You buy a hat, you gotta have shoes. It's a lousy business any way you look at it."

"So that's it!" I said.

"After all, a girl's gotta get married sometime. And she's gotta be attractive; otherwise, nobody's gonna ask."

"Oh!" I said.

"Wait, " she said, "you're too young to understand. But wait, you'll want to get married too, someday."

"Oh no, Tessie," I said, "I ain't ever gonna get married."

"Now I ain't saying it's easy, kid," she continued, oblivious to me. "It's pretty hard nowadays to get a guy to ask."

"I ain't ever gonna ask."

"But you gotta get married," she said.

"Why?"

"Because," she said, fumbling for words, "because *everybody* gets married."

"Never," I said, "I'll never get married!"

"Maybe, kid, you're not so wrong after all," she admitted. "Before you know it, you're knocked-up, and you're washing diapers, and you're carrying bundles. Why anybody wants to get married is beyond me! There's no percentage in it."

"I ain't ever getting married," I said. "I don't like girls."

And at this, she laughed as she pushed open the door and I took another look at her legs.

Into the darkness of the kitchen we came as I made out a tiny white object standing at the sink.

"Nu!" said the white object, wiping her hands on an apron.

As my eyes slowly grew accustomed to the lack of light, the tiny white object turned into Tessie's old lady. And tiny she was, no more than about four feet tall, dressed in a white kerchief and a white dress, so clean that they shone like radium-tinted dials.

"What's this?" she asked, looking at me from an old wrinkled face.

"It's nobody," answered Tessie as I felt a pang.

"What do you mean—it's nobody?" asked the old lady. "I see somebody."

"It's just a kid who helped me with the bundles," said Tessie.

"Oh!" said the old lady as she went to fetch her glasses from a drawer in the kitchen table, put them on, and then peered right into my face. "It's only a child," she added, disappointed. "I thought it was a man."

"A good kid!" said Tessie. "He saved my feet—carrying those bundles."

And here, she threw off her shoes, sat down at the table, and began to open the packages.

"Nu!" said the old lady.

"A dress," indicated Tessie as she opened a bundle and lifted a garment out of the box.

"Who cares about dresses!" said the old lady.

"A pair of shoes! A hat! A bag! Earrings!"

"Nu!" said the old lady, then turning to me, she added, "Here's a chair! Help yourself!"

I didn't know whether to go or stay, so I sat down. Now we all sat at the table: Tessie, her mother who was eagerly waiting for Tessie to speak, and me.

"I put on that black dress this morning," began Tessie, "just like you told me. You know, the one I bought in Macy's Department Store for two dollars."

"Who cares how much you paid!" said the old lady.

"I put it on and walked out of the house. I turned the corner. I walked pass the candy store."

"Nu!"

"It didn't do any good. He didn't even look."

"The bum!"

"I came back. The bundles were covering me up so much, I knew he couldn't see the dress."

"He's not looking at the dress!"

"So I got an idea. All I had to find, I thought, is a kid to help me carry the packages."

"Nu!"

"So at the station, I see this one standing there. And he looks like a good kid, so I ask him to help me carry the bundles, and he says, 'Yes!' Then I began walking."

"So!"

"I walked until I came to the candy store. And then I slowed down, and—"

"Nu!"

"This time, he looked."

"The bum!"

"He looked and then he turned away."

"How did he look?"

"From the corner of his eye."

"From the corner of his eye? May both of his eyes go blind and fall out of his head! That's all he did?"

"That's all."

"I'll fix him!" said the old lady as she took a needle from the drawer of the kitchen table and began to thread it in great anger. "I'll fix him so that he'll stay fixed forever! Take off the dress!"

"In front of the kid?" cried Tessie in astonishment.

"What does he matter?" said the old lady. "It's only a child! Take off the dress!"

I arose to leave.

"Say, kid, meet me tomorrow in the same place," said Tessie as she reached for the hem of her dress. "I'll probably have bundles to carry."

"O.K., Tessie," I said. "I'll carry."

And Tessie lifted her dress over her head; and as I went to the door, from the corner of my eye I saw Tessie's old lady begin taking the dress in at the seams of the hips, but at Tessie herself, I didn't dare look. And as I went down the stairs, my heart was heavy for reasons I didn't know why.

"Say," Bibi said to me as I went pass the candy store after coming out of Tessie's house, "Charlie's winning the game. Ain't you happy?"

I sat down on the bench behind Charlie's back without a word. There he sat leaning forward, his legs straddling the bench as he slapped the cards down. Through the lines of his always immaculate shirt, I could make out the immense span of his shoulders; and I knew that if he turned to face me, the open collar would show his big black hairs reaching right up to his neck.

"Ain't you happy that Charlie's winning?" asked Bibi as I rose to go.

"Sure, I'm happy that Charlie's winning," I said.

"You said that, but it don't sound as if you mean it," said Bibi, following me.

"Look," I said, "suppose I say I'm happy about Charlie winning. Is that gonna make Charlie win? Is it gonna influence the game any? The cards don't care whether I care or don't care."

"No," admitted Bibi, "it ain't gonna influence the game any, but dat ain't the right attitude to take."

"Why not?" I asked. "What's so important about Charlie winning? Suppose he loses; ain't the sun gonna come up tomorrow morning? Besides, one day he's losing, the next day he's winning. If he wins, he loses it back anyway."

"What are you so sore about?" asked Bibi. "Charlie ain't done nothing to you. Why, he never does anything to anyone. He doesn't even talk."

"I ain't got nothing against Charlie," I said. "In fact, for my money, he's a good guy."

"Oh," said Bibi, "you like Charlie then?"

"What do I have to like Charlie for? He ain't nothing to me."

"Then you don't like Charlie," said Bibi.

"I don't like him. I don't hate him."

"Now," said Bibi, "if everybody is going to take that attitude, before you know it, what's gonna happen to our street? The whole place'll be full of traitors and everybody'll be ratting on everybody else."

"As far as I'm concerned," I said, "they're ratting on each other already; besides, who the hell cares about this lousy street!"

"You just ain't happy about the idea of Charlie winning," said Bibi as I finally extricated myself from him and crossed the street to my house.

The next evening, exactly when Tessie was supposed to come home from work, I stood at the appointed spot. Before I knew it, a bundle of packages came right down on me, and I—eyes on legs—was following Tessie down the street.

Plunk! Plunk! Down the street went Tessie's legs.

"Anything wrong with my stockings, kid?" she asked, turning her head to gaze over her shoulder at me.

"Everything is all right, Tessie," I answered.

Left, right! Right, left! Up the curb went Tessie's feet.

"How do I look?" she asked as she stopped suddenly at the curbstone and adjusted her dress.

"You look wonderful, Tessie," I said.

Right, left! Right, left! Almost to the candy store went the feet.

"Hey, kid, a bundle—quick!" she said.

Right through the air flew a bundle as Tessie caught it and put it under her arm.

Forward march! One! Two! Three! This time, slowly, sinuously, when there in front of my eyes, the legs appeared to twist and turn, and down tumbled Tessie and the bundle with a bang right in front of Charlie's bench, and of course, in front of Charlie himself.

How terrible it all was! There was Tessie on the sidewalk, ready to cry; and there was Charlie on the bench, slamming the cards. And do you think that Charlie lifted a finger to help Tessie? No! Do you know what he did—he looked!

I helped poor, ashamed Tessie up as she adjusted her dress.

"Tessie, did you hurt yourself?" I asked.

At first, she walked slowly. Soon the redness of her face waned. Now she was strangely silent. Not a word out of her!

"Tessie, is anything the matter?" I asked, frightened.

"Kid," she said, her face deadly pale in anger as the legs walked, "remember what I say, 'I'm gonna kill that Charlie, yet!' "

And from the strange cold look in her eyes, the pale color of her face, and the slow, irritated motion of her feet as she rubbed them against one another, I realized she meant it.

"Ma!" said Tessie, weeping, as she flung herself into the kitchen.

"What's the matter, Tessie; what happened?" cried her mother, frightened.

"I did exactly like you told me. I was coming down the street. The dress was beautiful; I could feel how beautiful it was. Everything was all right, but I wasn't gonna take a chance.

" 'Say, kid,' I said, 'throw me a bundle!' "

"What for?" asked the mother.

"I was gonna drop the bundle in front of Charlie, right under his nose."

"Why?" asked the mother.

"To make the rotten skunk pick it up!"

"Say, Tessie," I said. "what's fair is fair! Why do you call Charlie a skunk? He didn't do nothing to you."

"Shut your mouth, kid, and mind your own business! You men are all alike!"

I shut my mouth.

"So!" said her mother.

"So I was gonna drop the bundle in front of him. Naturally, he'd have to pick it up."

"So," I intervened, "instead of only the bundle dropping, Tessie dropped and the bundle dropped—both. And Charlie—"

"The lousy skunk!" Tessie added.

"And Charlie—only looked."

"Pooh!" said her mother. "I thought something really terrible happened! It was only that you fell and he only looked. So what? Nothing in life comes easy. There will come a time when you will walk and you won't fall, when you'll pass by and not only will he look—but stoop! And when that time comes, you will step right on him!"

"Ma, I ain't getting nowhere with him."

"No," I echoed, "Tessie ain't getting nowhere with Charlie."

"Shut up, and mind your own business!" said Tessie.

"Don't let everything out to the child," admonished the old lady. "After all, he's not responsible. In fact, if anything, he tried to help you."

"What am I gonna do, Ma?" moaned Tessie.

"Sit down, my daughter, and listen," said Tessie's old lady. "After all, I've lived a little longer than you. See, look at all the gray hairs in my head I have to prove it."

So Tessie sat down and I sat down with her. Silent was that house as we sat and listened. Only the drip of the water from the broken faucet could be heard in this dark little kitchen, the walls of which were saturated with the odors and oils of countless cooking pots. Only the faint creaking of the floorboards came to us as the house moaned and groaned in its old age.

"Dogs!" said the old lady.

"Who? What?" asked Tessie as eager to know what her old lady was talking about as I.

"Men!" answered Tessie's old lady. "Who else? Yes," she continued, "dirty dogs, that's what they all are! Did you ever see a man who was clean? If they never shaved or washed, it would be all right with them. You got to push them into the bathroom to take a bath or force them to wash their hands."

I squirmed. The picture of my mother forcing me to wash came to my mind.

"And oh, how they sniff and smell fresh meat! You walk with them by your side on the street. Everything is fine, everything is nice, yes? But they're smelling already! First, they smell, then, they look! How is it possible, you say? You didn't see nothing, but they (may they all go to hell!) have already seen. They can be a million miles away but they're sniffing the air already, the dirty dogs! And they don't need much either—a shoe, a foot, a skirt—as long as it's new."

"Ma," asked Tessie, "how about my Charlie?"

"Your Charlie is the dirtiest dog of them all," said the old lady, "but we're not through with him! Here I have such a beautiful daughter, a brilliant diamond shining in the dark, and he's got to be pushed!"

I looked at Tessie—she was by no means shining in the dark.

"Stand up!" ordered the old lady, taking out her needle and thread from the table.

"In front of the kid?" cried Tessie.

"What kid, who kid?" said Tessie's old lady.

And Tessie took off her dress right in front of me as I turned around, but this time it was too late because now my ears were filled with an awful racket as the blood pounded from my heart. And as I turned to face the wall, there beginning on the kitchen sink and going up to the cupboard with the breadbox thrown in and the place for the knives and forks, burned the image of Tessie.

Truthfully, I felt Tessie in my back, knowing that she stood there in her pink slip with the light from the bedroom seeping through; and I felt Tessie in the front because she stood on the wall without her slip, so that I burned in two places: in the front and the back.

So there was Tessie in the back, standing in her pink slip with the light coming through, her firm round breasts high and full, with two roseate buds up in the air and the swell of her navel as it rose and fell between the beauty of her thighs, holding some dark and mysterious secret. While up in front of me on the kitchen sink and cupboard burned Tessie without the slip and without any secrets.

How my blood thundered! How I feared they would hear the noise in my ears that I heard! How glad I was to leave this awful, yet beautiful kitchen!

"Tomorrow, kid, I'll be waiting for you," came Tessie's voice.

"I'll be there," I managed to say.

And as I went down the stairs, glad to be out in the fresh air, it occurred to me that Usher was wrong—Tessie's knees were not crooked. And as I walked further down the street, I realized that her old lady was right—Tessie was a brilliant diamond that shone in the dark.

The next day as we came in, her old lady said, "Nu! What happened?"

"Nothing," said the crestfallen Tessie, "he didn't look."

"May black crows peck his eyes out!" cursed the old lady.

"He didn't even turn his head."

"May he fall and break his neck so that his head remains turned forever!" continued the old lady.

"All he did was play cards."

"May his mouth be filled with so many cards that he chokes to death!"

"It's all Ace of Spades and Ten of Clubs and Jack of Diamonds with him."

"A spade they should use to dig his grave with!" added the old lady for good measure.

"Ma," cried Tessie, "I go down the street and I see him sitting there. Ma, I'm going crazy!"

"You're going crazy—and he doesn't even look," said the old lady.

"No," said Tessie. "He doesn't even turn his head."

"No, Tessie's mother," I interrupted, "it ain't the bosom. It ain't the hips. It's only the cards with Charlie."

"Then," said the old lady to Tessie, "sit down next time and say, 'Hello, Charlie, nice weather we're having! How is the Ace of Spades today?'"

"I can't talk to him about cards," said Tessie. "I don't know nothing about playing cards. Suppose I say, 'How is the Ace of Spades today?' And he answers, 'The Jack of Clubs is giving me trouble!' What do I do afterwards?"

"Maybe the child will help you," said Tessie's old lady.

"How can he help me?" cried Tessie in despair. "Nobody can help me!"

"What d'you wanna know about cards, Tessie?" I said. "I can teach you."

"It won't help," said Tessie. "It'll go in one ear and out the other."

Suddenly the old lady's eye brightened as it fastened on me.

"It's clear as the day!" she said. "The child holds the key!"

"I'll teach Tessie anytime," I said.

"Dear young man," said the old lady, "you don't have to teach my Tessie anything. All you gotta do is sit. Sit next to Charlie and watch. See what it is that he looks at. It's not the bosom. It's not the hips—else, he would have risen a long time ago and asked. It's something else. You gotta find out."

"Kid," said Tessie, "do this little thing for me and I promise you, I'll never forget you."

"Tessie," I announced, "for someone else I'd never do this, but for you, I will!"

So there I sat outside the candy store, next to Charlie as he slammed the cards. The sun beat hot, the wind blew cold, and I sat. When Charlie leaned forward, I leaned forward; when Charlie moved to the right, I moved to the right; when Charlie turned his head, I turned mine. And then there was another problem: Charlie was so tall that I had to sit on my knees in order to align my eyes with his. Thus when Charlie looked, I would be able to look, too, at exactly the same spot as Charlie did. No good! Just as I would bring my eyes up to see what he was looking at, it was too late. And all I could see was perhaps a passing finger, a retreating nose, or the trailing edge of a coat. No good! And then there were other things he looked at: a dog across the street, an automobile rounding the corner at high speed, the cover of a garbage can as it fell into the gutter. No good!

I hated myself as I made my way through the cellar to our hut in the back yard. Like crawling vermin I felt as I knocked three times at the door.

"Who goes there?" came the voice of that lousy Usher.

"A friend!" I answered.

"If friend, say the secret password; if foe—go!" commanded the voice from the hut.

"It's a friend—siss-boom-bah!"

"Say it three times!" ordered Usher.

And so I repeated the secret password three times.

"Enter!" said Usher.

There he sat, the rotten skunk, lying stretched out on the mattress, smoking a cigarette as usual.

"Usher," I began, "it stinks in this here hut from smoke. Why don't you open a window?"

Usher puffed away without a word.

"Louie pulled a job in Richmond Hill and got away with a load o' dough," I ventured.

He puffed and puffed.

"Usher," I asked, "maybe you'd like some cigarettes?"

Usher stopped puffing, now he was all attention.

"Whatta you got?" he asked.

I announced the brand.

"Gimme!" he said.

And without even looking, he tossed them into his pocket.

"Usher," I said, "a favor!"

Usher puffed away without a word.

"Suppose," I said, "you had to find something out—about someone I mean, for someone about something; and you couldn't ask this someone anything. Suppose, it was all in that someone's eyes and all your job was, was to watch the someone looking."

"Anybody pack a rod on this job?" asked Usher.

"No—no rods, it's a clean job," I answered, "but no rods. Maybe it would be better with a rod. Bing! Bang! The whole thing's over in a one, two, three! This is much harder. You gotta follow the eyes—steady-like, and you gotta keep a firm grip on yourself; relax for a single minute, for one second, and you're through.

"So you see," I continued, "there's Charlie sitting on the bench and I'm watching the eyes. But he never takes his eyes off those cards; and when he does, it's only for a quick flash. And by the time I look up, he's got the eyes back on the cards."

"Who're you the fingerman for?" asked Usher.

"Usher," I cried, "do you think for one minute I would hurt Charlie? Charlie's a good guy, he never did nothing to me. This is strictly legitimate, it's a favor. I swear I'm not the fingerman for anyone."

"For whom?" persisted Usher.

"It's personal," I said.

So this is how far I had carried it—Usher lay on the mattress, I sat alongside him, breathing in the smoke, and we were now at the point where everything was balanced like a hair on a scale. It would go either one way or the other.

"Well, what're you waitin' for?" asked Usher as he made a dash for it.

Out of the hut, through the yard, into the cellar, up the stairs, we ran when suddenly, as I came out into the open sunlight of the street, I realized that Usher was not with me anymore.

"Sh," came his voice from the hallway as he put his finger to his lips, "how's it outside?"

"The coast is clear," I announced.

Crossing to the bench, I sat down next to Charlie who was slamming the cards as usual, when I realized that lousy Usher was missing again. With perfect aplomb, as if we were the last thing on his mind, he encircled us once, twice, narrowing the circle down each time he made a complete turn. It was clear—Charlie was the target.

"Hey, kid," said Usher to me without even an "excuse me" or "please." "Shove over!"

When who should come down the street but Tessie's old lady, and what should she do, as if we were not crowded enough as it was, but squeeze herself in between Usher and Charlie.

"How's it going, Good-Time?" said Usher to Charlie as if Charlie were a long-lost friend and ignoring me completely.

"Keep quiet, kid," said Charlie, "the cards are against me tonight."

"Mrs. Goldberg! Mrs. Goldberg!" called Tessie's old lady up to a window above. "Come down and have some fresh air. It's a hot night."

It didn't take long for Mrs. Goldberg to come down. "Sit," said Tessie's old lady to Mrs. Goldberg.

So the situation stood thus: I was on the bench pressed against Usher, who was pressed against Tessie's old lady and Mrs. Goldberg, who were pressed against Charlie and his partner, who were slamming the cards.

"How's Mr. Goldberg?" asked Tessie's old lady.

"His back!" indicated Mrs. Goldberg.

"How's your Hymie?"

"His throat!"

"And how are you?"

"I can die twenty times a day," said Mrs. Goldberg, "and nobody cares about me. And how are you?"

"Nothing to complain about," answered the old lady and, then turning in Charlie's direction, she added nice and loud, "A little money in the bank. A clean house. A daughter who is a blessing. What more can anyone ask?"

And at this, the old lady jabbed Mrs. Goldberg in the thigh as she made a complete turn of the eyes in Charlie's direction.

"And how is Tessie?" asked Mrs. Goldberg.

"How can I talk about her?" said the old lady, spitting out. "The evil eye might get her! Only you and God know what I have put into that girl. Sews, cooks, washes floors—just like her mother—respectable, educated, brings home the pay. To business school she went, sits in an office and takes dictation— they don't dare move until she tells them—five people work under her, the entire place she carries in her head, and on Christmas—a bonus! Even a doctor would not be good enough for her!"

"I hope," sighed Mrs. Goldberg, "my Hymie turns out to be as good as your Tessie."

"He ain't got a Chinaman's chance," interposed Usher.

"And they say," sighed Mrs. Goldberg, "it is an unlucky stomach that carries a daughter."

"I should have half a dozen daughters like my Tessie—it

wouldn't have harmed me in the least. She's got everything a girl should have, and more!"

"And—boy friends?" asked Mrs. Goldberg.

"Plenty boy friends—too many! And you think—ordinary ones? Only professionals come banging on the door: Doctors, lawyers—they all want her! And why not—they know what's good for them!"

"Well," said Mrs. Goldberg, "what are you saving her for?"

And as the two women rose to leave, Tessie's old lady said in a loud whisper, "She's particular!"

"Poor Charlie," said Usher, and turning to Good-Time, Usher took out one of my cigarettes and said sadly, "Here, Charlie, have a cigarette—you'll need it."

Charlie took the cigarette and put it behind his ear.

"What d'you think?" asked Charlie, leaning over confidentially and showing Usher the cards.

"Mmm—!" said Usher.

"This is the card I'm gonna play," said Charlie, pointing to his hand.

"Mmm—!" said Usher.

And before you knew it, Usher was gone again.

"Usher," I said as I found him lying on the mattress, "what is it?"

"Mmm—!" said Usher, puffing his cigarette.

"Well," I asked, "what?"

He puffed and he puffed and puffed some more, then turning to me, he said, "It's legs, kid!"

Yes, it was legs, all right! He had found out in five minutes what I couldn't find out in five days, and I was so glad to get the information that it didn't bother me that he had called me a "kid," and it didn't even bother me to know that no girl had passed by Charlie while Usher sat there. Because I knew, I just knew, that my friend Usher the Landlord's son was right.

"Tessie! Tessie!" I screamed as I entered her house. "It's legs!"

"My daughter," shouted Tessie's old lady as Tessie fled down the stairs, "give him everything! Let him push! Let him pull! But not the raisin—don't give him the raisin!"

Then turning to me, she sat down and looking very strange, she sighed.

"Ah, you think I don't know that this is no good," she said, "that he's a bum, that he'll never make a living for her?"

"No, no, Tessie's mother," I cried, "I don't think anything at all!"

"It's all right—you can hurt my feelings," she said. "I don't care. But my Tessie has no men. Who wants her—nobody!"

"Everybody wants her," I said. "Doctors, lawyers, teachers—professionals!"

"Where?"

"Everywhere!" I cried.

"Foolish child," she said, "who knows my Tessie better than I? She has no father, no money, no education, and no professionals. And pretty—she is not!"

I sat shocked at the words coming out of this old lady's mouth.

"As for brains, when God gave them out, He forgot about my Tessie."

"Tessie's mother," I said, "that's not a nice thing to say about Tessie. After all, she's your own flesh and blood."

"But it's a bum, she likes," said the old lady. "You think I don't know what that is? In my *shtetel* there was a bum, too! Charlie, at least, can make a living—playing cards. It will be a plague on me what a living he'll make! But this bum did nothing, only slept and ran after the girls—*shicksies*, gypsies, *Polatchkies*, Jewish girls; it didn't make a difference. And so I was ensnared!

" 'Ma,' I used to say to my mother (may she rest in a lighted Paradise!), 'he pushes against me.' 'So what?' she would say. 'As long as he doesn't throw you down!' 'Ma,' I would say, 'he pinches and pulls at me.' 'As long as he does it where it doesn't show!' she would answer. 'Ma,' I would say, 'he creeps to my bosom.' 'It's attached to you,' she would say, 'what are you worried about?' 'Ma,' I would cry, 'he wants to go under my dress.' 'Give him,' she would say, 'give the dog whatever he wants—they're all crazy anyway—give him anything, but not the raisin! Don't give him the raisin—because without it, you're lost!'

"Ah, what a crazy one he was," the old lady continued, her wrinkled face taking on smiles, "in the middle of the night, stones at my window. I would walk down the road, and suddenly from out of nowhere, he would appear and follow me, singing, 'Little girl, little girl, I love you! Little girl, little girl, be my bride!' Or else, he would jump down from a roof or a tree and throw his arms around me and cry, 'Marry me or else, I'll go crazy! Marry me or else, I'll die!' "

"What happened?"

"What happened—he died!" she said as the tears came streaming down her face. "In the Kishinev pogroms, they nailed his body to a cross and set fire to my wonderful one! He who set fire to my blood, they set fire to!

"And I sit here, and I remember what my mother said to me, and do you know—I'm sorry! Oh, how sorry I am that I listened to her—not to give him the raisin!

"So really," said she wiping the tears from her eyes with her hand, "why should I be so angry at my Tessie? She's the same fool I was! Maybe God deliberately makes us stupid so that we live, else the truth would be so terrible we would all have to slit our throats!"

And so Tessie took her place beside Charlie on the bench, and she did everything a woman in love does as she sat. She crossed her legs, she uncrossed her legs. She lowered her bosom, she raised her bosom. She powdered her nose, and she didn't powder her nose. She opened her pocketbook, she closed her pocketbook. She stood up, she sat down. And while she did all this, she sighed, and sometimes she did all this and she didn't sigh.

One very warm and humid evening, the kind when it was too hot to stay inside and too hot to stay outside, the candy store owner began to put out his lights.

"Charlie darling," asked Tessie, "how's the game going?"

"The cards're against me."

"Do you need any money?" asked Tessie, opening her bag. "Don't be bashful; ask!"

Charlie didn't say a word, but Tessie understood. Taking out some money from her bag, she slipped it into his left pocket while with his right hand he slammed down a card.

"Hey, what's the big idea?" cried Charlie to the candy store man. "It's only twelve o'clock!"

"I'm closing up," came the reply. "Tomorrow's another day."

"I gotta finish this game," said Charlie.

"With you," said the candy store owner as he turned off another bulb, "you're always either at the beginning, the middle, or the end. If you gotta finish, finish on your own electric. What am I supposed to do—pay good money for bills so that you can play cards with my electric?"

"Shut up down there and let a person sleep!" came a voice from an open window.

And so in the dark, with the light coming only from the street lamp, Charlie played. No good—too dark! So Tessie began to strike matches. No good—no more matches! It didn't take long when she got a candle from somewhere, and there Charlie sat, slamming the cards with the light on the bench.

"Poor Charlie!" said Usher.

"What do you mean—'Poor Charlie'!" I cried. "Tessie is giving and Charlie is taking, and you say, 'Poor Charlie'!"

"I remember a time," said Usher, "not so long ago when it was 'Good-Time Charlie'!"

"And what is it now, if you're so smart?" I asked.

"Now it's 'Charlie Darling'—especially when he walks home with her after the game."

"So he walks home with her after the game. He probably throws pebbles at her window and jumps off trees and roofs in front of her. And when no one is looking, he sings."

"You're nuts, kid," said Usher. "There's no pebbles in this street. A tree there ain't for miles around. And who would be crazy enough to sing or jump off a roof for Tessie? No one would do this for Tessie."

"And why not?"

"Because," said Usher, "he'd break his legs and besides, she's knock-kneed."

"So?"

"So if she's knock-kneed, Charlie's gotta take her into the hallway and give her the business."

"The way I see it," I said, "it's she who gives him the money—not he, her. If you ask me, she's giving him the business."

"That's just it! She's gotta pay him!"

"Then why do you say, 'Poor Charlie'? He's getting rich on the deal."

"Because," said Usher, "poor Charlie is getting no bargain."

All of a sudden Tessie was screaming.

"The rats are taking my Charlie away!" she screamed. "He didn't do no job in Richmond Hill! Everybody knows Louie did it! Why should my Charlie go to prison—he doesn't even carry a gun! It's only the Ace of Spades and Ten of Clubs with him!"

I looked up and saw a sea of startled faces peering out of windows as if from the balcony of a movie house. And down below, three police cars blocked off the street while six cops, with guns drawn, were in action—three to get Charlie into one of the cars and three to hold Tessie, who was scratching, spitting, and kicking.

"Charlie Darling," she cried, "they're taking you away from me! How can I live without you—how can I live!"

And Charlie was sitting in the police car, looking very calm and smoking a cigarette, while Tessie, now held by six policemen, was hanging on the bumper of the automobile and wouldn't let go.

"Nobody understands him," she pleaded to the street, "my poor baby! How can anyone know how sweet he is, how good! The shirt off his back he'd give you if you asked him! When he goes into a restaurant—a tip! Stops blind people on the street and gives them handouts! Takes bums into restaurants and buys them meals! Knows how to treat a lady! I say to him, 'Charlie, here's money if you're short!' and never, never, does he take it with his hand, I gotta put it into his pocket when no one is looking. Money doesn't mean anything to him!

"What was I before I met my Charlie—nothing! Worked in a factory, came home late, washed dishes, went to work early! Now that I have my Charlie, what am I—everything!

"Take me with him!" she pleaded, her voice weak from weeping. "Let me go with him to the same prison! Lock me up in the same cell! Feed me bread and water! Put me in the same electric chair! Arrest me, please! Only don't take my Charlie from me!"

"Well," said one of the cops scratching his head, "we'll just have to take her in."

"Thanks! Thanks!" cried Tessie. "Thanks for taking me in! You're a right kind of cop! Never will I forget you for this favor!"

And with this, our Tessie released her hold on the bumper, flung her arms about the policeman, kissing him and crying at the same time.

And before the astonished eyes of our street, lining the windows as if they were in the balcony of a movie house, Tessie got into the car with Charlie as the sirens began to blow, and the police cars sped away from our street.

Life was very fearful and exciting as I knocked on Tessie's door to tell her old lady the news.

"Yes?" came the old lady's voice from behind the door.

"Tessie, did you forget your key?"

"It's not Tessie—it's me!" I cried.

Slowly the door creaked open as the wizened old lady without her teeth and with a shaven head, looking smaller and older than ever before, looked out.

"Phew," she cried, spitting out, "may all my fears be driven into wild animals! So late at night, a child goes knocking at strange doors?"

"Charlie's in jail! Tessie's with him!" I screamed. "Never before in the history of the world has there ever been anyone thanking a cop for taking him in! Your Tessie thanked!"

"Sh," she said, closing the door after me, "don't scream—I hear you. You'll wake up the neighbors. And what they don't know, won't hurt them. Come in, come in."

I entered the dark kitchen as she put on the light.

"Didn't you hear what I said? The cops arrested Charlie, Charlie's in jail," I hollered, "and Tessie, your own flesh and blood, is with him!"

"I heard! I heard!" she said as she slowly went to the kitchen shelf and took out her false teeth from a glass, washed them under the faucet, and slipped them into her mouth.

"That Charlie's in jail doesn't surprise me," she added, covering her head with a white kerchief. "As for Tessie, the moment Tessie met Charlie, I knew she was in for a jail sentence. I'm not surprised. But God walks in mysterious ways. Sometimes, He lurks in the dark corners like a phantom and lurches out at you. Maybe with Charlie, God has a plan, the end of which is not in sight. So let's talk about Charlie."

She wasn't even excited.

"Does he have a mother?" she asked.

"A mother!" I cried, astounded.

"What's the matter? Don't you know what a mother is?" she said, pulling at the top of her nightgown in irritation. "A bum he is, we all know. But surely, even Charlie was once a child and nurtured at a mother's breast. Surely, he stems from a house and somewhere someone is concerned with him."

"Yes," I said, "he lives in a house."

"With a mother?"

"Yes—with a mother."

"Where?"

"Five blocks from here."

"Then go," she ordered, "bring her here!"

Tessie's mother was tiny but Charlie's mother was even tinier. Peering out of her door, I saw she, too, was without teeth and with a shaven head in Orthodox style. What's this business, I said, everybody tonight's got false teeth and bald heads with wigs. By the time the frightened old lady got to Tessie's old lady, I had told her everything; and whereas Tessie's old lady took it calmly, this one grew confused. Kissing the *mezuzah* outside the door, she followed me into the kitchen.

"Ah!" said Tessie's old lady, confronting Charlie's mother with her hands on her hips. "So you finally came! I wanted to see what kind of mother it was who produced such a bum!"

Spread out on the table lay a white tablecloth. The faucet had been polished and gleamed in the light. Pieces of cut glass had been set up on the bureau and on the table itself large ornate pieces of silver were displayed. And Tessie's mother, herself, was dressed in her Saturday clothes while on her head she carried a brown wig.

"My Charlie's no bum," cried Charlie's mother, defending him like a mother should. "We stem from rabbis and respectable people."

"Is that the reason he sits out on the bench and plays cards all day long?"

"My Charlie has an active brain," said Charlie's mother. "He's got to be doing something."

"Wait, I'll show you what respectable people are!" said Tessie's mother as she went into the bedroom, opened a bureau drawer and took out bedsheets, pillowcases, blankets, and towels, and piled them up on the kitchen table. "This is what my Tessie takes with her. I've been saving it up for her even before she was born."

"This was my mother's," she said, throwing a quilt in Charlie's mother direction. "My poor mother would turn over in her grave if she knew that it would be used to keep a cardplayer warm. See, real Russian goose feathers, not the kind you buy in the department store. Examine it—go ahead!"

"I'm satisfied," said Charlie's mother, looking greedily at the pile of linens on the table. "Anyway, it's time my Charlie got married. What's he sitting for?"

"Oh, what a marriage this will be!" moaned Tessie's old lady, taking the quilt out of the visitor's hand. "Already, the bridegroom's in jail! What a plague on my old and broken bones!"

"From jails—it's not the first time," sighed Charlie's old lady, then gathering up courage, added, "but I'm more than satisfied with the linens. And money?"

"Who has money?" cried Tessie's old lady, wringing her hands. "If he had a piece of a profession or a trade, it would be another story. If he were even a truck driver or a street cleaner, but this is a cardplayer. And not only a cardplayer, but a cardplayer in jail. For this, there is no money."

"And the girl?"

"A diamond! Sews! Cooks! Adds in her head without pencil and paper! Takes dictation! Educated!"

"Respectable?"

"No man has ever touched her!"

"Healthy?"

"I should only be so healthy! She'll have children by the dozen!"

"A diamond? Sews? Cooks? Adds in her head without pencil and paper? Untouched by men? Children by the dozen?" said Charlie's old lady. "What can be bad?"

At this, the door slowly opened and Tessie walked in. Oh, how bedraggled she looked! Her dress sat askew on her hips. Somewhere, she had lost a shoe and so she upped and downed as she walked across the kitchen floor. Her eyes were rimmed with red from weeping, and the dark mascara had run down her cheeks and was smeared over her face. And beneath the ruin that showed, her face glowed green and sickly in the kitchen light.

"This is the diamond?" asked Charlie's mother, suddenly growing bold.

"Ah Tessie," said her mother, running to the rescue, "you must have had a bad day today." Then turning to Charlie's mother, she said, "She generally looks much better, but today was a hard day. If she has to take your bum to jail, what do you expect her to look like?"

As Tessie's mother grew more and more frantic, Tessie added to the ungainly picture she presented by vomiting into the sink.

I led Tessie into the bedroom as she lay down on the bed. I helped her take her one shoe off. Legs! Legs!

"Zip me open, kid!" she said.

I zipped her open and there in the small dark bedroom as the light came through the half-opened door of the kitchen, her flesh lit up like electric. And from her person came an intoxicating odor, a heavy perfume that weakened me.

"Charlie," she moaned, "my Charlie Darling! It had to happen to me, kid," she cried as she pointed to her breast. "I've been hit right over here!"

"Tessie! Tessie!" I cried. "Don't take it so hard! Charlie didn't do the job in Richmond Hill! Everybody knows Louie did it! Thousands of people saw Charlie playing cards that day! He's got an alibi! If you want, I'll even be a witness!"

And there in the bedroom with her flesh looking so soft and beautiful and with the delicious odor of her body bathing my very soul, I wanted time to have a stop and to sit so beside Tessie forever and ever. And I saw myself going to the jailhouse and with a key opening up the door of Charlie's cell and saying to Charlie, "Good-Time, I'm springing you!" And Charlie saying, "Gee, thanks!" And then taking Charlie out of prison to Tessie and Tessie saying, "Thanks!" And Tessie's mother saying to me, "Thanks!" and Charlie's old lady, too. Everybody saying, "Thanks! Thanks! Thanks!"

All of a sudden, what should happen to spoil the picture, but the stupid face of my friend Bibi appeared as I heard him say, "You just ain't happy about the idea of Charlie winning! You just don't like Charlie to win! You just ain't happy! You just ain't happy!"

And it was true! I was just not happy! Why, I thought, why should this be? But before I could get an answer, Tessie's bedroom door flew wide open, the electric went up, and there were the two old ladies coming into the room.

"So—it's fated!" said Tessie's old lady with a tear in her eye.

"What will be, will be!" sighed Charlie's mother.

"Ah," said Tessie's old lady, "I recognized the rabbis and respectable people in you, now!"

"But one more thing," requested Charlie's mother.

"Yes?"

"Leave me alone with the girl!"

Happily closing the door behind us after shooing me out, Tessie's old lady sat down in the kitchen and with great vigor and gusto set to work sewing. From the bedroom came moans and groans, whisperings, and the creaking of the bedsprings; when suddenly everything went quiet, and all at once Charlie's old lady threw open the door and came out in a fury.

"What's this?" she raged. "I'm sitting in my house quietly! You send a messenger to knock at my door! You race me through dark streets! I run downstairs and upstairs! I come in here and you set upon me and insult me—my Charlie's a bum, I don't come from rabbis, my family's not respectable! From every corner, you dragged out cats to tell me! And this—for what?"

"God save you, old woman," said Tessie's mother, "what is it with you?"

"With me—nothing!" cried Charlie's mother and pointing to the bedroom, thundered, "She's not a girl!"

"Not a girl?" exclaimed Tessie's old lady. "Whoever spread this terrible lie should fall off a streetcar and break both legs!"

"Nobody had to spread it, it was as plain as the day! She doesn't have the raisin!" said Charlie's old lady. "She's worth nothing! A waste of good time!"

"Come back! Come back!" called Tessie's old lady as Charlie's mother rose to leave. "What is it you want—money? I was just joking before—if it's money you want, I'll be glad to give it!"

"Ha! Ha!" laughed Charlie's mother from the stairway as she ran down. "The woman is crazy! Without a raisin, even money can't help!"

Tessie's mother sat quietly. Taking up her needle and thread, she began to sew. Only the water dripped from the faucet. Only the floorboards creaked. Then looking in the direction of the bedroom, she sighed a terrible sigh.

"How monstrous is life!" she said. "You want to pick up your head once in a while and laugh a little and be happy, but it won't let you. Always, always, you think of the most terrible thing that can happen and hope it won't, and sure as I'm sitting here, it always happens. Yet, I thank God! I thank God that although I was born into affliction and misery, although I have known poverty and starvation, I thank God that I was born a Jew! I thank God that although even death has come into this house and that I have known it, and although in my sufferings and anguish I have known deep and bitter tears, that my well of God never ran dry—because if it were not so, if I did not believe in my God, I would cut my throat here and now!"

"Tessie's mother," I said, "don't worry! Everything will be all right in the end. Tomorrow is another day. Charlie will come home from jail and he will marry Tessie—with a raisin or without a raisin—and everybody will live happily ever after."

"Ah," she said, "you are still a child, but this is the way it should be with you. Nobody lives happily ever after!"

"And why not? Why shouldn't everybody live happy?"

"Because, child," she said wearily as she took out her false teeth, put them in a glass near the sink, lifted her wig from her head, and set it on the cupboard shelf, "we begin in darkness and end in darkness. And between the darkness of the beginning and the darkness in the end, we grapple and grapple with life. 'Ah,' we say, 'I got it! I got it by the throat! It can't slip away from me now!' And just as we say this, God pulls a string and everything falls away and we stand before the open pit that is everybody's grave! Yet," she said, "man is full of such vanity that he can't give up; until the end, he fights! Let them put eggshells on our eyes after we die, how can one give up the struggle?"

Tessie came down the street in a cotton dress. She had on no mascara, no high heels, and no packages; in fact, she was getting fat. In front of her—a carriage with a baby darling, a treasure chest, giving off blinding beams of light that hurt the eyes. Heads of our neighbors went in, heads came out! Hands went up, hands went down! Lips smacked together and spat out on the evil eye!

"Ga-ga!" said the treasure chest.

Curses for the devil, blessing for the child! A bright future for the child! A productive one for Tessie!

"Goo-goo!" said the baby. "Cluck-cluck!"

When, seeing Charlie on the bench slamming the cards, Tessie let out a roar that shook the very windows of our street.

"Goo!" said the baby.

"This is how a family man spends his time!" bellowed Tessie as she approached Charlie and began kicking him in the shins. "Bum! I'll give you Ace of Spades and Ten of Clubs! Babies you know how to make? Raisins you know how to take? But a living, you never heard of!"

Then turning to the baby, she said, "Look at him, that's your father! Some father! If it were up to him, the milk from your mouth, he'd be willing to gamble away! The pillow from under your head, he'd sell to the pawnbroker if he knew I'd let him! And all for cards!

"Go to work, bum!" she screamed. "Go to work, bum, and bring home the pay!"

"I see it's no more 'Charlie Darling'," said Usher.

"Charlie," I said, "didn't know what he was doing. It was dark in the hallway when he struggled for the raisin and ruined Tessie."

"It was Tessie who ruined Charlie, not Charlie—Tessie!" said Usher. "In the dark or in the light, she just ruined Charlie! And if you ask me, I wonder if she ever had a raisin to begin with! Besides, why did it have to be Tessie? What's wrong with Gussie the Beautician or Mary Contrary?"

"What d'you think, Usher," I said, "raisins grow on trees?"

Free the Canaries from Their Cages!

THINGS WERE NOT ONLY BAD ON OUR STREET, THEY were terrible. And not only were they terrible, they were worse than terrible. Just when we thought we had hit a new low, zoom, down we went further. "This is the bottom!" we would say. And zoom, we were below the bottom. "It can't get worse!" And zoom, zoom, darn it if we weren't below the bottom of the bottom. Yes! Things were really bad!

The men on our street had lost their jobs and were now making an appearance as housewives: marketing, cleaning, and taking care of the little ones. This was bad. But then they began, like their wives, to get into fights. This was terrible. And then it didn't take long before the electric companies began to shut off our meters. This was really worse than terrible. And when entire families sat around tables lit with candles because the electric was off, and all they had was a loaf of bread and tea, and when someone would invariably say, "It can't get worse!" this was near the bottom. But when they went to the corner grocery to borrow on the bills so that they could have carfare to go looking for jobs, this was the bottom. And as if that were not enough, this particular winter was extra cold, so that, without money, we sat around without heat. This was below the bottom. And when the pipes began to freeze and burst, this was further down. Really, there was no end to how far down things went. Even the bottom had a bottom.

One day my friend Usher was blessed by a visit from his "rich" aunt from Borough Park. "Your pots don't shine enough!" she said.

"Maybe it's the Brillo I'm using," said Usher's mother.

"Something smells here!" said the "rich" aunt, adjusting the tablecloth.

"I'll open the window," said Usher's mother.

"It's time the boy received a good Jewish education!" said the "rich " aunt, opening the closet to see if everything was properly arranged.

"And with what will I pay for it?" said Usher's mother.

"Israel will perish unless he gets an education!"

I looked at Usher sitting very sheepishly and turning his head from one speaker to the other. It was hard for me to connect the fate of Israel with Usher.

"Anyway," said the "rich" aunt, "I never heard of a Jewish boy not getting a Jewish education! It could only happen in Brownsville! Everything happens in Brownsville! It could never happen in Borough Park!"

"All right! I'll shine up the pots," said Usher's mother.

The next thing you knew, Usher's Uncle Simchie appeared, a tall, handsome man whom the women of our street doted on.

"No rabbi for the child?" asked Uncle Simchie.

"I see the post office is busy sending mail!" said Usher's mother, knowing there had been intra-family consultations about this.

"Wait! You'll die and he'll say *Kaddish* in English!"

"God forbid!" said Usher's mother.

"Just imagine!" he said. "It's raining and we're all standing dressed in black, and they lower your body into the grave and pile the sand on it. And yours, yours gets up to say *Kaddish!* '*Yisgadal veyiskadash shmey rabo!*' he should say. But he won't say it! Other Jewish boys will say it! But not yours! Yours will say it in English!"

"I'm a believer," said Usher's mother, perspiring freely. "But my husband is not. I fight with him all the time. When Passover comes, he says to me, 'Another set of pots she has to buy! We don't even have bread in the house, and she must buy more pots!' And he's right! God understands English!"

"God understands English, but will you?" said Uncle Simchie, and then bursting forth in his beautiful baritone, he sang, "*Yisgadal veyiskadash shmey rabo!*—We must keep Israel alive!"

"Keep Israel alive?" said Usher's mother. "We're having trouble keeping ourselves alive!"

Third visitor. The grandfather. The grandfather who owed them three hundred and thirty dollars. Unfortunately, Usher's father was home at the time.

"How's business in Bayonne?" asked Usher's father sarcastically.

"The child can't read a prayer book!" said Usher's grandfather.

"To work in a shop, he doesn't have to know how to read a prayer book!"

"Before the doubter criticizes the word of God, let him know more than those who speak the word of God!"

"There are those who say they speak the word of God, and further there are those who say they speak with God!"

"God is, no matter whether man speaks of or with!"

"When those who owe me money pay me it, I will be able to satisfy them about my son speaking of and with!"

The old man grew furious.

"Do you mean to tell me," he screamed, "that I'm responsible for the ignorance of this child!"

"That's exactly what I mean!" said Usher's father.

"And how am I responsible?" screamed the grandfather.

"You are exactly three hundred and thirty dollars worth responsible!"

"I'm insulted!" said the old man, raising himself to his full height. "You can expect a check in the mail every week providing the money is used for the child's education."

"Send the checks," said Usher's father, "and the child gets the education."

"It will be a good deed!"

"Will it be a good check?" Usher's father asked.

"Israel must be maintained!" said Usher's grandfather as he went down the stairs.

"The check will maintain it!" said Usher's old man, and then turning to his wife, added, "I'll get that money back yet, even if I have to send the kid to Hebrew school!"

If I've shown anyone in a bad light, I should like you to know that I don't mean to. If I've shown the apostate as a little stronger than the believer, it is only because we were living in a time of apostasy. Neither believer nor non-believer was a product of his own self, each was a product of different sides of our dark and alien, suffering street. And in spite of Usher's father's bad manners and hot speech, I think we must remember that as he had to worry so much about his bread, he had little time to worry about God. As for the grandfather, if I have shown him to be a little foolish, remember he was living in an alien land.

Now like clockwork, a check for fifty cents would appear in the mail every week.

"A rabbi in the house!" said Usher's mother.

"The Workmen's Hebrew School!" said Usher's father.

"A rabbi in the house!" said Usher's mother.

"The Workmen's Hebrew School!" said Usher's father.

"Why not a rabbi?" said Usher's mother.

"A question of principle!"

"What principle?"

"The principle that rabbis turn out only scoundrels and thieves!"

"A new kind of principle!"

"Well, look at your family. A father, a scoundrel; a brother, a thief! Living proof!"

"A rabbi in the house!"

"The Workmen's Hebrew School!"

Stalemate! Nothing moved!

We, Usher, his mother, and I, were sitting in Usher's house having tea and black bread. The electricity had been shut off and a pair of lighted candles stood on the table.

"I'll die of shame if anyone comes tonight," said Usher's mother.

"Dat's all right!" I said. "We've been sitting in the dark for two weeks already in my house."

"No electric for two weeks?" said Usher's mother, suddenly grown curious, and then as if she did not want Usher to hear: "Go down and hang up the sign."

My friend Usher departed from the kitchen with a "Furnished Room to Let" sign.

"It's nice to have no electric," I said, looking at the flame quivering at the top of the candle. "Everything is yellow. And shadows move up and down and ghosts come!"

I don't think she knew what I was talking about.

Then all of a sudden, in this kitchen while the yellow flame came from the candlelight, and ghostly shadows moved up and down, I began to feel old, so very old, as old as Usher's mother, for this tender and pious woman began to speak to me as if to an equal.

"Young one," she said, "things are really bad!"

"Yes," I said, "they're killing Jews in Hamburg!"

"It's getting worse!" she said.

"Yes," I said, "they're killing Jews in Frankfurt!"

"What does your mother do for bread?"

"She goes to the corner grocery. We got a bill there for seventy-three dollars and fourteen cents cash. They're killing Jews all over the world!"

Somewhere in the back of my head there glimmered the realization that I should have never said this, that if my mother knew what I had told Usher's mother, she would be very angry. But there was something about this woman that made me tell everything.

"Next week my Pop is going to put in an application for relief. We can't pay the rent. My old lady has no money for shoes. She says she'll have to go out and pluck chickens. We owe the iceman money. We owe the egg man and the milkman. We owe! We owe! We owe!" And then taking a sip of tea, I added: "Things are really bad. They're just killing, killing the Jews!"

Suddenly from the stairs there was the sound of people walking up and Usher's excited voice.

"Guests!" cried Usher's mother, running about the kitchen, setting the tablecloth right, wiping the table. "My rich sister from Borough Park! And me with no electric! How can I explain it to her!"

But in walked Usher, smiling and happy, followed by his father carrying a large package covered with a cloth, which he set down on the table.

"Look!" said Usher as he snatched the cover off. "A bird!"

And there on the table, in an enormous metal cage, jumped a tiny yellow canary.

"That's the only thing we're missing!" said Usher's mother. "In the middle of everything, you have to bring a chicken."

"It's not a chicken!" said Usher. "It's a gen-u-ine canary!"

"It's not even a chicken!" said his mother, screwing up her face. "A chicken, at least, we could eat!"

And then she sat down and cried as if her heart would break. "Sing, little bird, sing," she cried. "Sing at my misfortune!"

And as she cried, there in that room with the candles flickering yellow light, and the shadow of the bird looking black and large on the wall, the little yellow bird began to sing.

At first my friend Usher could not do enough for the bird. He fed it, bathed it, saw that it got enough exercise, and covered the cage at night. He even got books on birds and studied up on them. But it wasn't long before his interest lagged and his mother had to take over the care of the bird.

Chirp! Chirp! How that damn bird did chirp! All day long he jumped up and down in his cage, exercising on his swing. And eat! You should have seen him gobble up those seeds! And dirty! All day long you had to clean that cage! And money! Everything would have been all right but the seeds cost money! Because for five cents you could go to New York by subway to look for a job! Chirp!

"What are you working so hard, jumping up and down the cage?" said Usher's mother to the bird. "What are you so happy for?"

But it wasn't long before the bird stopped singing.

"Unhappy house! Unhappy bird!" said Usher's mother.

And now I knew that the bird belonged.

The decision was made one night while Usher's father was reading his paper. He looked up and said, "They're killing Jews in Germany!" By this time the expression had become a kind of salutation on our street, like "Good morning!"

"Just for that," he said, "my boy will get a good Jewish education! We've got to show those damn Germans!"

"A rabbi in the house!" said Usher's mother.

"Yes!" said Usher's father finally. "A rabbi in the house! *And* the Workmen's Hebrew School! Both!"

The pale canary gave a tiny chirp.

And so my hero Usher got more than he had bargained for. Twice a week there came a small, bearded man with curls hanging from his ears, dressed in a long, black gabardine coat and carrying a cane, giving Usher lessons from a book in which you read from right to left. And four times a week Usher put in an appearance at the Workmen's Hebrew School, where Yiddish was spoken.

And now under the most unlikely circumstances, my hero Usher would suddenly burst forth in Hebrew. I remember one Friday night we, Usher, my friends Bibi, Pickles, Robby, and I, were lying on the mattress in our hut, smoking cigarettes, when Usher said:

"There's to be no smoking in this here hut any more!"

"Why not?" said Bibi.

"It's Friday night! No smoking on Friday night!"

"What's Friday night?" asked Bibi.

"You're a Jew, ain't you?"

"Yes," answered Bibi.

"Well, Jews is not supposed to smoke on Friday night!"

"Why not?" asked Bibi.

"Because God said so!" said Usher.

"How do you know He said so?"

"Because Moses said God said so!"

"How do you know Moses said so?"

"Because the Bible says Moses said God said so!"

"How do you know the Bible says so?" asked Bibi.

"Because *Boruch atoh adonoi elohenu melech hoelum asheh*," said Usher.

I don't have to tell you that my hero Usher's Hebrew had nothing to do with the point in question. Later, when I began to study the language, I found out it was the first sentence in the prayer book. And even that had been quoted incorrectly. But it knocked the props from under Bibi.

"What's dat?" said the flabbergasted Bibi.

"Dat's Hebrew, stupid! Don't you know anything?"

"Don't call me stupid!"

"You're real stupid!" said Usher.

"I'm not stupid!"

"You're a Jew, ain't you?"

"Yes!"

"You don't know Hebrew when you hear it. Do you?"

"No."

"Then you're stupid. Every good Jew has to know Hebrew if he wants to get to heaven. Every good Jew knows he's not supposed to smoke on Friday night. And you're not a good Jew!"

"You mean I'm not going to heaven?"

"Dat's right."

"You mean you're going to heaven?"

"Dat's right. There's a place reserved there for me."

"O.K.!" said Bibi. "I'll put out the cigarette."

This was the influence of the rabbi who came to the house; the influence of the Workmen's Hebrew School was of another kind.

"I'm a worker!" announced Usher to his mother one day.

"I didn't hear you," said Usher's mother, shining up one of her empty pots.

"I'm a worker!" repeated Usher. "I'm the salt of the earth!"

"Isn't my Usher wonderful?" she said, turning to me and smiling. "He knows his family's in trouble and he wants to help out."

"But you don't understand!" cried Usher.

"What don't I understand?" said his mother. "What I've forgotten, you'll never know!"

"I'm a socialist!" said Usher.

"So?" said his mother.

"So, I'm a socialist!" said Usher.

"I'm dying!" said Usher's mother, beginning to understand. "A socialist! In my own house! Don't you dare say another word! The walls have ears!"

"Socialist! Socialist! Socialist! I'm a socialist!" said Usher. Bang! Right across the face she smacked him.

"Socialist fool!" cried Usher's mother. "Do you want me to sit out my days mourning for you when they deport you to the other side? This is what comes of the Workmen's Hebrew School. A plague on your father!"

Yes! They were killing Jews in Germany, but they were also killing Jews right on our street. It happened one night that right on our street corner someone shot up Louie the Lip.

"They shot Louie the Lip!" our street cried in awe.

"Louie was shot! Shot right in the back! Some coward shot him in the behind!"

"They shot him in the ass when he wasn't looking! They wouldn't dare shoot The Lip in the front!"

You should have seen the funeral. Old women and children wept. Young women threw garlands of flowers after the hearse. Young girls cried and threw their arms around Louie's henchmen, who followed in big black cars. They screamed, they pushed, they fainted. While our men stood by awed and respectful. Brownsville remembers that funeral to this day: the long line of cars, the streets crowded with people for blocks and blocks around, motorcycle cops preceding the hearse.

Yisgadal veyiskadash shmey robo!

Yes! Our sad and unfortunate street needed Louie the Lip!

Mr. Grossman's grocery. A large corner store. Bags of barley, onions, grits. Barrels of pickles, tomatoes, herring, lox. Windows full of butter and cheese and halvah. Bundles of grapes, bananas, dates, and celery. And right behind the cash register, hanging from a nail, not far from the canned goods (separate department), near the wrapping paper and the cord, hung the bills. And on those damn bills stood Goldberg, Goldblatt, Greenbaum, Greenberg, Feinberg, Feinerman, and Hammerschlag.

Early one morning Grossman himself, in a long white apron and a pencil behind his right ear, appeared in Usher's house.

"I picked you," said Mr. Grossman, "only because you and I belong in the same boat."

Usher's mother was all ears.

"I'm a businessman and you're a landlady. I would not ask anybody else on our block. Stop me if I'm wrong. I need a boy in my store for the two-week holiday rush."

"You mean my Usher?" asked the astonished mother.

"He's reliable, I hope?"

"Reliable? How could he not be reliable? He's learning Hebrew in two places."

"Two places!" exclaimed Grossman. "I've got to have him!"

"He'll probably end up a rabbi," said Usher's mother.

"There's no question. I've got to have the boy. And I'm giving him a fifty-cent raise even before he begins."

And that was how our socialist went to work at Grossman's.

I never knew how dependent we were on my hero Usher. Because with Usher working, there was nothing for my friends Bibi, Pickles, Robby, and myself to do. The lumberyard was monotonous. Sitting and smoking in the hut was boring. Our ball-playing lost its zest. Things were just no fun any more. We would pass by Grossman's, and putting our noses to the window, look in and see my hero in his long white apron and a pencil stuck in his right ear, looking busy and important.

"Look at Usher," Robby would say. "Who would have ever thought it!"

Usher himself would come out, looking at us in disdain as if he had never known us.

"Hey, youse kids!" he would say, without batting an eyelash. "Get a move on you! You're blocking traffic. Da customers can't get in."

"What's the matter, Ush? Getting too stuck up for your old friends!" cried Pickles.

"I ain't arguing with you," said Usher. "If youse kids don't move on, I'll call the police. So get outta here and don't argue with me. Go away, children. Go ahead and play with your dollies. I got work to do!"

"I hope he breaks his neck, that damn Usher!" cried Pickles, as we began to hotfoot it down the street.

"My mother says you're to give me ten cents so I can go to the movies," said a little child in front of the counter. "Put it on the bill."

"You can't get ten cents," said Usher.

"Why not?" asked the child. "My mother said so!"

"I don't care if your grandmother said so. You can't get ten cents until you go back and bring me a note, signed and sealed by your mother, telling me to give you ten cents," said Usher.

"O.K.," said the child as he began to thread his way out of Grossman's between the stacked bags and barrels of sour pickles.

"And remember—no monkey-business!" Usher sternly cried after the child.

"O.K.," said the child.

I was standing in line at Grossman's having an order filled for my mother. And I could see my friend Usher running up the aisle for canned salmon, down the aisle for tuna fish, into the back for eggs, up front for herring, down below for barley.

"My mother says you're to give me ten cents so I can go to the movies."

There was the child standing at the counter again.

"You got a note, signed and sealed?" asked Usher.

The child handed him a sealed envelope. Tearing it open and

reading it, my hero Usher finally looked up and said, "It's a fake! You're not getting no ten cents to go to the movies. In fact, you keep this up, you won't go to the movies, you'll go to prison, for free!"

The child retreated, stumbling over a box of eggs.

"The nerve of dat kid!" said Usher, turning to me. "Trying to steal ten cents!"

Down the barrel for a pickle! Into the bin for butter! Up the ladder for peaches! On the counter for cake!

And would you believe it, there was the child again at the counter, handing Usher another envelope.

"This is much better," said Usher, reading as he rang up the register, and taking out ten cents he tossed it across the counter at the child. "Here's the dime, and next time do it the right way. You have five minutes to get to the movies before the prices change. And remember, if you don't get there on time, you can't come back here for the other fifteen cents!"

Zip! Right out of the store flew the child!

"You gotta teach those damn kids a lesson!" said Usher.

Mr. Grossman nodded his head in approval.

"It says here," said Grossman, pointing to his newspaper, "that a milk truck turned over on the highway. Usher, put one cent extra on the milk."

And Usher ran to take out a small tab from below the counter, and sliding it into a slot on the milk bin raised the price one cent.

"Hey, Grossman!" cried one of the women on line. "What's this business? Raising the price of the milk a penny!"

"Milk shortage!" said Grossman.

A short silence. Mr. Grossman turned the page of his newspaper and continued to read.

"Hm! What do you know? General Motors is going on strike. Raise the tuna fish three cents!"

"What do you call this?" cried the woman. "Three cents more on the tuna fish! Your prices grow on the shelves!"

"Transportation tie-up. Don't you read the newspapers? Here! It says so here!" and Grossman proceeded to show the item to the woman.

"Oh, I'm dying!" he cried as he fell back from the newspaper. "They're killing Jews in Germany! Usher! Usher! Quick! Five cents more on the herring!"

"Yes," said Mr. Grossman to Usher's mother, "your son is real honest."

"That's because I used to bang him on the knuckles if he took anything when he was a child."

"I tested him the first day. I left twenty-five cents on the counter purposely. I threw ten cents on the floor. I hid fifteen cents in the potato sack. And would you believe it, at the end of the day he brought me fifty cents. It added up right. You can be proud of him."

"Yes," said Usher's mother, "he adds well. Got a good head."

And as Mr. Grossman left, she turned to me and said, "Thank God, I banged that socialist monkey-business out of his head."

But (and this I hate to say) it turned out that Usher had not gotten that "monkey-business" out of his head.

There I was behind Jakie the Snotnose in Grossman's grocery, waiting my turn. Up the aisle went Usher for canned salmon! Down the aisle for tuna fish! Into the back for eggs! Up front for a herring! Down below for barley! When suddenly (and I could not believe my eyes), after handing Jakie the barley, I saw, or at least I thought I saw, my hero Usher suddenly dart below the counter and coming up throw an additional fistful of barley into Jakie's bag. It happened so quickly I thought it did not happen at all.

Then I remember the time I was in line behind an old lady of our street who asked for a herring, and saw Usher wrapping it in a newspaper, when suddenly, looking both ways, what should he do but throw an extra tail into the package. God! A thief!

Now I began to see it all. Fistfuls of barley. Tails of herring. Slices of sour pickle. A loose onion. An extra potato. Cheese in the butter. Cereal in the milk. That crook, Usher, was practically giving the store away!

I remember the to-do in Grossman's grocery the day Usher was found out. Sooner or later, I knew it was bound to happen, but personally I would have preferred it to happen later. There was such shouting and screaming from Grossman that day you would have thought the world was coming to an end.

It must have been that dopey Jakie who was responsible. Or was it Usher's father? Or the Workmen's Hebrew School? Or the sad and beautiful Miriam, Jakie's mother? Or was it Grossman's grocery itself? Perhaps it was our unfortunate street that was responsible. However, no matter who, it was Usher who was caught.

There was Jakie the Snotnose asking for a dozen eggs.

Into the box for bagels. On the counter for lox. Up the aisle for salmon. Down for tuna fish. When plop, my hero Usher, shooting a glance at Grossman, threw an extra egg into Jakie's bag.

"You're givin' me thirteen eggs," said the Snotnose, who was very smart in school. "I only want a dozen."

Mr. Grossman began to glare.

"Sorry," said Usher as he carefully withdrew the extra egg. "Mistakes happen."

"My mother wants a half a quarter of a half a pound of barley," said Jakie.

Down below for the barley. And while Grossman wasn't looking, plop, there went an extra handful of the stuff into the bag.

"What's that?" cried Mr. Grossman.

"Sorry," said Usher as he put the extra handful back under the counter. "My hand slipped."

"You don't mean slipped! You mean slippery!" said Mr. Grossman, slowly awakening to the truth of things.

"My mother wants you to write it on the bill," said Jakie the Snotnose.

"Next!" cried Usher.

The line moved forward. And it was not long before that dopey Jakie returned carrying an extra egg in his hand.

"You made a mistake. You gave me thirteen eggs," he said as he put the egg on the counter. "My mother told me to give it back."

You should have heard Grossman screaming and hollering. You should have seen the expressions of the ladies of our street standing there in line as this deluge of words surged through the store. People stopped and looked into the windows. A little crowd collected outside the front door.

"What's happening?" asked one of our neighbors.

"Grossman caught a thief stealing from his store."

"A thief—on our street?" asked another.

"A thief—from our street!" echoed a third.

"You're fired! Fired! Fired!" screamed Grossman. "Crook! Giving away my store! Fired! Fired! Fired!"

There is no point in my telling you the rest. Suffice it to say that Grossman ranted so, he began to bring in things that had nothing to do with the situation. He even brought in his grandfather.

"My grandfather worked all his life!" he cried. "And in the famine he died with his legs all swollen and his stomach blown up! Oh! My poor, poor grandfather! How he would weep to see what happened to me here today—and in my own store! Ten years I worked in a shop to be able to save enough to buy this store! Ten years! And yesterday the wholesaler sends me a bunch of rotten tomatoes! Rotten tomatoes! Who can live from all this? And as if that isn't enough, eggs they give me with specks of blood in them! How can I sell this to Jews, without sin! Flies in the milk! Stale salmon, even in the cans! The barley with ants in them! And as if this isn't enough—a thief in my own store! Right under my own nose! God sits in His heaven and watches! Why, God? Why?"

The women in the store suddenly held their breath in fear.

"You're fired once! You're fired twice! You're fired three times!" screamed Grossman.

The women in the store breathed again.

Flushing red, ashamed, his head bowed, unable to walk erect, his heart bleeding, the end of the world, so full of shame that he was unable even to weep, the outcast put his apron down on the counter.

Down the aisle past the tuna fish. Out of the counter near the barley sack. Under the bunch of yellow bananas. Past the Greek salad, the potato salad, and the cole slaw, and out into the open.

Yes! The "socialist" was fired—but good!

I think Bibi, Pickles, Robby, and I were glad this happened to Usher, after he had treated us like dirt just because he had a job.

"That lousy Usher!" said Robby.

"He was a thief! He is a thief!" said Pickles. "He will always be a thief!"

"A crook! Dat's what he is!" said Bibi. "A no-good crook!"

We were sitting in our hut playing poker by candlelight when suddenly a big black cockroach ran across the mattress.

"Kill it!" cried Bibi.

When who should walk in, carrying a pack of cigarettes, as cool as you please, but Usher himself.

"Nobody is killing nothing!" said he, sitting down on the mattress and opening his pack of cigarettes. "There's no look-out watching on the roof. An enemy could easily surround you without a challenge. I knew I couldn't trust you guys the minute my back was turned."

And here our long-lost Usher took out a cigarette with a

flourish, bent down to light it at the candle, and began puffing away.

"How about a drag?" said Pickles.

Usher ignored him.

"Say, Ush!" said Robby. "Is it true that Grossman keeps a pack of money hidden in a barley sack under the counter?"

"The rumor is false," said Usher.

"How about his underwear? Is it true he hasn't changed his underwear in the last ten years?"

"The rumor is true," said Usher.

"Is it true," asked Robby, "that Grossman kicked you out?"

"The rumor is a rotten lie!" said Usher. "We just didn't see eye to eye. I believe everything should be free. Grossman doesn't."

"How about a cigarette, Usher?" asked Pickles.

"Buy your own cigarettes, you cheap chiseler," said Usher, then added, "Everything should be free! Like the birds! Like the bees!"

I must admit the idea of everything being free appealed to me. I saw pictures of a table spread with all kinds of delicate pastries topped with whipped cream. I saw chocolate cakes and roast duck with cranberry sauce, *gefilte* fish and horse radish, stuffed derma with roasted plums, rolled cabbage and meat, soup with *mandlen*. I saw and saw and saw.

"Everything should be free?" asked Robby.

"Yes!" said our fanatic.

"Like the birds?" asked Robby.

"Like the birds!" echoed Usher.

"Like canaries, maybe?" asked Robby.

"Like canaries!" echoed Usher.

"Is a canary a bird?" asked Robby.

"Canaries is birds!" said Usher emphatically.

It was too late.

"I know a canary that ain't free!" said Robby.

"Where's that damn canary?" cried the unthinking Usher.

"We'll free it!"

"It's in a big cage!" said Robby.

"Where? Where?" exclaimed Usher.

"It's in a big cage—hanging in your own house!" said Robby, springing the trap.

"What?" cried Usher. "You mean my bird?"

"Dat's what I mean!"

But Usher was not to be daunted.

"Well, let's free him from the prison! Everything should be free!"

And we all rose up and dashed out of our hut.

"Free the canaries from their cages!" shouted the fanatic as we raced down the street. "Free all the canaries from their cages!"

With what fury we raced up to Usher's house, I cannot describe to you. I remember the whole thing as impossibly insane. There we were, panting and racing; our eyes staring, our faces flushed, our bodies freezing from the winter cold. And as we ran through the streets and up the stairs, into our possession came pieces of metal, sticks, glass, string, and all sorts of things.

Before you knew it, we were thrusting our faces against the cage. There was the bird, near the window in the cold winter twilight, the lights of Usher's house out, the kitchen cold and forlorn, the house deserted. And suddenly he chirped (if you could call it a chirp), his little, sad chirp. I compared the enormousness of our feelings with the smallness of the chirp. And it did not make sense to me. Something is wrong, I thought to myself as I saw the bird looking oh! so sad and small, while about him glared the large ravenous faces of Usher, Pickles, Robby, Bibi, and myself.

Why so much fury? Why so much screaming, shoving, and pushing? For what? For the small, sad bird? Why? But I did not dare to say a word, while the hot breath of my compatriots, their chests heaving with excitement, their eyes brilliant with expectation, shot through the bars of the cage and seemed to fix the bird into a kind of trance.

Like a conquering hero, like the leader of a herd, it remained for Usher to make the decision to open the door of the cage.

"Come out! Come out! Come out, little bird!" he panted.

The bird retreated to a far corner.

"Come on, birdie!" coaxed Usher. "Here's a polly-seed! Doesn't the little birdie want his polly-seed?"

Deeper into the cage retreated the bird.

"He doesn't want to come out!" cried Robby. "Let me try!"

"Here, birdie, birdie, birdie!" called Robby, coaxing him with a seed as the bird fluttered wildly to an opposite corner of the cage.

"You dumb bird! Come on out!" cried Robby as he began to thrash his hand wildly about inside the cage. "I won't hurt you!"

But the more wildly his hand thrashed, the more wildly the canary jumped about the cage.

"Don't you understand, little bird?" cried Pickles. "We don't want to hurt you! We want to set you free!"

And here Pickles inserted a stick into the cage to drive out the bird. And the bird parried it, now this way, now that.

"Throw some glass on the floor," said Bibi. "They hate glass!"

And so pieces of glass came showering down. Sticks were thrown in. Water was splashed. The cage was shoved, rolled, and pushed. And still the bird would not leave the cage.

"What a stupid bird!" cried Robby.

"You dumb canary!" cried Pickles, banging his fists against the cage. "Don't you want to be free?"

We all began to shout angrily at the bird, but he would not come out.

"Say, Usher! What do you say we go back and have a game

of pinochle!" cried Robby. "This here bird is a moron! They cheated your old man when he bought this dumb canary!"

And just as we had raced up, so we raced down.

But the little yellow canary would not come out of the cage.

There was weeping in Usher's house the next morning.

"The chicken is dead!" cried Usher's mother. "Oh! Oh! The poor little bird has gone and left us!"

Aroused, my hero, the giver-away of Grossman's barley and Grossman's eggs and Grossman's herring-tails, the would-be emancipator of wingéd things, good pinochle player, confederate, and friend, ran quickly into the unheated kitchen.

"Sing, little bird! Sing!" wept Usher's mother to the dead canary. "Sing at your misfortune!"

But the little yellow bird would not sing.

"While you live," wept Usher's mother to herself, "you dare not sing; when you die you cannot!"

They took the bird out of the cage. Usher brought him down to the back yard. And if I know Usher, as he buried the stubborn bird he must have said *Kaddish*.

"*Yisgadal veyiskadash shmey rabo.*"

And that is how one canary was freed from his cage.

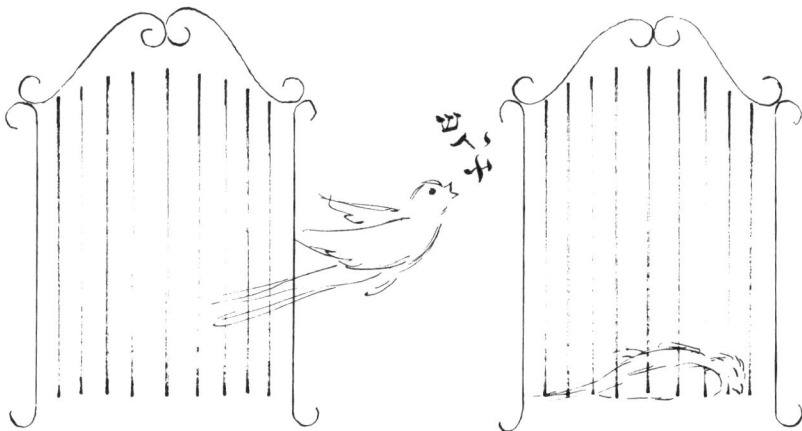

No Golden Tombstones For Me!

"TREASURE!" SAID USHER'S MOTHER. "COME HERE and look me straight in the face and tell me what you see."

"Nothing! I see nothing, Ma," said Usher.

"The truth, now, the truth. Tell me what you really see?"

"Nothing! Nothing!" said our hero, dangerously walking a precipice.

She was sitting over a mirror at the kitchen table and had been examining herself for a long time. The whites of her eyes were red from weeping. The lids were swollen.

"Don't you see, perhaps, a new gray hair?"

"No, Ma, I don't see no new gray hairs."

"Look over here, near the eyes! A new wrinkle, perhaps?"

"No, Ma, there's no new wrinkle there. It's clean as a whistle."

"Ah!" she said, wiping a bitter tear from her chin. "They come—so many of them. I look around, and before you know it another one has been added. Just when I get used to the last one, plop! comes a new stranger to my head! Where do they all come from?"

"Yes," said Usher, "you just can't stop 'em."

"But let's not worry," she sighed, lifting a gray hair. "Here, take this one and pull it out."

The gallant Usher set his teeth together and quickly extracted the hair, while his mother, with closed eyes, started under his hand.

"Usher," she said, digging into the pocket of her housedress, "I'm giving you ten cents to go to the movies. And I'm giving it to you for a special reason. Never mind what the reason is. Enjoy yourself!"

My friend Usher almost collapsed. Going to the movies was an event usually associated with cajolery, stamping on the floor, and even a tear here and there until the fortress capitulated and opened its pocketbook. You had to shout as loud as our Jews did to overthrow the walls of Jericho, employ cat-and-mouse tactics that would have done credit to any general. And now Usher was told to go enjoy himself!

"You don't have to give me ten cents to go to the movies because I pulled out one of your gray hairs," said the suspicious Usher.

"If I had to give you money for every one of my gray hairs, I'd go broke!" said his mother. "I got another reason."

"I ain't taking it!" said Usher.

"A stubborn mule!" said his mother. "Just like his father!"

"I ain't taking it!" said Usher.

"Please," she pleaded, as I watched, dumbfounded by this

reversal of things. "You're doing me a favor. Take the money and go to the movies!"

I could not contain myself.

"Do her a favor and take the money, Ush!" I cried, afraid she might change her mind.

"I ain't doin' nobody no favors," said our hero.

"Why not, if I may be so bold as to ask?" said his mother.

"I gotta know the reason you're givin' me ten cents to go to the movies."

"Listen to him!" said his mother, turning to me. "He's got to know reasons. I'm telling you—a real intellectual!"

Then turning to Usher, she said, "This a special picture. It teaches you."

"O.K.! Gimmie the ten cents!" said Usher, and then added: "Also, ten cents for him. And five cents for candy."

With infinite care the good woman dug into her housedress and came up with the coins. Examining each one tenderly, she slowly delivered them up to us.

"You're a good boy," she said to me. "It's a pleasure to give you ten cents to go to the movies. Your mother will bless me for the lesson it will teach."

As Usher and I began to make our way down the street, I felt an awful foreboding.

"It ain't right," I said.

"What ain't right?"

"It ain't right—getting the money so easy, without screamin' or hollerin'. Something is wrong."

"Nothing's wrong," said Usher. "What're you making a lot out of nothing for? She wants us to enjoy ourselves. Dat's all! We're doin' her a favor!"

Our movie house inside was Byzantine rococo with splendid spiral columns from which hung braziers and such. Mosques and minarets jutted out all over the place. And as if that were not enough, the Men's Room was adorned with a statue of Voltaire. Outside the Ladies' Room stood a bust of Marie Antoinette (as if she had sense enough not to go in). And while the inside of the theater was Byzantine, the outside was Brownsville baroque (and this I will not dare to describe to you). Yes, half-a-dozen architectural styles had been amalgamated for the benefit of our Jews. But it was all wasted on our lousy street, for in spite of everything it was known as "The Dump."

Yet I would not go so far as to say that the street was completely wrong. On warm days the atmosphere of that place would be filled with the odor of sweat and urine, while the harassed manager would come running down the aisles, spraying the air with essences from a flit-gun.

First we would wait on line, a thousand shouting, screaming, pushing children. Then the thousand would sit inside, stamping two thousand feet in unison, waiting for the film to go on. Here someone would let fly an orange, there someone's lunch would sail through the air.

"Who did that?" the sorry-looking manager would scream.

"Shut your face, you lousy little greaseball!" would come a voice (and this from a "greaseball" himself) as the frenetic manager would dash over to seize the culprit.

Bang! A bag filled with water would come flying from the balcony, bouncing against the Byzantine rococo (I swear it was the Hagia Sophia) and spilling out over the heads of at least ten victims.

"Hey, frog-face, why don't you put a roof on this damn dump!" would come a voice from the other side of the theater. "It's raining in cats and dogs!"

And now the poor manager would dash up to the balcony to see where that bag of water had come from.

Pop! Bang! Somebody down below would burst a blown-up paper bag with his fist.

"Fireman! Fireman! Save my child!" would come a high

falsetto from down below. "They're shooting him in the mouth!"

Finally the defeated manager would dash up to the projection booth and scream, "Start the picture! They're going to rip the house down!"

Screams! Stamping of feet! Hurray! The lights would go down. Suddenly a hush would fall and on the screen would appear an American flag.

Groans! Boos!

"Hey, manager, cut it out! What'd you think we paid ten cents for—to go back to school?"

Now the poor manager would be downstairs, banging against the back of a seat with a stick.

"Everybody up! Salute the American flag and sing 'The Star-Spangled Banner'. This is a free country!" he would scream.

"Hey, frog-face!" would come a voice from the darkness. "If it's a free country, why do I hafta pay ten cents to go to the movies?"

More groans and moans! The squeaking of seats as we stood up. The Pledge of Allegiance. "The Star-Spangled Banner" in a dozen keys.

The picture of an old lady flashed across the screen.

"A lousy picture!" groaned Usher.

Groans! Moans! Boos!

"Hey frog-face! I thought this was a cowboy picture. I want my money back!" would come a voice from out of the darkness.

"Mama! Mama! I don't want any castor oil today!" would come another voice.

"Hey, lady!" would come a heavier voice, this of someone older. "I don't need the bottle, but I sure could use the nipple!"

But soon enough silence fell and a thousand pairs of eyes were riveted to that screen.

First the old lady cooked and worked. It showed her with a

large family around her, how she took care of everybody, fed them, made the beds, washed the clothes. She worked real hard. And when the kids would fight, she would set everything to rights. And she never complained. She went right on working, cooking, washing, and all that.

You could hear a pin drop in the quiet of the theater. They like the picture, I thought, because everybody has stopped eating and nobody is going to the toilet.

Now the old lady's children were growing up. Some got jobs. Others went to school. But still the poor old lady worked and worked and worked, cleaning clothes, washing floors. And as if this were not enough, late at night when everyone was asleep, she took in sewing.

Suddenly guns began to roar. An army flashed across the screen. A bomb burst and a body flew up in the air.

Now why would they take somebody and shoot him up just like that? For me? Just to show it in a picture? Not on your life! They would not kill somebody just to show us! It was some kind of trick! Maybe a dummy! Yes, I decided it was a fake, but that did not mean I could look. I turned my head away, only to see behind me all the eyes lit up like electric bulbs, watching in the dark. Yes! Armies and killing we liked.

Now the youngest was going off to war. The old lady cried and waved a handkerchief at her son from the sidelines. She jumped out of the crowd and hung on to him as he marched through the streets. It was sad.

Sad? The eyes behind me told me it was tragic. Blinking lights, that's what they were, as children wept in the dark. Awful sighs and terrible moans rose from the audience, all the more agonizing because none dared do it aloud. I looked at Usher—he had gone off—weeping, weeping, weeping willows.

And still she washed and cooked and took in sewing until, would you believe it! No! you would not! Her lousy children, the traitors who stayed home, threw her out of her own house, so that she had to go over the hill to the poorhouse.

Our theater was enraged. Shouts were heard. The balcony

came to life as here and there children rose to scream imprecations.

Now the old lady was washing and scrubbing and cleaning all over again, over the hill in the poorhouse. Her hair is white. She is very old. When who should come home but her soldier boy!

Cheers! Cheers!

"Where is Mom?" he asks.

"Mom is over the hill in the poorhouse," says his brother, the traitor who did not go to war.

"What! My Mom over the hill in the poorhouse! How did you dare do this!"

Bang! He gives him a sock in the jaw, a left to the right, a right to the left, a left to the left!

Up rose the audience, Usher and myself included, to throw imaginary punches at our celluloid adversary.

And now the soldier boy throws the dirty dog to the ground. He drags him out on the road and over the hill to the poorhouse.

Cheers! Hoorays! Banging on the floor! Wild paroxysms! We were as one with the soldier boy.

Bang! He throws his brother right at the feet of his mother in the poorhouse.

But that dumb mother, instead of giving that dirty dog a kick in the face, smiles and forgives the traitor. Now, I ask you, is this a good ending? And with her two sons, hand in hand, she leaves the poorhouse to go over the hill to her own house.

Lights!

We had been wrung dry!

"It was a lousy picture!" said Usher, wiping a tear from his eye.

Now the manager was banging his stick against the side of a seat.

"All youse kids who saw the picture once, leave through the side exits!"

Excitement ran through the audience. A few cowards got up

to leave. Some hid under the seats, some ran to hide in the toilets, others just waited to be thrown out, as a crew of ushers went up and down the aisles to examine each individual stub. Here and there a child would attempt to rush through the cordon to an area of the theater that had already been screened. Plunk! Plunk! The ushers grabbed one here and one there and hauled them out amid loud protests.

How Usher and I managed to remain, I do not know. It was possible that it took so long to screen that crowd that "Frog-face" decided his schedule was in jeopardy and started up the movie again. Still, there we were, the lights down again, with the same old lady cleaning and scrubbing and sewing, and the same soldier boy, and the poorhouse over the hill. And the same children reacted in the same way at exactly the same moments. First the stillness, then the terror at the army scenes, the moans and groans as the mother went over the hill to the poorhouse, the cheers when the soldier boy returned, the bedlam when he drags the culprit over the hill to the poorhouse.

"A lousy picture!" said Usher.

"Not enough shooting!" I said.

We were coming up the stairs to Usher's house. It was now early evening and twilight was beginning to fall.

"Sh!" said Usher's mother as we entered the kitchen. "Not a word. Your father's asleep."

Then opening the nearly empty icebox, she took out some sour cream which she set on the table. Then taking a banana from the window sill and some black bread from the bread box, she said:

"Here, eat. It'll make you grow good."

"Don't eat in Usher's house," my mother had warned me. "Don't take the bread away from their mouths. They have nothing to eat as it is!"

"Well?" asked Usher's mother as he sat gobbling up the bananas and cream.

"Well, what?" asked Usher.

"You know," she said. "The picture? Did you like the picture?"

"Oh, the picture," he said, and quickly brightened. "It was a good picture!"

And as quickly as he had brightened, that was how quickly he unbrightened.

"Did it learn you anything?" his mother asked, moving cautiously.

"Yeh, Ma, it learned me a lot!"

"And what did it learn you?"

"It learned me: 'Don't give up the ship!' 'Remember the Maine!' 'Don't shoot until you see the whites of their eyes!' "

"Anything else? About fathers and mothers I mean?"

A piece of wood! It was as if she were talking to a piece of wood.

"Yeh! You gotta be good to your father and mother."

"That's a good son," and then after a thoughtful pause in which I could see a tear springing to her eye and falling down her cheek, she pleaded with that lousy Usher: "Usher, will you be good to your mother when she's old and gray?"

"Sure, Ma, I'll be good to my mother!"

"Will you remember that your mother worked and slaved for you and that she fed you?" she sighed. "Here, have another piece of banana."

"Sure! Sure, Ma!"

At that moment Usher's father came in from the bedroom, his eyes still red from sleep. Taking a glass from the cupboard, he went to the sink to turn on the faucet.

"What do you want?" he said to her, very irritated. "A promise that you'll get a golden tombstone?"

"I don't want no golden tombstone," she said.

"Don't you know there's a crisis in America?" he asked.

"I know, I know," she said. "If I didn't know the empty icebox tells me."

"Then what do you want—the child to give you a mortgage on the future?"

As he retreated back to the bedroom, she shouted after him, "In America they say, 'Mind your own business!' And what Usher and I have to say is none of your business!"

"Sure, Ma, sure," continued Usher. "I'll buy you a new dress and two pairs of shoes."

"You don't have to buy me two pairs of shoes," she said. "I'll be satisfied if you buy me one pair."

"I'll take you out dancing. And won't let you wash floors. I'll even get you a maid."

"And what would I do with a maid? I wouldn't even know how to speak to her."

"I'll give you money and let you go to the beauty parlor to bleach your hair red."

"Me—with red hair! Only whores go to the beauty parlor to dye their hair red," she said, then added, "And when I die?"

"A golden tombstone!"

"I don't want no golden tombstone. A plain one of stone is good enough for me," she said. "Will you say *Kaddish* for me, my son?"

"I'll say *Kaddish*. I'll say it for three years. I'll put lots of flowers on your grave. And every year I'll put up candles on the gas stove and light them. And on your tombstone I'll put stones to ward off the evil spirits. And you won't have to go over the hill to the poorhouse to wash floors."

"You're too good to me!" she said.

"And now," said Usher, "gimmie ten cents!"

Into her housedress she dug again. And as Usher and I sped down into the street, I remember she called after us.

"Don't forget to say," she called, "don't forget to say *Kaddish* for me when I die!"

"Where do you think you're going?" demanded Usher, blocking the path of a small child on the street.

"I'm going to The Dump to see a picture."

"What a waste of good money," said Usher.

"What do you mean—what a waste of good money?" asked the child.

"A lousy picture!" said Usher.

"Yes!" I said. "You're wasting your good money if you go! It's a lousy picture! It's all about an old lady! And all she does is clean, clean, clean! And nobody dies!"

They're Killing Jews on Sackman Street!

REB LEVI, A TINY MAN WITH EARLOCKS SHOWING from under his hat, with caftan long and black, was going from house to house on our street. He went up to see the Feather-Plucker, came down and walked by Fat Moe the Dope, walked to see Gussie the Beautician, visited Mandelbaum the Tenant, walked past Louie the Lip, visited Blickstein the Butcher, Parker the Barber, and now stood in front of my friend Usher the Landlord's house.

"Hey, Usher!" I said from the curbstone. "What's the rabbi doing in front of your house?"

"He's looking," said Usher.

"What's he looking at?"

"There's no law that says he can't look," said Usher. "If he wants to look, he can look."

"Hey, Usher!" I said. "What's the rabbi going up your stairs?"

"He's going up to ask for money," said Usher. "Don't worry—he'll be down soon. When my father sees him, he'll give him—but good! My father don't like rabbis. He says they're all crooks."

"Hey, Usher!" I said. "Why ain't the rabbi coming down out of your house?"

"You're absolutely right," said Usher. "He should've been down a long time ago. Maybe something happened."

Putting a rabbi with Usher's father in one room meant trouble, and so, immediately Usher and I went racing across the street and up into the Landlord's house.

Into the house we ran, expecting the worst; instead, there sat Usher's mother and the rabbi quietly at the kitchen table.

"Is this the way to come into a house when a rabbi is here?" asked Usher's mother. "Sit down and show some respect!"

And so Usher and I sat down at the table, but not before his mother took out a rag, wet it, and wiped his face amid loud protests.

"Sh!" she said. "Your father's asleep! No noise! Sit down and listen. Maybe you'll learn something."

And so Usher and I, Usher with his face nice and clean, sat down, staring into the face of the rabbi.

"You were saying—?" said Usher's mother to the rabbi.

"I was saying," said Reb Levi, "I was saying that the roof of the *shul* is caving in. Lumber, we need to fix it. Money, we need for lumber. And so I came to you."

Usher's mother's face was suffused with light.

"Is it right?" asked the rabbi. "Is it right that when it rains and Jews are praying down below that rain should come down upon them? Is it right, I ask you?"

"No!" she answered. "It ain't right!"

"And when the plaster from the ceiling begins to fall down, piece by piece! Is it right that we should get it on the head? You're a good Jewish woman—tell me!" he asked.

"A good Jewish woman! My sins are as full as the ocean is wide," she sighed. "But it ain't right!"

And she rose, went to the cupboard, and extracted from the deep interior a little metal box. Prying it open, she took out some coins and handed them to the rabbi.

"God bless you!" said Reb Levi.

"I wish I could give more," she said. "But now go, go quickly!" And to Usher she said, "Show Reb Levi the way downstairs."

Usher and I rose to lead him into the hallway. And I remember that just as the door closed behind us, I could hear Usher's father come into the kitchen, then the click of a switch.

"Electric cost money!" came his voice as the kitchen went into darkness.

At about this time, there lived a Pole named Big Pyotr not far from our street. And this Pole had a wife named Mrs. Pyotr, a son named Little Pyotr, and a daughter named Mary. And in our neighborhood they were the only Christians for miles around.

Big Pyotr had a house that stood removed from the street. Around this house was a big yard, where he kept all kinds of junk, which he collected God knows where and God knows how: old broken automobile parts, flat tires, pieces of lumber, broken baby carriages, plumbing for toilets, glass for windows, and all kinds of things. Once in a while, he sold something—a washer for a faucet, a seat for a toilet, a wheel for a carriage, or whatever you needed. You had only to ask for something, and he would turn up with it.

I remember standing outside of Usher's house when Big Pyotr became the subject of conversation.

"What's he doing on our street?" asked Parker the Barber.

"A *goy* is also a person!" Usher's father answered.

"I know what kind of a person Pyotr is!" Mandelbaum the Tenant said, standing outside his dry-goods store. "Eats, he eats like a horse! Drinks, he drinks like a fish! Steals like a wolf! A head like an ox! I trust him like I trust a snake!"

"One thing at least I can say for him is that he lives right next to the *shul*," Gussie the Beautician said, trying to be fair.

"Some recommendation!" answered Usher's father.

"He lives right next to the *shul*, all right," Mandelbaum the Tenant said. "Comes time to say prayers in the evening, then the Polack is banging away, fixing a washboard. A Jew goes to *shul* to say *maariv*. Is there anything wrong in that? Then, zip! zip! the Polack is sawing wood. He doesn't have time all day to saw wood, but when *maariv* comes, he saws. And when good people, all dressed up, go to *shul* on Saturday morning, what do they see as they pass but a drunken Polack standing outside his gate drinking from a bottle. Is this a sight for Jews to see right before they enter a Holy Place? If he were only a *goy*, I wouldn't mind. This is not a *goy*. It's not even a person. It's a Polack!"

"I won't hear another word against the Polack!" Usher's father cried. "It's true, he's a Polack, but the Polack is a worker too!"

"Some worker," Mandelbaum the Tenant jeered. "I know the kind of worker he is. He works hard stealing from us. Let him but smell out an empty house and hotch! potch! the plumbing is gone! Put something in front of your nose, and before you can breathe once, pish! pash! the Polack came! and the Polack took! and the Polack went! Whatever belongs to you, belongs to him."

"What's a *goy* doing on our street?" Parker the Barber asked.

"All I know," Blickstein the Butcher said, "is that his wife is a cash customer. She comes into the store, buys kosher meat— the best cuts. And she never argues about price."

"No wonder he likes her!" said Parker the Barber.

"And why shouldn't she buy kosher meat?" asked Usher's father. "Where else could she buy any other kind of meat?"

"And on Friday she comes into the grocery," said Grossman the Grocer, "and buys candles."

"Saving on electric," said Usher's father, the expert. "But I'll excuse her. She's a simple *shicksie*."

"Simple!" cried Mandelbaum. "Did you forget already how they burned us and killed us, left and right, in Poland? Did you forget? It was only yesterday! Because if *you* forgot, I still remember! The earth trembled from those hooligans, those 'simple' souls, those bastards! They were simple, all right. To kill a Jew was very simple to them—like killing a pig! What are those bastards doing on our street? Didn't we have enough of them in Poland?"

"The world is for everybody—even for *goyim*," insisted Usher's father.

"Yes, the world is for everybody—for everybody but Jews!" said Mandelbaum the Tenant.

"Even for Jews, even for Jews," persisted Usher's father.

"What's the Polack doing on our street? That's what I want to know," asked Parker the Barber.

Usher and I were standing outside the candy store, peering into the window.

"I wish I had a dollar," said Usher, with his face against the plate glass.

"What would you buy?" I asked.

"I'd buy that train, the one with the smokestack and the signal light in the front," said he, pointing into the window.

"If *I* had a dollar," I said, "I'd buy that metal racing car and the army with the tin soldiers for the other fifty cents. What's the good of throwing away a buck on only one toy when you can buy two for the same money?"

Usher thought a while, then turned to me and said, "Ask me again what I'd do if I had a dollar."

"Usher," I said, "what would you do if you had a dollar?"

"If I had a dollar, I'd buy the lotto game, the dominoes, the checkerboard, the pack of cards, the whistle, the brass knuckles, the handcuffs, the gun, the paper bullets, and the bull's-eye!" he said, counting on his fingers. "That makes ten. Ten cents each. Ten times ten is one hundred cents or one dollar. That way I would have ten things for the same dollar. When I get tired of the lotto, a little brass knuckle work would help out. When I get tired of the brass knuckles, bang! I'd shoot right into the middle of the bull's-eye. You never know when a gun comes in handy."

Suddenly, from below, our conversation was interrupted by a child's weeping.

"Hey, kid," I asked, "what're you cryin' about?"

No answer. The crying became more insistent.

Don't you begin crying, I said to myself. Whatever you do, don't cry in front of Usher just because the kid is crying. How would it look?

"Hey, kid! If you want to cry, get away from here and cry somewhere else," Usher said to the child, and turned back to the window. "It's your turn now," he said to me. "You're walking down the street. You know from nothin'. In front of you, you suddenly see somebody drop a buck. You look to the right. You look to the left. Nobody's looking. Bang! Down you go, and in a flash you slip the dough into your pocket. It's fair! The person who lost it had no right to lose it in the first place. Now, suppose the cops get you and begin to ask questions about that lost buck. How're you goin' to explain it? So you gotta get rid of it. It's burning a hole in your pocket. Now, what are you goin' to buy for that dough?"

Between Usher and the crying child I felt crushed, so bending down, I said, "Who are you, kid? Why are you cryin'? Did your mother hit you or something?"

All at once, the child stopped weeping and looked straight up at me.

"Who are you, kid?" I asked. "What's the matter?"

"It's the Polack's son, Little Pyotr," said Usher in disgust.

Then it was that Little Pyotr's face took shape, and I saw the high cheekbones, the tiny turned-up nose, pale blue watery eyes, and the white hair shining in the light from the candy store.

"What are you doing on this street?" Usher asked angrily. "You got no business here!"

"I'm lost," said Little Pyotr, the Polack's son.

"Lost!" cried Usher in amazement. "Now that's a hot one. You live only five blocks from here and you're lost! I never heard of such a thing. What are you—dumb? You're a real dumb Polack. Go on home!"

"How can I go home when I'm lost?" said Little Pyotr.

"Look, kid," said Usher, "you walk two blocks ahead, you turn to the right; walk one block, you turn to the left; walk two blocks, turn to the right; walk one block, pass the *shul*. And you're home. Now," said Usher, "do you know how to get home?"

"No," said Little Pyotr, the Polack's son. "I'm still lost!"

"What a dumb kid!" said Usher. "I tell him how to go home—I practically draw a diagram for him. And he don't know nothing! Just a dumb Polack!"

"Yeh," said Little Pyotr, "I'm a dumb Polack. I don't know nothing."

"Usher," I said cautiously, "let's take the kid home."

"I'm not taking no kid home!" said Usher.

"Imagine!" I said, thinking very rapidly. "A kid's missing. The mother's tearing her hair out, crying. The father is dragging the river for the body. In the middle of everything, you and I show up with their darling."

"They'd arrest us for kidnapping!"

"No—nuttin' like dat."

"What then?"

"A reward, that's what! Naturally, they're offering a reward for the return of the kid."

"Who would ever want such a dumb kid back?"

"Usher," I pleaded, "no matter how dumb a kid is, no father or mother throws him away. They got legal responsibility. It's a law!"

"How much?"

"Ten thousand dollars—at least!"

Usher looked into the candy store window. There stood the railroad train, with its tracks forming a figure eight, and railroad stations, and bridges, and all kinds of switches.

"All right," he said. "You talked me into it. But I'm not walking with any damn kid in the street. You take him and I'll follow."

At that moment, Little Pyotr, the Polack's son, put his hand in mine with a tremendous sigh as if his very heart were breaking and we were off—I, holding Little Pyotr's hand, and Usher following us in a very bad humor.

As we walked two blocks and turned to the right, the child's sigh went through his arm. As we walked one block and turned to the left, his sigh came through the palm of his hand, and I felt it in mine. As we walked two blocks and turned to the right, walked one block past the *shul*, I felt it come up my arm. And it was as if I was walking through the street with a little brother at my side.

"Hey kid!" said Usher as we came to the gate of Big Pyotr's yard. "Ain't you got no handkerchief? The snot is running down your nose so much—it's goin' into your mouth. Besides, what are you cryin' for? You're in your own back yard."

And then a strange thing happened. Usher took a handkerchief from his pocket, and with his own hands he wiped the kid's nose.

Through the darkness of the yard we crept, stumbling against the tin cans and baby carriages, while from the back of the house a dog moaned dolefully. From the window of the *shul* a pale yellow light fell across the automobile parts and flat tires, while the sound of the Jews singing in prayer filled the air with a strange, uneasy feeling that seemed to penetrate into the marrow of my bones. Even Usher was affected for he suddenly spat three times on the ground.

"What're you spittin' for?" I asked. "Don't you know it ain't sanitary?"

"Sh!" said Usher. "You gotta spit; we're in a *goy's* yard!"

Up the broken steps of the porch we mounted.

"Who's there?" came a voice, and the door of the house opened, disclosing the hugh frame of Big Pyotr the Polack.

"It's me," I said, quaking.

"What you want?" he cried.

"Nothin', I just brought back your son, Little Pyotr. He was lost!" I said.

"What—lost!" cried the father as he grabbed at the kid. "What you mean by getting lost?"

So there I was—Big Pyotr pulling at Little Pyotr and Little Pyotr holding on to my arm.

Crack! Down on the kid's head came the father's fist. Crack! Crack! And still the kid only sighed and sighed and wouldn't let go.

"You better let go, kid," I said.

With a final sigh, the kid let go as the father hit him one after another.

"Hey, mister!" cried Usher. "You ain't got no right to hit dat kid!"

"What's that?" cried Big Pyotr, forgetting about Little Pyotr and turning to Usher.

"I said, you ain't got no right hitting dat kid! Why don't you pick on somebody your size?"

The face of Big Pyotr turned red, then pale, and blew up into a big balloon. He threw the kid into the house and from the side of his belt drew out a gun.

"*Elohenu*," came the singing from the *shul, "v'elohai avosenu!*"

"Get off my property!" he roared. "Get off, or I'm gonna shoot you dead—you dirty sneak-thieves! I know—you're spying on me!"

"A fine how-do-you-do!" said Usher, and faster than you can blink your eyes, we were out of the yard, past the automobile tires and junk and at the gate. Out of the darkness jumped Mary, Little Pyotr's sister, with curlers in her hair, and threw herself on Usher and kissed him.

"You saved my brother!" she said.

Then she grabbed me, and said, "Thank you! Thank you! You both saved my brother!" And disappeared into the darkness.

Usher spat. "First," he said, "I spit on that lousy Pig Pyotr the Polack because he's an ungrateful stingy rat with a gun, who knows he's got to give a reward but welshes out of it! Then, I spit because I gotta wash out my mouth of those lousy kisses that skinny runt forced down my throat! Then, I spit because I was stupid enough to walk into a *goy's* yard, when everybody knows it's a sin!"

"*Boruch hu horuch shemo*," came the singing from the *shul*.

I was sitting with Usher in his kitchen watching his mother at the stove, cooking. She was obviously in a very bad state because every five minutes or so she looked at the clock.

"Oh! Oh!" she cried as she tasted the boiling water in the pot. "It ain't ready. And soon your father will be home."

"Ma," said Usher, always ready to give advice. "Why don't you open up a can?"

"Canned soup!" cried Usher's mother in horror. "How can you compare a good homemade soup to soup from cans? Your father would recognize it with the first spoon. Where's your head?"

Then turning to Usher, she said, "You see, I won't be able to eat this soup—it'll stick in my throat—unless I know that a certain person will have some."

"Oh!" said Usher. "Papa will have some. He'll eat most of it."

"No," she said. "Not Papa."

"Miriam who's poor?" asked Usher.

"No," she said. "Not Miriam."

"Who then?"

"Reb Levi," she said. "Who else? And when the soup's finished, I'll give you the privilege of bringing it to him."

"You mean I gotta walk five blocks with a jar of soup to Reb Levi?" cried Usher. "Some privilege!"

"Yes, my son," said his mother. "This is no ordinary rabbi!"

The sun was shining nice and bright that day when Usher with his jar of soup and me at his side made our way through the streets of Brownsville to Reb Levi's *shul*. The rabbi was the last thing on our minds.

"Yeh!" said Usher. "I heard all about it. My friend Bibi heard it from my friend Robby, who heard it from Pickles, who saw it with his own two eyes."

"You don't say!"

"Willie September stuck a shiv into the back of Fat Yernie. That lousy Yernie was trying to muscle in on Willie's territory. and Willie ain't goin' to allow no two-bit chiseler to horn in for a rakeoff on his crap games. You don't think Willie has been building all this up just to let Yernie come in and take over, do you?"

"I don't care about Willie keeping the territory," I said.

"Why not? He's real tough. Ain't nobody more entitled to it then Willie."

"I don't care if he's the toughest guy in the whole wide world," I said. "He don't give the kids no tips. Here we are."

Sure enough, there we were, and Usher threw open the door. Before us lay a large empty room, filled with wooden benches and a kind of closet up front for the ark. The room smelled of musty air, dried spit on the floor, and stale tobacco.

"It's just an empty store!" said Usher.

We had expected to find a host of graybeards, covered with long white shawls, moaning and swaying in the House of God (was this not the way a *shul* was supposed to be?); instead, there was a complete emptiness as if our Jews had forsaken their temple. And although I had little religious training, and Usher had even less, a terrible anger rose in us as we considered the backs of the empty benches. It was not right!

"You gotta put something on your head," said Usher as he proceeded to take out his handkerchief, knot the corners, and cover his head.

I did the same as we went through God's empty house, when all at once an awful din and clatter broke out above our heads, as if God himself in all His anger was beating down on us to punish us for our sins.

And there was Reb Levi, banging a stick with all his might on a table in the back room while two dozen kids were throwing things, fighting with each other, and stamping their feet on the floor.

Usher was furious. With one lurch, he put the jar on the table, picked out one kid (a small one), and bang! slammed him one right in the mouth.

"What's goin' on here?" he asked. "Where do you think you are—in your own house? Ain't you got no respect for the rabbi?"

There was instantaneous silence, as all eyes turned to him.

Then turning to the rabbi, he said, "Rabbi! Nobody says you gotta take any crap from these kids!"

"Ka-choo!" sneezed a child from the back of the room.

"What was that?" Usher screamed furiously at the trembling children. "Who made that noise? I double dare the lousy rat who opened his mouth to come out in the open! I'll separate his no-good head from his lousy body!"

The children sat petrified.

"My mother," said Usher to the rabbi, "sent you a jar of soup."

"Long may she live," the rabbi said. "Children, we have a guest," he announced, then turned to Usher. "Here, have a seat. Make yourself comfortable."

"O.K., rabbi," said Usher as he and I sat down on a bench before the window.

Suddenly Usher looked out of the window and gasped.

"Did you see what I saw?"

"What did you see?"

"Children! Children!" said the frightened rabbi as he rolled down the window shade. "Forget what you saw there! This is a House of God."

He rolled down the shade, but not before I saw Big Pyotr stealing across the yard, dragging a big piece of lumber that was supposed to go up on the top of the roof, so that no pieces of plaster would fall down on the heads of our Jews when they lifted their voices in prayer.

It was not the same Usher who came out of the *shul* that had gone in. His face was as in pain. His eyes, large and questioning.

"I don't understand it," he said. "Is it right? Look, my mother steals pennies from my father when he ain't looking and she drops them into the box. We don't have any money as it is, and she takes from the nothing that we got, and when the rabbi comes to ask, she gives. Is it right?"

"No!" I said. "It ain't right!"

"And when a mother steals from a father, it ain't the same like when a crook steals from someone else. After all, it's in the same family. Am I right?"

"Yes," I said. "You are right."

"Now if she wants to give the money to Reb Levi to buy lumber for the roof of the *shul*—it's her privilege. She's entitled to it. But when Reb Levi takes the money and buys lumber, and when I see with my own eyes that lousy Polack steal the stuff, right out in the open; and when with my own ears I hear the rabbi saying, 'Forget what you saw here!'—then the rabbi is as much a crook as the Polack himself. Right?"

"No!" I said. "Wrong! It makes him a bigger crook!"

"Then it's wrong!" he said. "It's wrong to give the Polack the lumber that rightfully belongs on the roof of our *shul*."

"That's right," I said, "it's wrong. But what're you goin' to do about it?"

"Plenty," said Usher. "Imagine—free presents to a Polack with my money! I never heard of such a thing."

That night it rained in Brownsville. Pools of water formed in the cellars as the sewers backed up. The empty cans in Big Pyotr the Polack's yard brimmed over, and Big Pyotr's yard turned into a sea of floating things. Unless a thing was tied down, it floated. And, of course, the broken roof of our *shul* got plenty.

"The weather is with us," said Usher as we waded into the slime of the Polack's yard.

"I don't care if the weather's with us or against us," I said as I felt myself sinking deeper into the mud. "All we need is for the rabbi to find out what we're goin' to do and we're through. And if the rabbi don't find out, there's always Big Pyotr and his gun. Let's go home."

"First," said Usher, "who paid for the lumber? My mother! Second, I don't care what that rabbi thinks. Whether he likes it or not, we're goin' to help him. If you ask me, I wonder if he's really a rabbi. Isn't a rabbi supposed to be against *goyim*? Isn't he supposed to be on the side of the Jews? And isn't there a war going on between the *goyim* and the Jews? Third, that Polack couldn't pull the trigger, even if we put his finger on it and showed him—he's always too drunk to know he's alive."

And with this, we pulled the piece of lumber out of the

Polack's pile and dragged it through the mud and dropped it in the back of our *shul.*

The next day it was back in Big Pyotr's yard.

How that Pyotr knew one piece of lumber from another, I do not know. It's possible that in dragging it through the mud, Usher and I left a trail. It's also possible that the Polack didn't know and thought it to be just another opportunity to steal.

In any case, he had a lot of nerve! So, without further ado, Usher and I went right back to Big Pyotr's yard and took that piece of lumber right back to the *shul* where it rightfully belonged. And sure enough, the very next morning Big Pyotr saw to it that it was back on his property.

I was standing outside my own house, minding my own business, when my friend Bibi came up greatly excited.

"Did you hear the latest?" he said.

"No. What's the latest?" I asked.

"They're beating up a kid on Sackman Street!"

And so Bibi, followed by me, began to run. We ran until we met Robby.

"Did you hear the latest?" I said.

"No. What's the latest?" asked Robby.

"They caught a kid on Sackman Street and they're beating him to death! Maybe they're even giving it to the rabbi!"

And so Bibi, followed by me, who was followed by Robby, began to run. We ran until presently we met Pickles.

"Did you hear the latest?" said Robby.

"No. What's the latest?" asked Pickles.

"They caught a kid on Sackman Street and beat him to death! The rabbi tried to stop the murder and they finished off the rabbi! Two dead! For all we know they have even burned the *shul* down."

We ran on until we met Willie September.

"Hey, Willie! Did you hear the latest?" said Pickles.

No. What's the latest?" asked Willie September.

"They're killing kids on Sackman Street! The rabbi's dead! The *shul's* on fire! The houses are burning! The police are out! Bodies all over the place—the lousy Polack is shooting his brains out like mad!"

All together we ran until we met Mary Contrary the Whore.

"Hey, Mary Contrary! Did you hear the latest?" said Willie September.

"No. What's the latest?" asked Mary Contrary.

"They're killing Jews on Sackman Street! A kid got it! The rabbi got it! The *shul* got it! Brownsville's burning! They're shoveling out the bodies—there's so many of them!"

"What's so strange about them killing Jews on Sackman Street?" asked Mary Contrary as we ran. "They're always killing Jews! If not on Sackman Street—then it's another street. What's the difference?"

By the time we reached the *shul,* Brownsville had sent forth her best. The street in front of the Polack's yard was black with people. And there was the Polack holding Usher by the neck, and there was the rabbi alongside of them. Nobody was dead!

"The child is innocent!" the rabbi was saying.

"Innocent!" roared Pyotr the Polack. "I catch the bum stealing my lumber, red-handed. And this is innocent?"

"In the first place," shouted the nervy Usher, "whose lumber was it? I know where you stole it from, you big crook! Didn't I see you, with my own two eyes, take that piece of lumber from the *shul* in broad daylight?"

"What!" cried the astonished Mrs. Goldberg from the crowd. "Stealing lumber from a *shul!*"

"I steal no lumber from no *shul!*" said the Polack. "I find this gangster in my yard stealing from me!"

The crowd parted as Willie September came forward.

"I've had a lot of business with this legal business," said the formidable Willie (and God knows he had) as he stepped into the yard. Turning to Usher, he said, "Did you or did you not come into this yard with the intention of taking off with the aforementioned piece of wood?"

"I didn't steal nothing," said Usher. "The Polack's the crook!"

"Ah!" came a voice above the murmur of the crowd. "The child says he didn't steal nothing!"

"Answer the question!" said Willie September.

"The child is innocent," said the rabbi.

"Rabbi!" shouted Fat Moe the Dope. "You stick to your business and let Willie take care of his."

"My baby! My baby!" shouted Usher's mother. "He's no crook!"

"Did you or did you not come into this yard with the intention of carrying away the aforementioned piece of wood?" asked Willie. "Answer the question!"

"I did," said Usher.

"Let's go home," said another voice from the crowd. "The kid has confessed. It's an open and shut case."

A few of the onlookers began to turn away.

"Yes," said Usher, "I was goin' to take the wood but this lousy Polack got there first!"

"Who's a lousy Polack?" said the Polack.

"You're a lousy Polack!" said Usher.

"I'm not a lousy Polack!"

"You're a lousy Polack, ten times over!"

"You dirty Jew!" cried the Polack.

"Hey, Polack!" shouted Mrs. Goldberg from the crowd. I'm not dirty—I just took a hot bath!"

"Did you hear what that Polack said?" came another voice from the crowd. "The dirt is an inch thick on his neck, and he has the nerve to call us dirty! But then again, what can you expect from a lousy Polack?"

"Who's a lousy Polack?" said the Polack.

"You're a lousy Polack!" said Usher.

"I'm not a lousy Polack!"

"You're a lousy Polack, ten times over!"

"You killed our Christ!" cried the Polack, crossing himself.

"What do you mean—I killed your Christ!" cried a voice from the crowd. "I wasn't even there!"

"Listen to the Polack!" another said. "Listen to him—how religious he's suddenly become!"

"Hey, Polack!" a man shouted. "What's happened to you? Don't you know Christ was a Jew?"

"Christ was no Jew—you dirty Jew!"

"Tell him the truth," came another voice. "Tell him that Christ was a dirty Jew—just like us!"

"By Christ," said the Polack, "those lousy Jews have even taken our Christ! First the lousy Jews take my lumber, and then they take my Christ!"

"Your Christ," another voice cried. "No wonder Christ died! He took one look at you and turned over!"

"Kill the Polack!" screamed Willie September.

"Kill the Polack!" screamed Fat Moe the Dope.

"Kill the Polack!" screamed Mary Contrary.

"Oh no!" protested the Polack. "You can't kill me!"

"And why not?" cried Mrs. Goldberg. "Are you made of special stuff?"

"It says," said the Polack, "that Jews have been put on the face of the earth so that the Christians can kill them."

"Where does it say?" screamed Mrs. Goldberg.

"So," continued the Polack, pausing to consider as he began to scratch his head, "shall I shoot the kid in the feet until he begins to dance? Shall I shoot him in the mouth until he sings? Or shall I just bang his brains out against a stone?"

"You see," said Mandelbaum the Tenant, "the world is for *goyim*—not for Jews!"

"It's very simple," said Parker the Barber. "Let's all become Christians and kill the lousy Polack!"

"Who's a lousy Polack?" said the Polack.

"You're a lousy Polack!" said Parker the Barber.

"I'm not a lousy Polack!"

"You are a lousy Polack, ten times over!"

"Dirty Jews!" snarled the Polack.

"Polack pig!" screamed a woman's voice from the crowd. "Go home and eat pork and bacon!"

"Enough!" cried the rabbi.

And now the rabbi stood up, looking strange and angry in his black caftan, and without knowing why, goosepimples formed on my body as he turned to face the crowd.

"Children of Brownsville," he said. "Children of God. I sit in my empty *shul* and wait. I wait and wait. I say it's not possible—these are the Children of Israel, the Chosen People."

"Yes!" called out a voice. "A great honor! Chosen—to be killed!"

"It can not be," continued the rabbi, ignoring the interruption, "that they have forgotten what they are. And so, I wait. The floor creaks. The mice run around. And once in a while, a child makes an appearance—to throw stones at the windows and to break them. Tomorrow, they'll come. Maybe, the day after. We cannot even get ten together for a *minyan*, let alone to fill the *shul*. If this is what I can expect from Jews—what should I expect from *goyim*."

"Death!" came a voice. "Death is what you can expect from *goyim*!"

"So the Polack steals a piece of lumber. What do you really care? You never go into the *shul* anyway. And if the *shul* even caved in, you wouldn't bat an eyelash. Now, all of a sudden everyone is concerned with a piece of wood. Shame!"

"Rabbi," came a voice. "Who are you working for—the Jews or the *goyim*?"

The rabbi paused. He took a deep breath and began all over again. But this time it was not the same. For from his lips there poured forth a strange combination of ch's and sh's that originated somewhere in the back of his throat. And mixed with these harsh guttural sounds were interspersed soft liquid l's, cajoling ah's, mysterious oy's, so that it appeared as if sweet and sour were mixed together.

And the rabbi was not the same rabbi any more. Small as he was, he now seemed big. Pale as he looked, he was now dark. Mild as I knew him, now he was terrifying.

"What's he saying?" I asked Usher as I felt him by my side.

"Search me," Usher said.

That night Usher asked his father a question.

"Pa," he said, "what was the rabbi saying?"

"Who knows? Who cares?" came the answer.

"The child asks a question and this is the answer you give him?" Usher's mother said. "He's asking his own father for the word of God, and this is how his father answers!"

"A crazy rabbi makes a speech, and I'm supposed to know what he says?" Usher's father retorted.

"It's O.K., Usher," I said. "I have a prayer book at home."

I was down, I was up, I was down and up again, and in Usher's house with a prayer book. Then after much fumbling to find the place, I read.

"By the rivers of Babylon," I read, "there we sat down, yea we wept when we remembered Zion. We hung our harps upon the willows in the midst thereof."

"Well," interrupted Usher, "it *was* raining."

"For there they that carried us away captive required of us a song; and they that wasted us required of us mirth, saying: Sing us of the songs of Zion! How shall we sing the Lord's song in a strange land?"

"For crying out loud," interruped Usher again. "That lousy Polack wanted me to sing! But I fooled him!"

"If I forget thee, O Jerusalem, let my right hand fail. If I do not remember thee, let my tongue cleave to the roof of my mouth, if I prefer not Jerusalem."

"That—I don't know the meaning of!"

I finished and stood with the open prayer book in my hand. I looked at Usher, and Usher looked at his mother, and she looked at his father, and he looked at his newspaper. There was nothing I could say. But suddenly I felt something inside me—something small that grew bigger and bigger until it was ready to burst like a balloon.

And so I said, "*Adenoi! Adenoi!*"

Fire Is Burning on Our Street!

THERE WAS THAT BAD YEAR ON OUR STREET THAT I told you about when people began losing their jobs. One after another the men began to be familiar on our stoops, and what had been a street of women and children during the day now became more varied, as fathers I had never seen before appeared, going to market, carrying baskets, rocking baby carriages, and sweeping hallways.

It was at this time that a new boarder made his appearance in the front room of my friend Usher's house, but this one was for free. It happened very simply. Usher's grandfather appeared on a visit, set himself up in the front room, and that's all there was to it.

"It's a pleasure to have you, father," said Usher's mother.

"When is he going to leave?" asked her husband.

"The house will have a real homey feeling with his white beard and skullcap," said Usher's mother.

"He's not paying any rent!" said Usher's father.

"The child will get discipline," said Usher's mother.

"He ought to go back to his own house and give discipline to the three he has left at home!"

"Have some respect for my father!" said Usher's mother.

"The moment he puts his foot out of the house," said the husband, "I'll have respect for him!"

This grandfather was an old patriarch, a breaker of chairs, a shaker of tables. When he first came to America he had had a long fleecy beard, but as time Americanized him, his beard became shorter and shorter, until he wore it à la Van Dyke. A carpenter by trade, he had bought three houses in Bayonne and a lot in Jersey City and had stopped working. He was "retired." I do not think he was more than forty at the time.

"Someday," he used to say, pointing in the direction of Bayonne, "they'll build a bridge over there and buy my three houses."

He read his newspaper and took an enormous interest in the weather. He would put his head out of the window, and as if sensing the barometric pressure, would say:

"Business is bad in Coney Island!"

"A real business man," Usher's mother would proudly say.

"Pa!" Usher's father would interpose. "They're going to build a bridge in Bayonne."

"Apostate!" Usher's mother would mumble under her breath.

But the old man never heard what he did not wish to hear; and on the assumption he was not responsible for what he did not hear if his head was not present, he would deliberately put it out of the window and return, saying:

"Business is bad in Coney Island!"

"Don't you think," Usher's father would say, "that you ought to be in Bayonne? They'll build that bridge and you won't be there."

Then the old man, carpenter that he was, would stand, walk over to the wall, and begin banging on it.

"What's he doing?" Usher's father would ask as the ceiling plaster would start falling, and the insides of the inner wall would start rumbling. "He'll bring the house down on our heads."

"Sh!" Usher's mother would say. "He's testing the construction."

"Do you remember our house in Kalenkovitch? That was a house!" the old man would say.

"Pigs used to run around in the back yard," Usher's father would answer.

"What a house! And what a stove it had!"

"Too hot in the summer! Too cold in the winter!"

"And the apple tree in front of the house! And the road leading to the village!"

"Yes!" said Usher's father. "To the village on one side! To the cemetery on the other!"

"Apostate!" said Usher's mother.

"Papa!" Usher's father would plead. "They're going to build the bridge in Bayonne."

"Apostate! Apostate!" said Usher's mother under her breath as she would jab him with her knee.

Day after day, the old man sat at the window reading his paper.

"What does he want?" asked Usher's father.

"I don't know," answered Usher's mother.

One day, Usher's father returned looking very tired and sad.

It was with the utmost of effort that he was able to face his wife and family.

"I've lost my job," he announced without looking at his wife. "I've been laid off! No work!"

"There's a crisis in America," the old man said, looking up from his newspaper.

"Old man," said Usher's father, turning on him furiously, "can't you see I'm unable to keep you? You've left a wife and three children alone in Bayonne. A bridge will be built there. You have sat yourself down on my shoulders, and you won't get off. What do you want of me?"

"Nothing, nothing," said the old man.

The day came when the old man announced:

"I'm leaving!"

"Good-by!" said Usher's father.

"But Simchie is coming in my place!"

"What place?" asked Usher's father.

"One would think that you didn't want me here," said the old man.

Usher's mother kicked her husband in the shins.

"Apostate!" she said.

"All right," said the weary husband. "Let him come."

And so Usher's Uncle Simchie, a tall, handsome-looking man with whom women were delighted, made his appearance. Thereafter, the old man and the uncle alternated every week or so. First one, and then the other, occupied the front room.

"What do they want?" asked Usher's worried father.

"Only God knows!" said Usher's mother, for even she was beginning to get leery.

And in response to questioning as to what they wanted, the old man and his son would answer, "Nothing, nothing." Or else, "Who could want anything from you!"

Yes, it was as if they had set siege to the house, and in spite of their refusal to admit they wanted anything, it remained for my friend Usher to discover what it was.

I had just finished having my black bread and coffee in Usher's house when Usher's grandfather appeared and walked into the front room.

"Sh!" cautioned Usher.

I was not aware of having said anything, but realized soon enough this was merely a sign for me that Usher was listening. We could hear the old man whispering to the uncle.

"They're changing shifts," observed Usher.

We walked into the front room.

"Don't say another word!" warned Usher's Uncle Simchie, looking directly at Usher.

"Before the apostate's child you can say anything you want," said the old man. "The child has nothing upstairs. What can you expect from such a father!"

Now I could see my hero Usher putting on a particularly imbecilic expression.

"We must have seven hundred dollars!" said Uncle Simchie.

"I know! I know!" said the old man. "But go draw blood from a stone!"

"Give him a proposition, then. Make him a partner."

"What!" said the old man. "Make that hard head a partner! Impossible! He's got no business sense! I'm not giving him any propositions!"

"He's got the money!" said Uncle Simchie.

"Maybe he has, and maybe he hasn't!" said the old man.

All this time, my friend Usher was acting out a part. First he walked with his arms hanging loosely like an ape, then he put his tongue out from the side of his mouth and let the saliva drip out like a idiot; he took to cleaning his ears with his fingers, then sending them up into his nose and mouth, and as he sucked on his fingers he closed his eyes in delight.

I could not stop laughing. He looked like a real idiot, but I knew that he was only a detective.

Finally his uncle could not take it any longer.

"Papa, I can't go on any further," he said and then looking

directly at Usher, added, "not while we're surrounded by a spy."

"Spy?" said the old man. "You mean the young one? Don't mind him. He's like his father—carries a heavy head."

Indeed, it was "heavy" information the "spy" carried to his father.

"They want to give you a proposition," said Usher to his father.

"Me—a proposition! I'll give them a proposition—to get out!" said his father.

"The proposition is going to cost you seven hundred dollars," continued Usher.

"Crazy," said Usher's father, matter-of-fact.

"The old geezer's store is empty. So for the seven hundred, they're going to go into the grocery store business. It will be split three ways. Uncle Simchie will be the manager," continued Usher.

"A manager with my money!" exclaimed Usher's father in amazement.

I suspect the old man was much shrewder than I took him for, because this was exactly what he had intended. Just as he had calculated, it was Usher's father who came to him, rather than he to Usher's father.

"Papa," appealed Usher's father, "I have no money. Don't you understand?"

"Who's asking you for money!" said the old man.

"No money! No propositions! No nothing—not even a job!"

"We're going into business. You, Simchie, and I," announced the old man. "And I'm sitting here until I get seven hundred dollars."

"Then, sit!" said Usher's father.

Yes, I am sorry for the old man; it was out of desperation that he did this. I am sorry for Usher's father; he was not collecting rent. Sorry, too, for Usher's mother; she was at a loss. And the truth of the matter was that Usher's father had no seven cents, let alone seven hundred dollars.

The house in which my friend Usher the Landlord lived was an attached, box-like affair, with an apartment above which his family occupied and a store below with three rooms in the rear which was occupied by a tenant. Long and narrow, it contained rooms where no provision had been made for windows. As a result, the place was studded with constantly corroding skylights, blazing hot in the summer and freezing cold in the winter. And so my hero Usher and I, every spring for fifty cents apiece, would be assigned to the important task of painting the skylight green.

It was, therefore, only natural that Usher and I, "detectives" that we were, should put our ears to an open skylight one day to hear what was going on down below in the tenant's apartment.

"Business is bad!" said a voice down below.

"Dat's Mandelbaum!" whispered Usher.

A plate banged on a table. A water tap ran. Someone walked across a floor.

"Yes, business is bad!" echoed a woman's voice.

"Dat's the wife!" whispered Usher.

And so we put in our few strokes with the brush, rested a little, listened a little, put in another few strokes, and listened again when Usher said:

"They're at it again, listen!"

"It's getting worse!" said a voice.

"Dat's him!" whispered Usher.

Someone snorted.

"Yes, it's getting worse!" said the woman's voice.

"Dat's her!" whispered Usher.

"We gotta do something!"

"Yes, we gotta, but what?"

"Only one thing!"

"Never!"

"It's the only way!"

"Never!"

"I got somebody to do it—for ten dollars!"

"We'll go to prison!"

My hero Usher jumped.

"Quiet!" I said. "They'll hear you!"

Someone coughed. A chair moved.

"Nobody will know!" said the first voice.

"Never, never! I'll never let you make a fire!"

"Yes!"

"No!"

"Pop," Usher announced. "Mandelbaum is going to make a fire and burn our house to pieces!"

"Such discipline we're getting," said Usher's father, looking sternly at the grandfather. "The lad has gone crazy."

We were all seated in the kitchen. It was one of those rare occasions when the old man had come out of the front room. Usher's mother had finished cleaning her pots and pans, and they were distributed about the kitchen, hanging from hooks or displayed in closets.

"Pots! Pots! All day long, she cleans pots," said Usher's father, unable to give vent to his ire. "Your pots are blinding me."

"Leave my pots alone," said Usher's mother. "Eat something instead."

"Eat? How can I eat when our lad has gone plumb crazy," said Usher's father between mouthfuls of some bread the mother had baked. "Wash his mouth out with soap."

Usher's mother took my hero to the kitchen sink and, letting the tap run, pretended to soap his mouth.

"That'll refreshen you," said his mother, using water instead, then closing her eye in a wink, she raised her voice in great indignation for her husband to hear, "Now you won't go around with such stories."

You should have seen the performance the "spy" gave as he came out gasping.

"What was that you said?" asked Usher's grandfather, coming out of deep thought. "Repeat it again!"

My hero Usher began again:

"I was paintin' the skylight, and I heard Mandelbaum talkin' to his wife. 'Business is bad!' he said. 'It's getting worser and worser! We gotta make a fire!' 'I won't let you make a fire unless it's a big one,' she said, 'with flames creepin' up the stairs, with windows blastin' out, with lots of heat, and hooks and ladders, and crowds of people, and water from the hoses!' "

"I heard nothin' like dat," I said.

"Shut up!" said the grandfather. "Go on, Usher."

"Dere's nothin' else to tell. Da place is goin' to go up in flames any minute now. It'll be burnin', burnin', burnin'!"

"God save us!" cried his mother, aghast.

"God save us, nothing!" said the old man. "Mandelbaum will save us!"

Then tapping Usher gently on the cheek, he said, "That's a good lad." And turning to Usher's mother, added very pointedly, "He takes after our side of the family."

"I won't have it!" cried Usher's mother. "I won't have a fire in my house!"

"You're not going to have a fire," said the old man. "Mandelbaum is going to burn."

"I work to keep the place clean. I won't have my pots and pans blackened. I scrub the hallways, the windows, the stairs. What will happen to it all? Where will we all go?"

"You're not my daughter," said the old man, and then turning to Usher's father, he added, "She has no business sense!"

Things were getting worse. Entire families were being evicted with their furniture out on the sidewalk. Businesses were going bankrupt and stores were emptying out, one after another. Thus the season for fires began. First the delicatessen store, then the restaurant, then the candy store. Even the Feather Plucker had her fire. My friend Usher was torn between the joy of watching windows crack and fire engines coming down our street and the fear of the portending doom to his own house.

"It should happen to us," said the old man.

"Bite your tongue!" said Usher's mother.

"What's the matter with that coward Mandelbaum?" asked the old man.

"Lord protect us!" said Usher's mother.

"How long! How long! O Lord!" cried the old man.

Now the entire family took to going to bed with their clothes on.

"I'll watch!" said the old man.

He would sit up all night waiting for the thing to happen. And as he viewed the street from the window, he would announce, "Kaufman is burning!" or "Goldberg is going up in smoke!" or "Feigenbaum is next!"

One night he was startled by loud screams coming from the daughter's bedroom.

"At last," he sighed.

"False alarm!" said Usher running in. "It's only Mama! A bad dream!"

"A real lummox the lad is!" said the old man, disappointed. "No wonder; he doesn't take after our side of the family!"

"I can't sleep," moaned Usher's mother. "I dreamt the house was burning."

"A sign!" said the old man. "It's coming closer!"

It was now Gussie the Beautician's turn to go up in flames. And my friends, Pickles, Bibi, Robby, Usher and I, were watching the conflagration without any interest. So many fires had occured in our immediate neighborhood that the whole business had become routine. Nevertheless, Gussie was not on the street wailing.

"Up in the air goes my business!" cried the Beautician.

"They don't have no right to call her the Beautician," said Pickles, the observer of life. "She's no beaut!"

"What's she cryin' about?" asked Bibi.

"She's gotta cry," answered Usher.

"Why?" demanded Bibi.

"She's gotta cry to show that she didn't make no fire!"

"Oh," said Bibi.

"Everything is going up in flames!" wailed the Beautician, shaking her head done in three colors. "I'm ruined! My curlers! My machines! My expensive dyes—all are burning!"

"What a shame!" cried one of the women of our street. "Aren't you insured?"

"Mind your own business!" said the Beautician, snapping angrily at the woman. "Do I ask you if you're insured?"

Then she began again, "O my curlers! My cabinets! My mirrors! My hair nets!"

"She's insured," said Usher.

"How do you know, smart-guy?" asked Bibi.

"She's insured," said the all-knowing Usher. "If you're not insured, you don't have a fire. Listen to her—her hair nets, her hairpins, her nail polish! What do you think she's doin'?"

"What?" asked the astonished Bibi.

"She's countin' the money!"

"O my combs!" moaned Gussie the Beautician. "My fine combs! O my imported scissors! My Italian marble tables with gilt legs! Three hundred, the terrazzo floor alone cost me!"

It happened when they least expected it. I remember our group slouching around the candy store bench across the street, Usher's mother coming from the market carrying a loaded shopping bag, and the old man seated at the window. All of a sudden, the front windows of Mandelbaum's store caved in with a loud blast, and Mandelbaum himself, followed by his wailing wife, came running out on the street.

"I'm ruined!" he screamed. "My dry goods! The socks! The dresses! The handkerchiefs!"

Upstairs the old man opened the window and looked down to see what was going on. Like lightning he began running through the house, opening up all the windows and doors.

"Papa, come down!" screamed Usher's mother, pale as a ghost.

"I'm airing out the place!" he called down to her.

"What's he doing?" asked Pickles.

"Papa, come down! You'll burn to death!" cried Usher's mother as the black smoke began to roll out of the windows.

"We're saved!" called back the old man. "Happiness! Happiness! This is happiness!"

"O my chenille bedspreads!" cried Mandelbaum. "And those women's nightgowns I just bought! And that new shipment of house shoes—very expensive!"

You can imagine the commotion! The fire engines! The hoses dripping water! The crowds! The firemen with their heavy boots, banging on the floor, wrecking with their crowbars, throwing furniture out of the windows, smashing plate glass!

"There's an old nut upstairs singing and dancing who won't come down," said one of the men.

"Send the ladder up for him!" said the captain.

Up went the ladder, but the old man still would not come down.

"Flush him out with the hose!" ordered the captain.

Into the window went a stream of water, and still the old man would not come down.

"Throw him out of the window!" said the captain.

A large hoop opened, and at the window appeared a group of firemen, struggling with Usher's grandfather.

"Cossacks!" he screamed at them.

Down he went bouncing into the hoop, with his limbs outstretched, his small beard flying in the wind, his skullcap intact.

"Is this the way to treat a rich man?" he asked.

Out he spilled from the hoop with as much dignity as he could muster, and running over to his pale frightened daughter, cried:

"At last! A new world opens up!"

I admit that to watch someone else's fire is great fun, but your own is another matter. To Usher and his mother, it was as if part of their life had been burnt away. These were things to which they had grown accustomed. Now, all was a shambles.

As the pale and shaken mother walked through her charred house, she cried: cried as she looked at her pots and pans, hopelessly cried at her linens strewn over the floor, cried at the immense havoc that had been wrought.

The house became public property. Complete strangers entered to examine the damage, lines of people poked about, looked into cupboards and closets, touched and read documents. Even the lousy Feather Plucker, the troublemaker of our street, entered.

"Anybody killed?" she asked.

"What are all these people doing here?" asked the irate grandfather.

"Dancing on my grave!" said Usher's mother.

"Everybody out!" cried the grandfather, taking command, and turning to the pale, woe-begone Usher, he said, "Throw them all out! You and I have work to do!"

"Everybody out!" shouted Usher as the crowd began slowly to drift down the stairs. "Nobody is allowed in here! Fire Department's orders! Hey, you, take your dirty hands off that china! That's private property! Where do you think you are?"

"Everybody out?" asked the old grandfather.

"Everybody," reported Usher.

"A smart lad!" said the grandfather. "Takes after our side!"

With this, the old man grabbed a lamp and threw it at a mirror smashing it into a million bits.

"Not enough damage!" observed the old man. "Come on, young ones, break everything you can!"

"Enough! Enough!" cried Usher's mother.

"I'll save you in spite of yourself," said the grandfather.

Usher and I began smashing everything we could lay our hands on; Usher, half-heartedly, at first, but with more enthusiasm as he fell into the spirit of the thing, while I waxed ecstatic from the first throw. Yes, it was a joy to smash with nothing to hold you back, and even to be urged on.

And I can not remember how many countless dishes, mirrors, clocks, lamps, and assorted items went down to their doom that day.

Yes! Other streets, other peoples let their ire out differently. Some inflicted damage on themselves with knives. Others took it out in drink. Still others beat their wives and children. But ours sent everything up in smoke. And it was as if the more unhappy we were, the more we burned. Today, as I think back, and as I see Mandelbaum's windows blasting their way out into the street or the flames shooting out of the Beautician's shop, I say to myself, "Unhappy Mandelbaum! Unhappy Gussie!" And if I remember a particularly disastrous one like Goldberg's where the entire house caved in, I say, "He must have been very unhappy, indeed!" And even when I think of Usher's grandfather, I say, "Poor, poor grandfather! You were probably the unhappiest of the whole lot!" And, so it came out.

Up the stairs came a tall dignified man with blond hair. He held his hand to his nose, as if assailed by bad odors. He walked without touching the banister, and even pushed the door in without touching the knob. With a notebook in one hand and a handkerchief held against his face with the other, he carefully and systematically went through the house, noting all the damage. This was the Adjuster.

"How much do you want for this?" he asked Usher's mother.

"Seven hundred dollars," said Usher's mother promptly as her father beamed at her approvingly from the kitchen door.

"My limit is three hundred," said the Adjuster.

The old man began motioning frantically to his daughter.

"Excuse me," said Usher's mother as she walked out to the kitchen and closed the door.

"He's too low," whispered the grandfather.

Usher's mother returned.

"Too low!" she said as the old man nodded in approval.

"Three hundred and ten then," said the Adjuster. "The ten is for nuisance value."

The old man began to motion again.

"Excuse me," said Usher's mother.

"The thief is still too low," said the grandfather.

Again, Usher's mother returned.

"Still too low!"

"Three hundred and twenty," offered the Adjuster.

Again, the old man waved frantically. Again, his daughter went out into the kitchen.

"Tell him we're suing."

"Have it your own way," said the Adjuster, as he proceeded to pick up his notebook and leave.

"Are we really going to sue?" asked Usher's mother.

"Nah, it's just to scare them," said the old man and then, looking after the retreating figure of the Adjuster, he said, "It would be our luck to get an anti-Semite!"

What with the letters that went back and forth, and the half-dozen adjusters, all looking officious and important, who came and went, and with the hope of money coming in, Usher's house took on a different aspect. For the first time in their lives, people were coming to them pleading, while they held on. I often think they would have preferred never settling the "case" for all the joy it gave them.

"I have a proposition for you," said Usher's grandfather.

"Don't do me a favor. I don't want no propositions," said Usher's father.

"When the 'case' is settled, we'll go into business in Bayonne."

"When thumbtacks will burst into bloom, that's when I'll go into business with you!"

"There's enough for three."

"I'll never pasture pigs with you in the same meadow," said Usher's father.

"Golem!" said the old man. "In every country, money is another word for freedom!"

"All right!" said Usher's father. "Then remember, I'm free and you're not!"

"What's three hundred dollars!" asked Usher's mother.

"Three hundred and twenty!" corrected the old man as he turned to Usher's old lady. "People will say as you go by, 'She's stuffed up to the neck with money! A business woman—in Bayonne!' Isn't that something?"

"Goodness is better than riches!" said Usher's mother.

"In America," answered the old man, "nobody asks you if you're good. They say, 'How much money have you got?' And if you have money—you're good, you're smart, you're even stylish!"

"Wait until the 'case' is settled."

"What else have I got to do?"

"You've got the bridge in Bayonne!" said Usher's father managing to slip one in.

Here, the old man looked up and sighed; and for the first time, I felt sorry for him.

"It will never be built," he said with the utmost finality.

And it was as if a blast of cold came through the air. And I could see that even Usher's father squirmed uneasily.

"All I want," said the old man, "is a little bread and a little happiness!"

And the blood came to Usher's father's face as he flushed red with embarrassment.

The day came when Usher said:

"You know, you're going to Bayonne."

My mother had spent the best part of the morning scrubbing my neck. I got into my best clothes, even wore a white shirt and tie. Before I left, she made sure I sneezed and then put the handkerchief into my pocket.

"Be sure to use it," she called after me. "Don't wipe on your sleeve."

It was a joyous morning. The air was brisk and clear, and it was with the keenest of anticipation that I hurried to Usher's house. Sure enough, there was Usher in a starched white shirt, looking as unreal as myself.

"Blow!" said Usher's mother as she held a handkerchief to his nose.

In less happier circumstances my hero Usher might have protested, but now he blew.

Full of excitement, we preceded his father and mother down the stairs.

"Hey, Usher!" cried Bibi from across the street. "What're you all dressed up for? It ain't no holiday!"

"I'm going to my store in Bayonne!" screamed back Usher for the entire block to hear.

We were so happy that soon we were singing at the top of our lungs when, as luck would have it, that plague of our street, the Feather Plucker, passed by.

"What's she looking so angry at me?" asked Usher's mother. "It's a bad omen!"

"Let her go to hell!" said Usher's father.

But we had only to walk half the block to find out why the Feather Plucker was so angry at the landlords.

"My God!" said Usher's mother. "Shivers are running down my spine!"

I looked up and saw Jakie the Snotnose, Miriam's son, sitting on a chair near the curb. And while one of his brothers was lying in bed right out in the open on our street, another was curled up on a dining-room table; and Miriam herself, the beautiful unhappy Miriam, with one child at her side and another in her arms, was alongside it all, looking lost.

"She's been evicted!" cried Usher's mother.

And evicted she was! For there on the sidewalk, piled high, mattresses, pillows, furniture, and all, were all of Miriam's worldly goods.

"My blood runs cold!" said Usher's mother.

"Don't worry! Don't worry!" said Usher's father, pushing his reluctant wife by. "Everything will turn out for the best."

"Avrum!" she shouted. "A crime has been committed!"

We soon forgot the unwelcoming sight. All I could think of was that we were going to take a ferry. And it was not long before we, Usher and I, were lost in the sights and sounds of the boats as New York fell behind us, and the world became a fantastic succession of whistles, chains, tugs, and docks.

"Dat's the Woolworth Building," said Usher, pointing out the sights to me. "There's the Statue of Liberty with her torch, lighting up the land of the free and the home of the brave."

Suddenly, a huge black vessel loomed up ahead of us.

"What's da matter?" asked Usher.

"We're gonna hit dat boat!" I said in fright, feeling neither brave nor free.

"We're not gonna hit any boats. Watch how da ferry slows down."

And just as he said this, the ferry stopped churning, its motors went dead, and the vessel steamed by.

"You see!" said the well-seasoned traveler. "What did I tell you?"

I looked at him with respect. He knew almost everything.

"Da ship is going to Greece," he said.

"How do you know, Ush?" I asked in amazement.

"Can't you see dat flag?" he said. "White and blue! Dat's Greek!"

He was, indeed, a hero.

"What's the matter?" I heard Usher's father ask.

"My mother is spoilin' da trip," said Usher. "She's crying."

"Avrum!" she said. "I can't forget it! The picture is still in front of my eyes! My heart is bleeding for that woman!"

"Here's an ice-cream cone," said Usher's father.

"*Schlemiel!*" she said angrily, pushing it away. "Haven't you any feelings?"

It remained for Usher and myself to finish the delicacy.

"You can only take the same amount of licks I do—no more!" said my hero Usher.

And that was how we divided the ice cream evenly between us.

I shall never forget my first view of Bayonne. Even now, when I think of a "factory town," or when I go through the Pennsylvania "coal towns," it is Bayonne I see. Bayonne, with its oil refineries and black, old-fashioned windowed factories, its ugly railroad yards, its air heavy with the noxious odor of chemicals, and the utter, utter sadness of its factory workers going to work.

"Those are the customers," indicated Usher.

"It's just like Brownsville," I remember saying.

"Jerk," said Usher, "this is Bayonne!"

Down the street we ran to the store.

"There it is!" said Usher, proudly.

I looked at the shabby grocery with its bags of potatoes and flour on the outside and its towering strings of onions and hanging cheeses on the inside.

"The 'spy' is here!" said Uncle Simchie, standing in the doorway.

Usher's grandfather came to the front.

"What did you come for?" asked Uncle Simchie of Usher's father.

"What do you mean—what did I come for?" said Usher's father, beginning to stutter. "I came to see the business!"

"What business?" asked Uncle Simchie.

"Why, why! My third!"

"His third!" laughed Uncle Simchie the Manager. "You'll be lucky if you see a hundredth!"

"What does he mean?" said Usher's father, appealing to the old man.

Slowly, the old man wiped his hands on his apron.

"Things are bad," said the old man. "The factory workers are not buying. They're being let go."

"What do you mean—not buying? They were buying last week!"

"Last week, they were buying! This week, they're not!"

"Liar!" screamed Usher's father. "You're trying to steal my money!"

"Your money went down the drain a long time ago," said Uncle Simchie.

"Come, let's go home," said Usher's mother. "We'll sleep on it. Tomorrow, we will see it with a clear head."

"We have no home!" wept Usher's father. "Besides, we have a right here just as much as they have—even more!"

"Go home! Go home!" cried Uncle Simchie. "There is no money here—nothing! The business is on the rocks!"

"Rocks! Last week, the business was going good! This week, it's on the rocks! I'll give you rocks!" cried Usher's father, his face flushed and angry. And he bent down, picked up a rock from the street and hurled it into the window of the grocery.

Before you knew it, Usher's father, with Usher caught in the middle, had thrown himself on the unlucky Uncle Simchie and was flailing away.

"Stop it!" shouted Usher's mother. "You'll get killed! It'll cost us more in doctor bills!"

But it was really Usher who was getting "killed."

Finally, Usher's mother managed to grab hold of her husband.

"Come away!" she said. "You'll end up in prison, yet!"

"Police! Police" shouted the old man.

The trip back was like a funeral. Usher and I were hushed. The ferry trip had no effect on us.

"Here, have an apple," said Usher's mother to her husband.

"Food—at a time like this," said her husband, "when I've been robbed!"

"We had nothing before," she said. "We have nothing now. At least, we're not out on the street."

"Nothing? Is three hundred and thirty dollars nothing?"

His wife looked out on the harbor with the skyline of New York approaching and the ships going by.

"Money is like water!" she said.

"Money is like blood!" said Usher's father.

And right out in the open, in the middle of the harbor, with the windows of the skyscrapers shimmering electric, and the bridges bent like strings of pearls, and with the Statue of Liberty all lit up over the land of the free and the home of the brave, he bowed his head in his hands and helplessly wept.

We followed Usher's father and mother as if they were leading a funeral cortège. It was cold and darkness had fallen. A piercing wind was sweeping through our now-deserted street, and suddenly everything looked to me like Bayonne.

"I can't stand it!" said Usher. "My old man is drivin' me crazy with his crying!"

And horror of horrors, as if Bayonne had not been enough, there were Miriam, her five children, and all her worldly possessions, still standing there on our street.

"Avrum!" moaned Usher's mother as she began to run. "A judgment has been delivered on us!"

"Miriam!" cried Usher's mother, grabbing the youngest child and taking him into her arms. "You're still here? How is it possible!"

"My husband has left me," whispered the beautiful Miriam.

"The bum!" sneered Usher's mother. "There is no other bloom that shines like you on this street!"

"It's not the first time," said Miriam. "He'll be back."

"The drunkard!" jeered Usher's mother. "He should have been strangled before he was born!"

And then Usher's mother, unable to contain herself, unloosed a cascade of tears. And now Jakie the Snotnose began. And then Usher and I. And Miriam's other children. And Usher's father. All crying! All sobbing on our sad and unfortunate street!

"There's no question!" said Usher's mother. "We're taking them in!"

"Are you crazy?" asked Usher's father, his eyes widening. "We have troubles of our own."

"Miserable wretch!" cried Usher's mother. "I'll kill you here right on this street in another minute if you don't take them in! Then I'll kill myself! It'll be in all the newspapers tomorrow, how an unfeeling husband was responsible for the death of his wife!"

"And what will we eat?" asked Usher's father.

"Your insides!" screamed Usher's mother. "I'll take in an extra boarder! One in front and another in the back!"

"And where will we sleep?"

"We'll sleep in the kitchen on a folding bed!" said his wife.

"Grand Central Station!"

"A judgment has been delivered on us!"

"Not on us!" said Usher's father. "On me!"

And so we began. Usher handed me a stick of furniture. I handed it to Jakie the Snotnose, who handed it to Usher's mother, who handed it to Usher's father, who took it into the basement. In no time, Miriam's furniture was put away.

"Free storage!" said Usher's father.

"Break your head!" said Usher's mother.

"I can't!" said Usher's father. "I have a judgment on it!"

"Dirty apostate!" said Usher's mother.

Up the stairs, we dragged Miriam's mattress and placed it in the living room.

"May you live to a hundred years!" said Usher's mother, thanking me as we parted.

And as everyone in Usher's house went to bed, except the two women, who stayed up all night, talking, I ran home to tell my mother everything that had happened.

The next morning, bright and early, my mother awoke me.

"They'll need food," she said. "Take this to them."

And there were packages of bread and bottles of hot soup and jars of fish.

And so I quickly dressed and carried the bundles to Usher's house.

You should have seen that house! Children and mattresses all over the place. People walking about with clothes and without clothes. Bottles being warmed. Diapers being dried. Crying. Screaming. Fighting. And Usher's mother soothing this one, hollering at another, patting a third, admonishing a fourth.

"Tell your mother, she'll be rewarded in heaven," said Usher's mother.

When who should make his appearance but Usher's father, carrying Miriam's youngest.

"This is not a child!" he cried, lifting the child up in the air. "This is a treasure!"

And then one of Miriam's children hid behind a door as Usher's father pretended to search for him, while another went to hide under the table and squealed in delight as he was found out.

"There he goes spoiling the children!" said Usher's mother

and then, turning to Miriam, added, "What can you do with him?"

And there was the sad and gentle Miriam standing at the stove, preparing a bottle while a ray of light came through the window and lit up her chestnut hair so that it appeared as if there were beams shooting out. And she stood so, without tears, looking confident and self-assured, her every motion beautiful and exquisite. And I realized that she was the first woman I ever truly loved. And it was as if because I loved her, I loved everyone else—Usher's father, Usher's mother, Jakie the Snotnose, Uncle Simchie and the grandfather, and even that lousy Feather Plucker! That is, everyone but Miriam's husband, Moishe! Him, I could never love! And as I stood so, I thought I could hear the fire engines coming down our street, and I realized they were coming for me; for not only were fires burning on our street but there was fire burning in me. And I was burning, simply burning up!

Come into the Hallway, for Five Cents!

O NCE UPON A TIME, WE JEWS HAD A PRINCESS, named Berenice, who was affianced to the Emperor Titus. Bedecked in her jewels, attended by her slaves, and with gongs and cymbals clashing, this Jewish Princess made her appearance in the court of Rome, only to find that the King of the Romans had gone mad. For the Emperor Titus insisted there were flies buzzing in his ears. How the Jews throughout the Roman Empire must have prayed for this marriage! But it was not to be.

Once upon a time, we, too, had a Berenice, who was affianced to a king among men. Bedecked in a housedress, her stockings bulging with money, this Berenice appeared in Usher's house in Brownsville, only to find her king had flies in his nose! There the parallel ends.

My friend Usher had an aunt named Berenice, on his mother's side. I suppose you might call her "simple." The story was told that when she came to America she was naturally examined by the immigration authorities.

"Do you suffer from epilepsy?" asked the official. She did not answer.

"Do you suffer from epilepsy?" asked the official again.

"Your honor," she said, "I do not understand."

"Do you have the 'falling sickness'?" repeated the official.

"Sure," she said, "I fall."

"You do?" said the official.

"Sure, in the winter when I walk on the ice, I fall."

"Pass her," said the official.

As "simple" as she was, that is how beautiful she was. An olive skin, with almond-shaped eyes that slanted ever so slightly upward at the ends. You sat and searched and searched and saw a thousand things in those eyes, that is, until you realized that there was nothing there. Her nose was straight and ended in the most fascinating nostrils that seemed to quiver constantly. And you watched spellbound, thinking that the quivering expressed a profound sensitivity until it dawned on you that her nose moved for everything from soup with almonds to soup without almonds; such was the gamut of her philosophy. As for her lips, adorable as they were, housing the straightest, whitest teeth you ever did see, everything was as raisins and almonds until she opened them up. And then, all illusion, all hope was destroyed. Yes, she was a true Oriental beauty.

"I'm here!" she would announce as she would sit herself down in the kitchen and begin to cry.

"What are you crying about?" Usher's father would ask.

"Idiot," Usher's mother would answer, "she wants to get married."

"That's easy," Usher's father would say.

"In Bayonne, it's not so easy!" Berenice would say.

"What's wrong with Bayonne?" Usher's father would say.

"There are no men in Bayonne. All the men are in New York!"

I am afraid she was not very particular. She would sit outside Usher's house and watch the crowds go by and say to Usher's mother, "Look at that one with his fine long nose. Such character in that nose. A real professor!" Or else, she would say, "Look at that one—the small one, with that tiny bit of a nose. Oh! What a darling he is! Such excitement in that nose! Such life!" And then suddenly she would cry out, "Oh! I'm dying! What a nose that one was that went by! A sort of in-between one! Not too big! Not too little! Just right! A prince among men!"

Usher and I decided she was crazy.

"Usher," she would say, "I'm here. Sit down!"

Usher would sit down.

"I want you to write me a letter," she would say as she opened her enormous handbag, so enormous it was that it almost looked like a market bag, and then turning to Usher's mother, would add, "Everything goes on in Bayonne. The stories I could tell you about that place!"

Then she would take out a post card and a pencil, hand them over to my hero Usher, and say, "Write!"

"What should I write?" my hero would ask.

"Say that Mrs. Beinstock is carrying on with the man who takes care of her stove."

My friend Usher would write.

"Add to the bottom," she would say, "that the stove is not the only thing he's taking care of."

Usher wrote. "Where should I send it?"

"Send it to the FBI!"

Usher wrote.

"Next!" she would say as she took out another post card. "Say in this one that Schwartzkopf is making whisky in his bathtub."

Usher wrote. "Where should I send it?"

"To the FBI, of course! Where else?" she would say handing Usher a nickel. "Thank God for the FBI!"

"Have some bread; I made it myself," Usher's mother would say.

And then taking the bread, our Oriental beauty would say, "Everything is better in Brownsville! Even the bread!"

There appeared in Usher's house a new boarder. Bounding up the stairs two at a time, he burst into the kitchen carrying the "Furnished Room to Let" sign.

"You gotta room?"

"Front. Very clean," answered Usher's mother.

"I'll take it!" said the man.

"Don't you want to take a look, first?"

"Nah, I don't have to look," he said as he walked in and took possession.

I noticed he carried no luggage.

"What a nice young man," said Usher's mother. "He makes such a fine appearance."

Immediately, from the front room, there came the sound of someone banging rhythmically, and soon there followed a "One! Two! Three! One! Two! Three!"

"What's goin' on dere?" cried Usher as he raced into the front room.

And there was the new boarder in his underwear, moving his arms up and down, bending at the knees, exercising to beat the band.

"Look!" said Usher.

Then the boarder did a few more bends, stood on his head, and looped his body in the air in a quick somersault.

"He's great! The greatest we ever had! The greatest of them all!" cried Usher.

And so my friend Usher and myself found a new hero in Benyomin. We would sit enthralled in the boarder's room as he went through his exercises. One! Two! Three! One! Two! Three! And while the boarder would remove his shirt, the better to show his muscles, we would sit with mouth open, watching the fine motions of his musculature. One! Two! Three! One! Two! Three!

First, he would work his arms, and we could see his enormous biceps rise and fall. One! Two! Three! Then, he would work his shoulders as his magnificent flesh would crawl with animation and life. One! Two! Three! And while the sweat from his armpits and neck would run down his hairy chest, he would heave, thrust, and practically burst his ribs for us, as we would look at this wonder of wonders, this prince among men. One! Two! Three! Then, he would tighten the muscles of his limbs into hard knots and lift Usher, or myself, onto his shoulders. One! Two! Three! And as our heads touched the ceiling, George Washington and Louie the Lip and every hero we ever had went down the drain. Two! Three! One!

We could not do enough for our boarder. We would sweep his room and fix his bed. We would tie his shoelaces and polish his shoes. When he entered the house, we would hasten to remove his coat. We would run the water for him in the bathtub and would sit with him while he bathed, handing him his towel and covering him with his bathrobe so that he would not catch cold. And when he was finished, we would clean the tub out after him.

"Say, kids," he would say, "get outta here! I gotta use the toilet."

And we would stay outside the bathroom door while we could hear him moaning and groaning on the inside.

And when he came out, we would say, "Benjy, did you go good today?"

For everything about him was of the utmost concern to us. And my friend Usher, in the midst of playing ball, would suddenly remember Benyomin and say, "Benjy didn't sleep good last night; he wasn't snoring. He snores every night; last night I didn't hear a peep out of him."

He was, indeed, the greatest thing that had ever entered our lives.

"Avrum," cried Usher's mother to her husband, "he's wonderful; so young, so full of life!"

"A bum!" said Usher's father.

He was the greatest, the greatest of them all. One! Two! Three!

Strangely enough, it was not only Usher's father who delivered such a cynical observation on Benyomin. I remember Miriam, our neighbor, was visiting Usher's mother in the kitchen when the boarder passed through to his bedroom. Passed through, did I say? He passed through, took one look at the beautiful Miriam, and stayed without saying a word. Electricity was flying through the air.

"What's the matter, Benjy? You sick?" asked the worried Usher. "You want some medicine?"

And there he stood, a changed man. His movements slow and graceful. His eyes looking through narrow slits. And oh! how sad he seemed, yet, how strangely happy. And without saying a word, as if in a dream, he poured her a glass of tea in slow motion.

"Thank you," she said, "but I do not want any tea."

Slowly, insinuatingly, like a cat, he took out a cigarette and offered her one.

"Thank you," she said, "I don't smoke."

Lightning was flashing! Thunder was rolling in the kitchen!

And then, as if impelled by inner voices, he put his strong hands on her wedding band and twisted the ring around. With great fury, her eyes flashing, she pulled her hand away.

"Ah," he said banging his fists against the muscles of his thigh, "one can live, but they don't let you!"

Soon, there emanated the rhythmic noises of his exercises from the bedroom.

"Isn't he wonderful? Did you ever see such a man?" cried Usher's mother. "Did you ever see such life, such energy, such joy!"

"He's no good," said Miriam in a flat voice as she turned to leave.

But, of course, everyone knew Miriam was stupid.

It happened that Usher's Aunt Berenice appeared one day when the boarder was exercising in his bedroom.

"What's this?" cried the amazed Berenice as the floor of the kitchen began to shake. "Is this a crazy-house?"

"Sh!" said Usher. "It's the new boarder, he's exercising!"

"You should see him!" cried Usher's mother. "A joy! A happiness! A treasure!"

"Usher, darling, dear," said his aunt opening up her large bag, "here's a nickel. Call him out!"

"Give Benjy another five minutes," said Usher pocketing the coin. "He's gotta finish the exercise!"

One! Two! Three! How the floor did shake! How the windows rattled! How even the plaster in the walls rumbled!

"What's he so quiet for?" asked the aunt as the noise stopped.

"Breathing exercises," said Usher.

"Exercises for breathing?" cried the astonished Berenice. "Who needs to exercise breathing?"

And there was Benyomin suddenly standing in the kitchen and breathing with all his might and main.

"My sister," said Usher's mother.

"Pleased to meet you," said Benyomin.

I noticed the loud and garrulous Berenice´ standing as if struck dumb.

"Benjy boy," said Usher, "show my aunt an exercise."

The boarder moved his arm.

"What did I tell you?" cried Usher to his aunt. "And it's real!"

"I can't believe it!" said Berenice.

"Believe it! Believe it!" cried Usher and then, turning to Benyomin, he said, "Benjy, can I feel dat muscle in your arm?"

"Go ahead, kid," said the obliging Benyomin. "Feel!"

And now, we, Usher and myself and his Aunt Berenice, were at Benyomin's arm checking on that muscle.

"Hit me in the stomach," said Benyomin. "Go ahead, hit me!"

And then, we, including the aunt, began to hit him in the stomach.

"Harder! Harder!" he cried.

I hurt my fists banging him in the stomach.

"Feel that thigh!" he ordered.

And now, we, including the amazed aunt, were examining the muscles of his thigh.

"That's all for today, folks," said our athlete as he retreated into the bedroom.

"What did I tell you?" asked Usher's mother. "Such a dream! Such a diamond! Such a joy!"

"I swoon from ecstasy," said Berenice. "Such character in that nose! I'm smitten! A prince among men! I'm moving in!"

It came to pass that Usher's father brought home a dog.

"A dog!" exclaimed Usher's mother. "I don't have enough to clean, I've got to clean from a dog, too!"

"He's got a dog-brain, that's the reason he brings home a dog!" said Berenice stretched out on the couch, preparing to go to bed. "If it were a dog, this is not a dog."

I looked and saw that Berenice was right. The head was one dog, the tail was another, the legs were a third. He was all mixed-up.

And would you not think this dog would be only too glad to find a home? Would you not? But this stupid dog, the moment Usher took his hand off his neck and turned his back, took off across the kitchen floor, his nails scratching the linoleum, and ran whining to the door. Not only a mutt, but a real crybaby, too.

"I ain't lettin' him escape! The last dog we had ran out of the door and never came back. Here, Brownie! Have some milk. It's good for your intestines," said Usher as he proceeded to tie the dog to the drainpipe under the kitchen sink.

That night, a great snore rose in Usher's house. There was Usher's father snoring a kind of long steady snore without any interruptions. There was Usher's mother snoring a tired, staccato one that came out like machine gun fire, ceased, and then began all over again. Then Usher, a whizz that seemed to rattle from the throat. Then Benyomin the Magnificent, a beautiful sonorous sound that came out like a clear bell, or like the cantor's singing in the synagogue. And then Berenice on the couch, loud but nervous (and she was to have plenty to be nervous about). As for Brownie, he did not snore, he was awake.

"Help! Help!" cried Berenice.

And everybody came rushing out in his long underwear to the screaming Berenice.

"Berenice, my darling, my dear!" cried Usher's mother. "What happened?"

"What happened?" cried the frantic Berenice, clutching her enormous handbag. "What didn't happen! I was asleep on the couch, when I dreamt somebody was over me and putting his face toward my cheek. And when I awoke, sure enough, there was somebody, or something, over me, and would you believe it, he was licking my face!"

"I don't believe it!" said Benyomin in astonishment.

"Fool! Since when is that something to scream about," smiled Usher's father and then, looking at Benyomin knowingly, added, "Next time, if someone kisses you, don't scream; kiss him back."

"What do you mean 'since when is that something to scream

about'? Of course, it's something to scream about!" cried Berenice.

"If you gotta scream, scream about something worthwhile," said Usher's father from the bedroom.

"It was Brownie," said Usher.

"Who's 'Brownie'?" asked Berenice.

"Don't you know who Brownie is? Brownie's our dog."

"I shouldn't know from a harmful disease; that's how much I know from 'Brownie'!"

"Look!" said Usher. "Come into the kitchen. Dat dog tore the string in half and ran out of the kitchen. He was doin' all the kissin'!"

"A dog kissing me!" cried Berenice in disgust, wiping the palm of her hand against her face and looking in Benyomin's direction. The prince began to laugh.

"Oh!" screamed Berenice as she raised her hands to cover her bosom and ran to the couch, still holding on to her bag. "I'm undressed!"

The prince laughed even more heartily.

Then Usher grabbed the dog, slapped him once or twice across the face, and said: "You dumb dog, I'm gonna teach you! When I get through with you, you'll be the best watchdog in the world. Now, here's another cord. And this one, you won't be able to break loose from. What's the matter with you? Ain't you got no brains—kissin' dat Berenice!"

"False alarm! It was a false alarm!" he shouted as he prepared to go back to bed.

"Put out the lights and go to sleep!" cried his father from the bedroom. "Respectable people don't stay up all night. This is a respectable house!"

"Help! Help! Help!" screamed Berenice. "I've been robbed! Somebody has taken away my money!"

They were all there in their long underwear again.

"My money! My money! Somebody has stolen my money!"

"Money! Somebody stole your money!" cried Usher's father frightened.

Money was a serious matter.

"I work hard!" she cried. "I slave in the shop! Where else would I expect to be safe? Not in Bayonne, but here! And here, even in Brownsville, there are thieves crawling about! Look! Look! Look at my empty pocketbook!"

And sure enough, the pocketbook was completely empty.

"How much money did you have?" cried the wide-awake father, who was really a philosopher when he slept but did not know it.

"Four hundred thirty-two dollars and twenty-seven cents!"

"What?" cried the wide-awake mother, who was really dumdum bullets when she slept but did not know it.

"So much money!" exclaimed Benyomin the Magnificent, who was the widest awake of all, and who was a cantor when he slept but did not know it.

"How can you trust the bank?" cried the FBI, now alerted.

And there in their underwear, their knees shivering in the cold, they all knew she was right, for the débâcle of one great bank was something everyone on our street had felt.

Then Usher, who was really nothing at all when he slept, bent down and picked up a dollar bill and gave it to Berenice, who immediately threw it into her empty pocketbook.

"The crooks left one behind," he said.

And then, suddenly the distraught Berenice began screaming at Usher, "I know! Here is the one who took the money! Last week, I gave him a nickel, and he wouldn't give it back! He's the thief!"

The eyes of his mother's face opened up; her hands became molded into fists.

"Search the monster!" cried Berenice.

Search the monster. What could you search? Poor Usher was standing in his underwear as it was.

"Torture the thief! Find out where he hid the loot! I swear I'll squeeze the truth out of him!"

And then, reluctantly, Usher's mother began to shake my friend Usher.

"I didn't steal no money!" he began as the tears formed in his eyes and began racing down his cheeks like Niagara. "She's crazy. Why should I steal her money? I ain't no crook!"

"Stop!" interrupted Usher's father. "Unhand that child! This is no way to treat a human creature! The child has his rights, too!"

And the mother retreated, only too glad to do so.

"Kill the beast! Kill him! He stole my money!" cried Berenice.

"Let me handle it," said the father, brushing them all aside with a wide sweep of the hand and turning to Usher, added, "Sit down! Over here!"

The "beast" sat down on the couch.

"He's liable to steal the only dollar I have left!" cried the crazed Berenice as she grabbed her bag away from him. "I won't even have carfare to go back to Bayonne!"

"Let me look into his eyes," said the father. "I can tell if he took it, just by looking."

And so Usher's father looked while they all stood about with bated breath, waiting without a sound. Not only did he look, but he looked and looked.

Then falling back, the father gave forth a sigh.

"Well!" demanded Berenice as she released her breath.

"I can't tell. But there's no question there is something hidden in those eyes!"

Now Benyomin the Magnificent stepped forward.

"Let me try," he said.

Usher's father stepped aside.

"Stand up, Usher!" said the Magnificent as he began to motion with his arms. "Would you like to do some exercises with me?"

Usher nodded his head in silence.

"That's where the real brain lies," said Usher's mother referring to our boarder and looking angrily at her husband.

And so Benyomin and Usher, Usher and Benyomin, began to exercise. One! Two! Three! Arms out! Arms in! Leg out! Leg in! And as they exercised, the tears fell from Usher's face to his neck and down his chest under his underwear.

Then Benyomin gently said, "Usher boy, did you take the money?"

Cascading waterfalls! Summer rain! Rivulets and brooks!

"Usher boy," he repeated, "the money! Did you take the money?"

"No," persisted my friend Usher, "I didn't take no money! I ain't no crook!"

"He didn't take the money," said Benyomin turning to Berenice.

"Then who did?" cried Berenice.

Benyomin turned to Usher, "Who took the money, Usher? The truth, now."

My friend Usher tightened his muscles, closed his eyes, drew in his breath, and said as quickly as he could:

"You took the money!"

"You're kidding!" cried Benyomin, aghast.

And now everyone turned to face our Benyomin.

And here I must interrupt. I'm not going to apologize for Usher. I know he took the easy way out. But put yourself in his place. Would you be any better? There was Benyomin, the strong, handsome Benyomin. Surely, he could go to the electric chair better than Usher. And if you love someone, such as Usher loved Benyomin, should not the one you love help you out in an emergency once in a while? After all, what is the sense of loving someone, unless he can do you a favor? And if you do not have a big brother, and a "brother" like Benyomin enters your life to fill in the empty spaces, should he not fight for you when you are in trouble? After all, whom else can you get into trouble but the one you love? The one you hate will not let you. And not so oddly enough, the treatment a Benyomin the thief would get would not exactly be the same as an Usher the thief would get. And so it happened, as you will see.

"Benyominal, darling! You're not the thief, are you?" asked the incredulous mother, all sugar and spice.

"The kid's crazy!" exclaimed Benyomin.

"Good people! Wonderful people! Friends! Neighbors!" cried Berenice suddenly springing to life and standing up. "It must be told! Let everyone hear! This money was my dowry. I worked and worked to save it up, so that I could go to my husband with respect and with dignity. After all, why shouldn't a good Jewish girl bring her husband some money to help out. A few extra dollars never hurt anyone. Since it was my dowry, and since Benyomin took it, I'm willing to forgive and forget. And here, I want everyone to listen closely. Usher darling, are you listening?"

"I'm listening, dear Aunt Berenice," he said returning into the parlor.

"Listen, everybody! Listen, extra special! My Benyomin can have the money. I give it to him as a dowry," continued Berenice, now all smiles, as Usher began to turn all colors.

"What's the matter, Usher?" cried his mother.

"I think I'm going to vomit!" said Usher.

"Don't vomit! Listen to your Aunt Berenice!" said his mother, and then, turning a beaming face to Benyomin, said, "It looks as if we're going to dance at somebody's wedding. I'm going to break that floor dancing!"

"Nobody is dancing at my wedding, yet!" said Benyomin, a little frightened, his breath heaving, his shoulders caving in.

"Benyominal, darling! I love you like my own son," said Usher's mother. "I want to break dishes at your wedding. You got the dowry already. We trust you. Only give us the wedding!"

When at that very, very moment, what do you think happened? There was that stinking mutt Brownie entering the room from the kitchen with a batch of the green stuff in his mouth.

"Look!" cried Usher. "The dog!"

"My money!" cried Berenice as she made for the dog's mouth and tore out her hard-earned dollar bills.

Now it became clear. Money lay on the kitchen floor. There was money under the couch, under drainpipes and radiators, under tables and chairs. A dollar bill here. A five-dollar bill there. Money! Money! Everywhere!

Now Berenice began to scream. And everybody, for the next half hour, showed his back to life, as he got on his knees to help find that green stuff: Usher's father, Usher's mother, Benyomin, and Usher himself. And as each bill was found, they turned it over to the frenzied Berenice, who counted and threw it into her bag. It seemed as if it would never end.

"Well?" asked Usher's father. "Do you have enough? My knees are falling off."

"The twenty-seven cents is missing!" said Berenice.

They continued to search. I think they spent more time looking for the twenty-seven cents than for the other four hundred and thirty-two dollars until Usher went over to the dog and cried,

"Brownie, come over here! Where is the twenty-seven cents? Where did you hide the money?"

And Brownie sniffed the air, and wagged his tail, and pawed the linoleum in the living room.

"Where, Brownie? Where did you put the twenty-seven cents? Did you put it under the sink?"

And Usher ran to the sink and looked, but there was no money.

"Did you put it in the stove?"

And Usher ran to look in the stove, but there was no money.

"In the toilet maybe? Did little Brownie put the money in the toilet?"

And Usher ran into the bathroom, and sure enough, there lay the twenty-seven cents on the bathroom floor.

Then Usher banged the dog in the face with his hand and

said, "You dirty crook! That'll teach you a lesson!"

"Let's go to bed," cried Usher's father, "it's enough for one night."

And Berenice began to extract her money from her pocketbook.

"Pocketbooks are not safe, anymore," she said, as she raised her nightgown and began to push the money down her stocking while Benyomin the Magnificent looked slyly from the corner of his eye. Then when she could not fit in any more, she began to push the money down the stocking of her other leg. And when this failed her, she started to fill up the bosom of her nightgown.

"To bed! To bed!" cried Usher's father, putting out the light.

That night, Brownie made his getaway.

And so Usher's Aunt Berenice, on his mother's side, was now a sort of walking pay station. When she had to pay her rent, she dug. When she had to give Usher a nickel for running some errand, she went for it in the most outlandish places. And then she was always embarrassing you by feeling to see if her assets were intact. Thus the Berenice that had existed before was still there, only more so. Yet no one in Usher's house, or on our street for that matter, felt that she was doing the wrong thing by carrying her money on her person, for they had all lived through an unhappy experience with a bank, all as one.

There had once stood a great bank on one of our streets. It had marble columns, and porticoes, and piazzas. On the front of this bank hung its name—in marble, of course. "Bank of the United States" it was called, or at least, its real name was almost as good.

"How can such a bank fail?" cried the Jews of our street. "It's America's own bank!"

Recommendation, good enough. Is it not?

And as if the entire civilized world had been culled for the enlightenment of our Jews, murals depicting Hammurabi, the

Phoenicians, and Benjamin Franklin hung on its walls. Yes! There was even one of Moses beckoning his Jews across the Red Sea.

"How can such a bank fail?" cried the Jews of our street. "Moses himself asks you to come across!"

A real production.

And as if this was not enough, the tellers in their marble cages all had straight noses and spoke in whispers when they took your money.

"How can such a bank fail?" cried the Jews of our street. "It's a pleasure to give them the money. They take it with such respect."

Take my money. And give me a whisper in return.

But when this bank failed, it was not whispers that were heard. There were loud, raucous cries. There was screaming!

And so Usher's Aunt Berenice went about with her dignity unquestioned.

It happened one night that Usher and I came running up into his house. Finding the kitchen empty, Usher began to attack the icebox, and finally tiring of this, he said:

"Where's dat Benjy boy? He isn't exercising today. I'm going in to say 'hello' to him and see what's going on with his muscles."

When from the boarder's room there came the sound of a woman squealing in laughter.

"What's this?" cried Usher. "Something new here?"

And leading me by the arm, he went into the hallway and quietly climbed up the metal ladder to the roof.

It was cold and dark up there. And from the open skylight of Benyomin's room, there came a bright light that lit up the roof like a jack-o'-lantern.

"Do you hear anything?" whispered Usher, putting his ear to the skylight.

"No, I don't hear a sound."

"Dat Benjy is wasting my old man's heat with his skylight

open that way. Do you see anything?"

I put my eye to the corner of the open skylight and looked. My head was twisted and my neck was forced into an uncomfortable position when, with one eye, I could make out a piece of our boarder and help! help! would you believe it! another piece of Berenice and both pieces were put together like one as Berenice sat on our boarder's lap. And Benyomin had one hand extended about her waist, while the other was pawing her thigh, just where her stockings ended.

I fell back, shocked that our Benjy could do such a thing, when Usher proceeded to contort his head and place his eye to the opening in the skylight.

"That dirty Benjy!" cried Usher as he fell back in astonishment. "Kissing a girl! That no-good traitor!"

Like the dead weight of a hammer was this traitorous blow to Usher.

"Usher, darling, finish your breakfast," said his mother.

"I ain't hungry."

"Eat! Don't those bananas and cream look delicious?" said his mother.

"I ain't hungry."

"Ain't hungry? You must be sick. Castor oil, it'll be!"

Usher fled from the kitchen.

Like a bad dream that had to be blotted out.

"How's Benjy boy?" I asked by mistake one day.

"What boy are you talkin' about?" said Usher.

"You know—Benjy boy!"

"I don't know nobody by that name," said Usher.

"You don't know nobody by that name! What's the matter? You sick in the head or something! Don't you know Benjy boy—your boarder?"

"We ain't got no boarder by that name," insisted Usher as he turned away.

Even the name of the Magnificent had become anathema.

Yet, slowly, insidiously, in another fashion, Benyomin the boarder was to creep back into Usher's life.

On our street, there lived at this time an "American." Her distinguishing characteristics were that she wore high heels, kept herself aloof from our neighbors, and had packages delivered by the Macy truck.

And when that truck from Macy's appeared on our street, it was even better than one of our perennial fires, for from the houses and the stoops issued children, and from the windows peered our women to see this outlandish sight.

"Rich! Macy's truck!" came the impressed voices from the windows.

Her husband was a cop. Thus with that Macy truck coming to deliver packages, and that big six-foot wielder of a night stick, it was enough to earmark this "American" in a pale all her own. And the fact that this woman had only one child, a girl named Dora, served further to isolate her from our world of women who bore children in more fruitful quantities.

"One child! A real high-tone lady! Rich!" said the voices from the windows.

What this family was doing living on our street, I will never know. It was as if they had gotten lost; or maybe the rent was just cheap. But when the "American" fearlessly walked by our houses, every Saturday like clockwork, with her Dora on their way to the child's dancing studio, eyes followed them, fingers pointed. And, indeed, it took courage to walk the plank surrounded by peering eyes on both sides.

"Rich! Dancing lessons for the child! Rich!" said the voices from the windows.

"Look how that child carries herself! Such grace! A real dancer! A Hollywood actress! Rich! Rich!"

"Hey, Dora!" said Usher one day as we were standing outside his house. "You wanna make a nickel?"

I swallowed spit at the nerve of that Usher talking to our Dora.

"What did you say?" said the dancer of our street as she stopped.

Yes! She was human. It suddenly occurred to me that this Dresden china doll was only too glad to have someone talk to her. Human, all too human!

"Come into the hallway, I'll give you a nickel."

"Gimmie the nickel, first!"

"First, come into the hallway."

"The nickel, first!"

"Into the hallway!" ordered Usher and then, turning to me and giving me the coin, he added, "Let him hold the nickel. He's honest!"

And that cheap, nickel-plated Dresden doll went into the hallway with Usher. Human, all too human!

I did not recognize that hallway. Mysterious squeaks came from the stairs to frighten us. The walls sent forth a tidal wave of moisture that seemed to match the anxious perspiration that cascaded from us. And the steam fitting on the radiator hissed and hissed like some awful witch hurling steady imprecations at us for what we were about to do.

And would you believe it, instead of my hero Usher doing the kissing, that Dresden Dora pulled Usher to her, clasped her arms around his shoulders and kissed and kissed and kissed. Then as if that was not enough, our china doll turned to me, and before you could say, "Hello, Mama! Papa's here!" there she had her pouting lips planted on mine, and she was kissing away to beat the band.

The Stars and Stripes Forever! Anchors Away! Onward Christian Soldiers! In Dixieland, I'll Take My Stand! Hooray! Hooray!

Kiss! Kiss! Kiss!

"Hey!" cried Usher. "He didn't pay! He ain't entitled to no kisses!"

And so she turned back to her breadwinner and planted her lips on his.

On the Shores of Tripoli! By the Waters of Minnetonka! Tipperary! O Tipperary! Tipperary! O Tipperary!

Kiss! Kiss! Kiss! How that Dresden doll did kiss!

"Stop!" cried Usher. "Gimmie a minute to catch my breath."

And while Usher held her off to synchronize his breathing, that dancing Dora turned to me and began all over again.

"O.K.!" she said finally. "Give me my nickel!"

"What do you say, Ush? Does she get the nickel?" I asked.

"She gets the nickel! It's hers! She worked for it!" cried the satisfied Usher.

"You would have had to give me the nickel, anyway. My Pop's a cop!" said Dora as she took the coin and very gracefully began to walk out of the hallway. "Pleased to make your acquaintance."

She was a good dancer!

Yankee Doodle Went Uptown! Riding on a Pony! Yankee Doodle Went Uptown! Went Uptown!

She was a good dancer!

Naturally, Usher became a steady visitor in Dora's house.

"How do you do, Dora's mother," said Usher as he and I made our entrance one day.

"Won't you sit down and make yourselves comfortable," said the "American" who was all dressed up to go out.

Usher and I sat down, ill at ease.

"Dora, I'm going to Macy's," said this Queen of the department stores as she went to the door. "You stay home and watch the house."

"Yes, Mother."

And as soon as we heard the high heels of this mother descend the stairs, we were galvanized into activity, and Dora did the honors by allowing us to search the house. We went through closets and drawers and found all kinds of fascinating things: brass knuckles, policemen's uniforms, guns, bullets, torn socks.

"Your Pop ever shoot anybody?" asked Usher.

"Of course, you ninny! He shoots somebody at least once a day."

"If he shoots somebody," Usher challenged, "let's see the medals."

"Medals! Medals! The whole place is full of those medals," said our dancer as she opened a drawer and pulled out a host of medals. "My mother says if he brings home another medal, she'll scream."

But Usher and I were deaf to this girl as we gazed fascinated and stirred beyond human comprehension at this fabulous sight before our eyes. It seemed to me as if these were not mere medals, but preciously woven jewels that could be regarded only with an emotion of religious awe.

"Can I touch it?" asked Usher as this emotion slowly thawed.

"Yes! But be careful to put it back," said Dora, "otherwise he hollers, and when he hollers, watch out, because he's liable to do anything, like breaking the dishes, or spilling out the chicken soup into the garbage pail."

Carefully, tenderly, with the greatest of humility, Usher took one of the medals and hung it on his chest. I could almost see the tears forming in his eyes, while drums beat, and armies marched, and mothers tearfully bid their boys good-by as they went off to war. This was happiness.

Yankee Doodle!

What, with nobody coming into that house, Usher and I were, indeed, very welcome. Upon entering, he would immediately make a dash for the medals and in a few short moments adorn himself with row upon row of the hardware.

"Wife," would Usher, metallically adorned, cry as he sat down at the table, "bring me my hat!"

And Dora would run to her father's closet and bring out a policeman's hat.

"Wife," Usher would cry, putting on the policeman's hat and banging on the table, "bring me my club!"

And Dora would run and bring my hero a night stick.

"Wife," Usher would cry banging the stick on the table, "where is my supper?"

And Dora would run to the closet and bring back an empty plate.

"Wife," Usher would cry, "you didn't give me a kiss!"

"Gimme a nickel, first!" Dora would say.

And Usher would take out a coin from his trouser pocket and give it to our dancer, who would immediately throw the coin into a glass which she kept on top of the kitchen stove. And it was not long before those coins in that glass began to mount up and up.

I told you, she was a good dancer.

It happened one night when Usher and I appeared in Dora's house that Usher, adorned with his medals, equipped with a night stick, and bedecked in a policeman's hat, began to bang on the table.

"Wife, gimme my gun!"

The dutiful dancer ran and returned with an empty holster which she proceeded to tie around Usher's waist.

Bang went the stick on the table!

"Wife, gimmie my supper!"

Over to the kitchen closet. Out came the empty plate. Down it went in front of Usher.

Usher looked and looked.

"What's in that plate?" asked Usher.

"Ham and eggs," said Dora.

"Ham and eggs!" shouted Usher. "I ain't eatin' no ham and eggs! What do you think I wanna do—poison myself? Gimmie horseradish and bread, instead. I ain't no *goy!*"

The enduring dancer skipped to the cupboard and returned with "horseradish" and "bread."

Usher began to eat.

Bang went the holster on the table!

"In one minute, I'm gonna shoot up this place with my gun!" he cried. "You didn't give me no horseradish!"

"I gave you horseradish!" cried Dora.

"Where is it, then?"

"There—on the plate! You're going blind from screaming so much! That's the reason you can't see the horseradish!"

"Where's the horseradish?"

"There—can't you see it?"

Usher looked suspiciously at the empty plate.

"Well! What do you know! It's horseradish, all right!" said Usher and then added, "Wife, give me a kiss!"

"Five cents, please!" said Dora as she put out her hand and took the coin from Usher.

Plunk! Into the glass went the nickel.

"Wife, it's getting late," said my hero, "let's go to bed!"

"Ten cents, please!" said Dora.

Plunk! Into the glass went the dime.

Soon my hero was on the couch, holster on his hip, cap on head, night stick at his side, and medals dangling; and there sat Dora on his lap, as he entwined one hand around her waist and with the other began to paw her thigh.

I was terrified. Suppose someone should walk in! The medals on Usher's chest clinked musically. Once in a while a titter would come from the dancer. Otherwise, the room was quiet, except for my own busy breathing.

Somewhere, someplace, it occurred to me I had seen this before—a piece of Usher and a piece of Dora, and both pieces put together for a kiss. And I saw myself going up the ladder to Usher's roof, and peering down the open skylight into Benyomin's bedroom, and seeing Benyomin with Usher's aunt on his lap.

Life! It was life itself that beckoned to Usher and me. And I was frightened. In Dora's house! In Benyomin's bedroom! Life was beckoning to me!

And there was Usher kiss, kiss, kissing. Usher, who was usually so awkward and ungainly, and who was, now, possessed with confidence and fearlessness, while I sat trembling, fearful of a black cloud.

And the black cloud came, because just at this very moment, dressed in a garb representing everything that was lawful and orderly, appeared Dora's father, who hovered over us, and who stamped out everything in an instant and turned all to despair.

With one full sweep of his arm, he tore the unsuspecting Usher from his kisses, and with one full kick of his leg, he hit my hero in the rear, to send him sprawling across the floor.

"If I ever catch you in this house again," roared the cop, purple with rage, "I'll send you up for twenty years! Get out of here, you dirty gutter-bum, you filthy sewer-rat!"

Yankee Doodle went uptown! Riding on a pony! He stuck a feather in his—and out came macaroni.

My hero Usher, sprawled on the floor, sought the protection that tears could bring, and began to cry. And how we managed to get out of the kitchen, and how we managed to make our way into the hallway and down the stairs, I swear I do not know. But as we went I cringed, I shut my eyes, I closed my ears to the awful screams that came from Dora's kitchen as her father was laying it on thick on that dancer.

Thus denuded of the medals, without his hat, the night stick returned to its original owner, the holster now gone, my hero limped slowly down the stairs, weeping.

Yankee Doodle went downstairs! Went downstairs!

"That lousy Benjy!" cried Usher sitting down on the stoop. "He's to blame for everything!"

Benjy! What did Benjy have to do with it?

When suddenly, from nowhere and everywhere, people began running down the street.

"Must be another fire," I said not even moving from my perch.

"It's a fire, all right! My crazy Aunt Berenice!" cried Usher, his eyes popping.

In a flash, we were running in the direction of Usher's house, and there was his Aunt Berenice, attired in her nightgown, surrounded by a multitude and screaming her head off.

"Good people! Honest friends and neighbors! Jews of Brownsville!" screamed Berenice. "A terrible thing has happened on our street!"

"What happened? What happened?" cried Mrs. Goldberg in agony.

What happened? For God's sake, I screamed within myself! What terrible thing happened?

"Worthy brothers and sisters! There are thieves walking around free on this street! And worse than thieves, there are murderers, murderers who victimize innocent young girls!"

"Still a girl?" cried the incredulous Mrs. Feinerman.

"Listen to me!" cried Berenice. "Listen to my story, so that you will know enough to guard the virtue of your daughters! Listen to my tale! Hear me out!"

"Dear child," cried one of the old ones of our street, "I'm listening."

"He told me he would marry me," cried Berenice, the tears streaming down her face. "And I, like a fool, was going to give him the money. Benyominal darling! I said to him, here's my money, and we'll get married. And we'll open up a delicatessen store and buy a little house, and we'll be happy, so happy!"

"What else did you give him?" cried Mrs. Rosenstein.

"And he said to me, gimmie the money, and I promise you we'll both stand under the canopy. And he even threw a glass on the floor and stamped his foot on it. Good people! Honest friends and neighbors! Jews of Brownsville! Never believe these fortune hunters, these monsters! Sign the marriage contract first, I said, and then, I'll give you the money!"

"Good girl!" cried Mrs. Needleman. "Good girl! A real Jewish head!"

"Neighbors! Friends! What do you think he did?"

"What? What?" cried Mrs. Finkelberg.

"These snakes do not stop at anything. They creep! They

crawl! They slide! Once they smell money, they fasten themselves on their victims, and you can't shake them off."

"If you didn't keep the money in your bosom, he would never
get to it," said Mrs. Eisenberg.

And now Usher's father came out.

"Get out of here!" he shouted scooting the crowd away and,
turning to Berenice, he cried, "Get upstairs, you fool! So what!
You and your money are still intact!"

"I'll marry you without money!" cried Mr. Mandelbaum the
Tenant laughingly.

And Berenice, her hair disarranged, tears streaming from
her eyes, went up the stairs.

"A free show!" said Mrs. Greenblatt.

"It's better than the movies!" said Mrs. Haegerman.

"But no samples!" said Mandelbaum the Tenant. The street
roared.

Frightened, I began to run up the stairs. What did this mean?
Was Benjy leaving us? Was he gone? Who's going to give us
that One! Two! Three! if you go, I cried? Who's going to show
us his big strong muscles, or lift us into the air to hit the ceiling?
And didn't you have fun with us, too? Didn't you laugh when
we opened up our mouths in amazement when you did those
famous somersaults? Benjy boy, you wouldn't leave us now,
would you? You are the greatest! The greatest of them all!

And the higher I got up the stairs, the worse it got.

Benjy boy, I cried, don't leave me! I don't know what I'll do
without you! Take her money! Take all her money! She should
give it to you with pleasure! Take the whole world's money, if
it's money you want! And if that's not enough, I'll go out and
steal some more! Only don't leave me!

And running like two lost rats into the boarder's room, we
suddenly came to a halt. No Benjy!

"He's gone!" cried Usher. "He's gone! And he didn't even say
good-by!"

"Not only is he gone," said Usher's mother, "he took my best pillowcases with him!"

"Not even a good-by!" cried Usher stamping his foot on the floor. "He didn't even say good-by!"

"Who was that man I saw downstairs yesterday, standing in the crowd?" began Berenice the next morning, all dressed up, sitting in the kitchen, drinking tea and lemon.

"Which one?" said Usher's mother. "There were thousands of people standing in that crowd yesterday."

"You know the one I mean," said Berenice, "the one with the long, distinguished nose. So refined! So cultured!"

"Do you mean Mexile?" said Usher's mother.

"Such a respectable appearance! Such an intellectual look! A prince!"

"A pushcart peddler," sighed Usher's mother.

"Now who would have thought that Benyomin would turn out to be such a disappointment," said Berenice, all dressed up, sitting in the kitchen, drinking tea and lemon. "He had such an honest nose!"

Three! Two! One!

"When We Produce Prostitutes and Thieves, We Shall Be a Normal People!"—Jabotinsky

THOUGH I HAVE RANDOM MEMORIES OF THE KID—and I exalted him!—they remain significant as the symbols of a dream to which I return again and again. And in it I ride a horse pursued by a phantom Jabotinskyite with whom I conduct an interrogation that never ends.

"Where are you going?"

"We're going to Palestine by way of Gallipoli. We'll be led by Trumpledor, he who left his arm in Port Arthur."

"And what will we do there—in Palestine and Gallipoli?"

"We will render useful service bravely and honestly. It will not be all heroism; there will be many kitchen difficulties."

"And after we've rendered useful service?"
"We'll lie in our graves under the Star of David on the mountainside of Eleom."
"Whom have you recruited?"
"Tailors! Only tailors: from England, France, Austria, Russia, and America. It'll be a babel of crossed stitches; they sew in fourteen languages."[1]

> *"Good-by, girls, I must leave you.*
> *Something tells me I must go.*
> *For you know I can't deceive you.*
> *To Gallipoli I go."*

I would have given anything to have been Kid Itzik's friend, even though he and his brother Pal Pesach had unsavory reputations, but the Kid never knew I existed. No, he must have been aware of me, but in a limited way. It was strange that I should have had an affinity for the Kid because he could barely read or write; and although I was much younger than he, I could read and write well enough. However, if one is poor in one area, there is usually compensation in another. So if anyone saw the Kid as a failure, I never did.

I was sitting on a stoop checking out our street. Pickles was throwing dice, Robby was cracking nuts, Bibi was dealing cards, and Baruch, who was very religious, was in his house, praying. And while Pickles was throwing and Robby cracking and Bibi dealing, had Baruch come out of his house and given one little *adenoi*, the entire street would have run for cover. That is how religious our street was! In short, nothing was happening on our street.

Suddenly I saw the Kid approaching. He had his head down,

---

[1]   Adapted from Vladimir Jabotinsky, *The Jewish Legion* (New York: Brith Trumpledor Organization of America, Inc. [1941?]), p. 8.

aligned with his arm, as he sent forward imaginary jabs into the air. Then he straightened up and began to skip as if jumping rope. Training already, so early in the morning? Without stopping he continued to dance until he came up in front of me.

"Kid," I said, "since you're in training, I thought I'd watch your house."

"Yes," he said, giving the air a few extra jabs, "I like to know my house is protected while I'm away." Then plopping down beside me, his face lit up as he continued, "My brother Pal Pesach! The things he's got going for him! I say, 'Pal, you got no business fooling around with girls when you're in training. How're you gonna get to be the champ?' When my mother is not in, he drags the girls up into the house. I keep a count—thirty-five girls already, sometimes two a day. He's gonna drain off all his strength if he continues so, but no! you can't stop the Pal no ways!"

I knew the Kid's elder brother Pal Pesach was also a fighter, but for the life of me, I could not figure out what he was doing with the girls. All at once my heart began to pound as I realized something extraordinary was going on in that house. I pictured the Pal dragging a girl by the hair up the stairs to the fourth floor. She would get up and start running around the table. Then just as he put out his hand to catch her, she would evaporate into the air. The pounding of my heart became so unbearable that I had to erase the picture and begin all over again. Into the hallway the Pal dragged another girl up the four flights of stairs. This one, too, stood up and ran around the table. And because the Pal was chasing girls around the kitchen table, the Kid became something special, too.

"You idle bums! You worthless thieves! Make way so that a person can get through!"

It was Hannah Sarah, the Conjurer of our street, she who was summoned whenever our neighbors were in crisis or had secrets to fend off. Quickly the Kid and I separated so that the old, wrinkled crone with her wig askew and her black dress dragging on the ground floated through like the weightless wraith she really was.

"From how many pushcarts did you steal today? First it's the pushcarts, then it'll be the savings banks, and finally the U.S. Treasury! Do America a favor and drop dead! Prize fighters, you call yourselves! Bums, you are! Why aren't you in a shop working like normal people?" she cried racing into the dark hallway.

"She's probably going upstairs to my house," sighed the Kid. " 'Head of an ox!' she screams at my mother. 'How do you expect lightning not to seek you out and strike you dead if you don't keep a glass of water on your window ledge? Do you want to be boiled in your own blood? Put a glass of water on the ledge and the water will boil, not you. You'll have plenty of time to boil in hell, so why encourage early invitations?' "

What was that crazy Hannah Sarah doing here? Before she appeared, only the Pal and the girls were running, but now the Pal was running, the girls were running, and Hannah Sarah was running, too—around the table in the kitchen on the fourth floor.

And so the Kid began to sing:

> *"I came to a house and I knocked at the door,*
> *And the old lady says, 'I have saw you before,*
> *Why don't you work like other men do?'*
> *'How the hell can I work when there's no work*
>   *to do?'*
> *Hallelujah, I'm a bum!*
> *Hallelujah, bum again!"*

Mrs. English was teaching English.

"Boys and girls," said Mrs. English with her pointer to the blackboard. "At the dinner table, cultured people never say, 'Gimmie the salt!' They always say, 'Please may I have the salt?,' The former is considered vulgar; the latter, cultivated."

In my head I saw nothing wrong with Pickles, Robby, and Bibi passing salt with a "may I?" or a "please?" even if Baruch was *adenoi*-ing, but I had reservations about a Mrs. English teaching English.

At that moment the door opened and a hushed silence fell over the class as the Kid walked in. His face was white as a sheet, he was breathing heavily, and across his cheek was a red splotch as if someone had laid it on, but good. Something was up. The Kid did not belong in my class. Nevertheless, he walked slowly down the aisle between the transfixed class and the transmogrified Mrs. English, his eyes transformed into narrow slits. Now the burly Mr. Friedman, our gym teacher, appeared after the Kid, remaining at the door with his hand on the knob. His face, too, was white as a sheet, and he, too, was breathing heavily. You could hear a pin drop in that classroom.

Mr. Friedman watched the Kid going down the aisle and did not take his eyes off our amateur boxer until the boxer sat down. Then the gym teacher turned and left the room as silently as he had made his appearance.

It was not difficult to figure out what had happened. The truant officer had picked up the Kid on the street and brought him in. The Kid was a boxer, first and foremost, and they kept insisting he was a truant. And a boxer was a special kind of person like no one else. How could anyone who was not a boxer understand that? Was it, therefore, not right for the Kid to accept the gym teacher's challenge to put on the gloves and go down to the boiler room? That is exactly what a real boxer would do. There was a conspiracy against boxers, and in that conspiracy stood Mrs. English, the truant officer, and our gym teacher.

It was with the utmost speed that I bounded out of my seat when the bell rang. I raced after the Kid, but the hordes in the hallway and then on the stairway kept me from the light in front of me.

"Hello, Kid!" I said as I finally caught up with him on the

street. "Still training? You look in good shape to me."

I excused him for not answering. He was jumping.

"How's your mother?" I asked.

He did not answer.

"And the Pal? Is he catching any girls lately?"

No answer.

"And how's that Hannah Sarah?"

This, he answered.

" 'Face of a dead mackerel!' she says to my mother. 'Why do you keep the windows sealed? I can tell from the smell in the kitchen that there are six dead souls imprisoned here. I'm not looking into your cupboards and cracks. God only knows what's doing in there! I'm sure they harbor countless dead ones. I could save you by calling on them, but there must be so many hidden away that even I can't be expected to clean them all out. God in heaven! There's one peering out of the mirror at us. Quick, open a window! How do you expect him to escape if you don't present him with a passage to the fire escape?' "

"Yes," I said. "Things are tough all over. The chorus girls are kicking! The firemen are in the red! The subways are in a hole! The fish market stinks! And Alcatraz is on the rocks!"

But the Kid only bent down and said, "Are you gonna be anywhere near Powell Street and Livonia Avenue tomorrow night?"

"I'm gonna be there—right on the corner."

"O.K.!" he said. "Nine o'clock."

I was sitting on the curbstone checking out the street on Powell and Livonia and waiting for the Kid. It was night and all the street lights were on. I thought, if I asked that one where he was going, what would he say? He would say, "I'm going to the Livonia Avenue Theatre to see a movie on the silver screen." And I would say, "You may pass!" If I had asked that one crossing the street where he was going, he would answer, "I'm going to the clothing store to buy a pair of pants so that I can sign up for the army tomorrow." "Pass!" I would have said. Then as a man carrying a ladder appeared on the opposite corner, I thought of asking him, "And what do you intend doing?" "I'm gonna make a speech," he would have answered. "On that ladder?" I would have asked. "On that ladder," he would have answered. "Do you have a permit?" "It's in my pocket." "O.K.!" I would have finally said. "You have my permission to make a speech."

So there I sat on the curbstone waiting for the Kid and listening to a speech by a Jabotinskyite.

The Jabotinskyite began:

"A Russian peasant once propounded this mathematical theory: 'Four and four make eight, with this I agree; some say five and three also make eight—but that's a Jewish plot!' "

"Speak to the point," interrupted one of the listeners. "You got your countries mixed up. We're not in Russia; we're here in America."

"Precisely," said the speaker. "Joining a new community is first a question of reception and then of assimilation. What kind of reception or assimilation do you have in Brownsville— we are all Jews? Jewish assimilation in Brownsville has obviously failed in bringing Jew and America together."

"The only ones we can assimilate with," came a voice from the crowd, "are the bums and the gangsters."

"What's the question again?" came another voice. "I don't trust that answer."

"Don't write off the bums and the gangsters," said the Jabotinskyite. "They may come in handy to oil the wheels of progress!"

At that moment a big, black, open truck appeared, careening wildly down Livonia Avenue with the Kid on top; and before I knew it, he had thrown down a pile of newspapers at my feet, and the Jabotinskyite was shouting at him and at the departing truck.

"Stop! Stop! We need you bums and gangsters for the Jewish army to defend Palestine and speed up the redemption of *Eretz Israel!*" he shouted. "Your character is endowed with *Hitlahavut*—so says the Baal Shem."

"Extra! Extra!" I began shouting. "Read all about it! Feds Club Reds at City Hall! Extra! Extra!"

"Listen to the little gangster!" continued the Jabotinskyite. "Come over to this side of the street. We will make a general of you."

"Extra! Extra!" I shouted. "Slobs Drop Jobs in Garment Strike! Extra! Extra!"

"Little gangster!" cajoled the Jabotinskyite. "The prophets and the sages hold out grace and redemption for you sooner than for me. For the love of Zion, for that unquenchable, ecstatic fire, for that still and steady flame of grace, take your gun and bring it to the Jewish army and your life will be sanctified with holy significance."

"Extra! Extra!" I shouted. "Read all about it! Socialists Refused Seats in State Legislature! Extra! Extra!"

"What's new in Gallipoli?"
"It's a failure."
"And our Jewish soldiers?"
"Wonderful! First class!"
"And Trumpledor?"
"The finest man I ever met! He is in command of our unit."
"The Mule Corps?"
"The Mule Corps! One must begin somewhere."
"And what else is there—in Gallipoli?"
"Lord Kitchener does not want any campaign in Eretz Israel *and does not desire any Jewish regiment."*
"What remains to be done?"
"We'll flood the regiment with recruits."[2]

---

[2] Adapted from Vladimir Jabotinsky, *The Story of the Jewish Legion*, (New York: Bernard Ackerman, Inc., 1945), pp. 69-70.

"Mademoiselle from Armentières, parley-voo!
Mademoiselle from Armentières, parley-voo!
She washes the soldier's underwear.
Hinky-dinky, parley-voo!

"My Froggie girl was true to me,
She was true to me, she was true to you,
She was true to the whole damn army, too!
Hinky-dinky, parley-voo!"

My pockets were bulging with money as I ran into the poolroom looking for the Kid. The place was full of tables covered with green felt, and the men were playing "Chicago" as they tapped the score on chips wired above their heads. In the rear of the poolroom, I found the Kid practising in a small gym.

He was dressed in boxing shorts, was wearing laced shoes, and had on regulation gloves. I piled the money on top of the nearest pool table and watched him.

Still practicing, he danced over to me and pulled out two dollars from the pile of money with his teeth and gave it to me; then he tapped me on the shoulder with his glove—gently, oh! so gently! I feinted first and then gave him a jab. He pretended to fall back as I gave him another jab. It was a dream in slow motion that I was to dream all the days of my life. It was a dance of bliss such as David and Jonathan might have danced. He received my blow and tapped my cheek. I held firm and gave it to him under the chin. With a loud bang, he deliberately fell to the floor and lay flat on his back.

Dear Kid, wherever you are: You danced with me as if at a wedding. You made me *shicker* as a *goy*. You jumped off the screen of the Livonia Avenue Theatre on a horse. You asked me to go for a ride with you.

Then from the floor, the Kid began to speak:

"That witch Hannah Sarah! 'Tail of a black cat!' she says to my mother. 'The souls of three wild geese are crying from your pillowcases. 'Have mercy on us!' they cry. 'Give us back our clothes so that we can ascend to heaven. They have cut our throats and plucked our feathers and we can't get out. We have been murdered and imprisoned in pillowcases. Imagine, in pillow cases—the final humiliation! Even the chickens are laughing at us. Mercy! Mercy! Without our feathers, we can't fly.' "Then the witch orders my mother to throw out the pillows and the pillowcases."

I took the two dollars, laid it on his chest, and quietly tiptoed out of the poolroom. He had done everything right.

"What's up?"

"It's the Second Jewish Brigade, the 39th, an American battalion, commanded by Colonel Margolin. Jewish volunteers."

"Whoever heard of such a thing! How many are there?"

"Two or three thousand; indeed, there's a whole lot of them."

"Splendid young men, and they know how to march from Powell and Livonia. They go to meet General Allenby in Palestine, he who salutes the Hatikvah.*"*

"Will there be kosher food at the front?"

"Of course! We shall negotiate with the butchers' union."[3]

"Did you ever think as the hearse rolls by
That the next trip they take, they'll be layin' you by,
With the undertaker inscribing your stone?

"Oh, the bugs crawl in and the bugs crawl out,
They do right dress and they turn about,
Then each one takes a bite or two,
Out of what the War Office used to call you."

---

[3] *Ibid.*, pp. 115-16.

"Extra! Extra! Read all about it! Gang War Leaves Punk Fighter Dead! Extra! Extra!"

Yes, the Kid was dead! He went out like a light! He was shot down like a dog, his body riddled with bullets, in a dispute over the newspaper route; and I shouted the headlines on Powell and Livonia.

O weep for the Kid! He is dead! Close his eyes and strap his chin. Wash and perfume him, dress him in white, prepare him for his wedding. Overturn the chairs, break the pots in celebration. He is dead! And after the candles are lit, dance the seven circuits around the body. Do not forget his feathers. Enclose his boxing shorts, his laced shoes, and his regulation gloves in his wooden coffin, and remember the sachet of earth from Palestine. And the canopy—do not forget the canopy over his grave. Wrend the garments. Throw a handful of dust over your shoulder.

"Extra! Extra! Kid Itzik Gets a Grand Send-Off! Extra! Extra!"

And as the Kid went to his long home, and the mourners went about in the streets, his mother cried, "Have pity on me! Have pity on me! O my friends, for the hand of God hath touched me!"

And Hannah Sarah? She must have stolen into his house to do her dirty work, for it is forbidden for a woman to touch a dead man's naked body. There was a glass of water on the window ledge. The windows were open for the dead souls to depart. She even saw to it that the pillows were taken care of.

And when I got to the corner of Powell and Livonia, I looked up and saw feathers falling.

And so all the night long, I ride by the side of the Kid! the Kid! my life and my pride!

"Extra! Extra! Goose Feathers Are Falling on Powell and Livonia! Extra! Extra!"

"Oh, your eyes drop out and your teeth fall in,
And the worms crawl over your mouth and chin,
They invite their friends and their friends' friends, too,
And you're chewed all to hell when they're through with
*   you."*

"Extra! Extra! Goose Feathers Are Falling All over the
World! Extra! Extra!"

Hello, Lenin! Hello, Stalin! How's the Revolution Today?

NOW IF AN ITEM COSTS A DOLLAR AND ONE CENT, everybody knows the one cent is more important than the dollar. For the dollar is the cost of production and the one cent is profit, and profit can make or break the capitalists, especially if their name is Meltzer. This is known as the theory of surplus value. And for that one cent, the workers will march down Blake Avenue and turn into Junius Street, singing, *Arise, ye prisoners of starvation! Arise, ye wretched of the earth!* And for that one cent, bloodsucking capitalists like Meltzer will hide inside their factories, trembling, only to call the police.

And while the police cordon off the factory, the workers will assemble to make more speeches and add to their song, *For justice thunders condemnation! A better world's in birth!* Doesn't this prove that the capitalist class is a bloodsucking class, trying to keep the workers on a starvation level? How does the capitalist class dare to do this when everybody knows, *'Tis the Final Conflict; let each stand in his place; the International Soviet shall be the Human Race?*

"Ma!" cried Usher the Landlord's son. "I need twelve dollars!"

"Ordinarily," observed his mother, "you don't recognize my existence, but when you want something from me, suddenly I become your mother. Now that I have received full recognition, do I have the right to ask what you need twelve dollars for—not that you're going to get it?"

"I need twelve dollars," announced Usher, "to go with the Boy Scouts to Canarsie to shoot Indians. A uniform costs money. How do you expect me to shoot Indians without a uniform?"

There I was, sitting and drinking tea in Usher's house. The candles were burning. The pots and pans were glistening. The food was on the table.

"I never get nothing in this house!" shouted Usher.

"What do you mean, you never get nothing?" answered his mother. "You get everything. You go to school. You can read and write. You're an American. What have I got? I can't even spell my name."

Who should walk in but a lady, dressed in lace and wearing a wig, carrying Usher's "Room to Let" sign before her!

"Is this the family that wishes to rent out a room?" she asked.

"Yes," answered Usher's mother. "This is the family that wishes to rent out a room. You came to the right place. Truthfully, we've never taken in boarders before," she lied, "but I said to my husband, 'Avrum, why should an extra room go to waste when someone could put it to good use?' 'Do what you want,' said my Avrum." Then she sighed, "My husband lets me do whatever I want."

"Yakov!" the newcomer called into the hallway. "You can come upstairs. This it it!" Then turning to Usher's mother, she asked, "Do you keep a kosher kitchen?"

"What kind of question is that? My enemies shouldn't live so long—that's how kosher my kitchen is."

"Is there a synagogue in the neighborhood?"

"Plenty synagogues! If you don't believe me, ask witnesses."

"Yeh!" attested Usher the Witness. "I go to Hebrew school there in the basement. It's on Blake Avenue. Plenty synagogues! Plenty rabbis! Plenty Hebrew schools! That's all they have in Brownsville is synagogues."

"Yakov!" said the woman, turning to her husband as he entered. "The kitchen is kosher and there is a synagogue nearby."

"Minsk!" he huffed. "Pinsk!" he puffed. "Omsk!" he said. "Tomsk!" he tried once more. "My Mashie! My Bashie!" he began again.

"My husband is trying to explain that it was the revolution that forced us to come to America."

She was tall and he was short. He was thick and she was thin. She was dark and he was fáir. When he was asked a question, she would answer. When she was asked, he would answer. They had one voice. And from the way she spoke for him, and the way he answered for her, it was a love affair. Although ordinarily it was nice to see a love affair, this one I did not approve of: Older people were not supposed to have love affairs. And even though I sat drinking tea, I had to admit something new had entered the kitchen: A happy assortment of musical sounds that made me want to look up names in the geography book.

"We lived in Minsk," began the wife, "and kept a cow in the back yard. One cow—for milk! Is that so terrible?"

"It's not so terrible!" admitted Usher.

"It was for Mashie and Bashie," added the husband.

"Those are our daughters."

"Beauties!" said the husband.

"With the revolution," began the wife, taking a deep breath, "it did not take long, but the cow lost its name and was not a cow anymore. It was designated as a means of production. Further we were individual entrepreneurs who had stolen a cow that belonged to the people. I tell you, to be called capitalists for once in our lives was an elevation, but to say we were exploiting the masses was a deflation. So we slaughtered the cow and went to Pinsk."

"In Pinsk," continued the husband, "they took one look at my hands and said, 'The hands are wrong for Pinsk. No calluses!' 'I'm a scholar,' I explained. 'No scholars in Pinsk!' they insisted. 'Scholars are counterrevolutionary! In Pinsk are only workers! Go to Omsk, there you can be a scholar!' So we went to Omsk. In Omsk, they said, 'Why do you wear a beard?' 'I'm a Jew,' I answered. 'No Jews in Omsk!' they said. 'Religion has been abolished! You had better go to Tomsk—there, beards are permitted.' 'Yes,' they said in Tomsk, 'that is correct, beards are permitted, but not for being Jews. If a Jew has a beard, or a beard has a Jew, it hides a Trotskyite. Out of Tomsk, and back to Omsk!'

"A capitalist in Minsk! A counterrevolutionary in Pinsk! No Jews in Omsk! A Trotskyite in Tomsk! So we ran! Who had time for correct definitions!"

"And now Mashie and Bashie are coming," announced the wife.

"It has to do with immigration officials and filling out papers," explained the husband. "Ten years, we haven't seen our daughters. Do you know Meltzer?"

"Which Meltzer?" asked Usher's mother. "Meltzer with the pocketbooks or Meltzer with the fish?"

"Meltzer with the pocketbooks."

"Of course, I know Meltzer with the pocketbooks! Who doesn't know Meltzer! Rich! Rich!"

"A blood brother from Minsk," the husband went on. "We came together on the same ship. Plenty of money goes from him into synagogues. Does favors for people in predicaments. Hired my daughters, sight unseen, and the government officials are letting them in."

"You are friends of that Meltzer!" exclaimed Usher's astonished mother. "Don't you want to see the room? God only knows how spotless it is. You can eat from the floor. Mattress, brand new. If you don't believe me, I'll show you the sales slip. That is, if I can find it. The bed has been slept in only once. Usher dear, do you know where your mother misplaced the sales slip? The bureau, just painted. The pillows, from my own dowry. Even a radio. Call me a liar, if it doesn't play in three languages. Only come and see for yourself. God forgive me, if I'm not telling you the truth."

It was too late! Usher's mother had them in the bedroom. The pillows were being trounced. The mattress was being bounced. And the radio was playing Russian music.

"You know," observed Usher, after a long pause. "She's really not my mother!"

"You just committed a sin, Usher!" I protested. "Of course she's your mother. Why else would she feed you bread and water, and give you a place to sleep?"

"She can't throw me out. There's a law against throwing children out into the street. She can't be my mother. My mother would give her son money if he asked for it. She would take out her last cent from her pocketbook, and say, 'Here's a penny! Please take it!' "

"I think the reason she doesn't give you twelve dollars is because she doesn't have it," I said. "The Jews are poor in Brownsville!"

"The Jews are poor," repeated Usher. "In Minsk! In Pinsk! In Omsk! And in Tomsk!"

Now if a cow is a cow, and has always been a cow, and suddenly turns into a means of production, it means a cow is not a cow anymore, but a factory, and has grown metal tubes in place of udders. And if Trotsky is a Trotskyite and not merely the name of a restaurant, it means that in restaurants as well as other places, there may lurk left-deviationists, counterrevolutionaries, and traitors to the working class. This bears watching! And if a Jew in Omsk has no beard and a beard in Tomsk is counterrevolutionary, it means there are no Jews left anymore. This is impossible! And if it occurs in places called Minsk and Pinsk and Omsk and Tomsk, it means the Russian Revolution has entered Usher's kitchen, and that one must wait for the two new boarders to arrive, since only their appearance can resolve the inner contradictions.

It didn't take long. Usher's mother was at the sink as usual, washing dishes. I was waiting for the Landlord's son, and he was eating an egg in slow motion. Suddenly, like a clap of thunder, the door flew open, the windows began to shake, and the new boarders made their appearance.

"I am Mashie!" announced the first.

"Hello, Lenin!" said Usher, trying to be nice. "How's the revolution today?"

"I am Bashie!" announced the second.

"Hello, Stalin!" said Usher. "How's the dictatorship of the proletariat?"

"Workers of Brownsville!" began Mashie. "We bring you fraternal greetings from your comrades in the Soviet Union. We have come to forge a chain of freedom and solidarity around the world. Europe burns at both ends and America is next!"

I looked around to see whom she was addressing.

"Hello, Trotsky!" said Usher, still trying to be friendly. "How's the counterrevolution?"

"Shut up, you American dope!" cried Bashie, taking offense. "Go and play football!"

later, the two daughters would begin to scream; and the poor
man was required to leave. He would pay the rent in silence,
and with the utmost dignity, proceed down the stairs.
And how that radio blared. Drunken peasants stamped their
dirty boots on the kitchen floor. Wild gypsies cracked their
whips and smashed champagne glasses into the kitchen sink.
And while Moscow skies sailed across Usher's ceiling, the
Volga flowed on Usher's floor. But for me, it was "Down with
the Czar!"
They would play, "O my horse, you are my old pal, my
Maruska. By the roadside, you must rest, loving years behind
us. Friends we are, as always, to the end, O horse, I love thee!"
Usher would answer with, "Mine eyes have seen the glory of the
Lord. He is tramping out the vintage where the grapes of wrath
are stored." "Down with the Czar!" They would play, "I had a
wife who was unfaithful. Ha! Ha! Ha! After I beat her, she ran
to the stable to make love to her German hussar. I love vodka!
Ha! Ha! Ha!" "O beautiful for spacious skies," Usher would
reply, "for amber waves of grain, for purple mountain majes-
ties above the fruited plain." "Down with the Czar!" They
would play, "Farewell, beloved mother country, farewell, my
dear old Moscow. Shall I ne'er hear again the happy music of
Kremlin's bells cascading down?" Usher would counter with,
"My country, 'tis of thee, sweet land of liberty. Of thee, I sing!"
"Down with the Czar!"

Usher came running breathlessly into the kitchen.
"Ma!" he announced. "Your worries are over! I was coming
home from Hebrew school, and I saw a crowd pushing; so I
pushed, too. When I got in, I asked the man, 'Hey, you got a job
for me?' You know, I always need money. So the man said,
'Sure, I got a job—but not for kids; it ain't legal. Do you know
any grownups who's willing to work?' 'Sure, I know—my
mother! She loves to work—that's all she ever does, is work.
She needs a job badly.' 'Tell your mother,' said the man, 'she's

hired! Send her here immediately!' "

"A job for me? You're joking!"

"No, Mom. For once in my life, I'm not joking. It's some job as a manager. You'll probably get paid as much as twelve dollars a week for it. But you must go immediately."

"You don't have to push me, I'm running already. But where am I running?"

"You go to Meltzer's factory."

And before Usher had the words out of his mouth, his mother was out of the house.

That night, Usher's mother came home, looking very tired.

"Well, Ma!" asked Usher. "Did you get the job?"

"I got it."

"Did they make you a manager?"

"Me? A manager! But I'm not telling you anything. You'll go and tell your father, and he is not to know. He makes nothing out of everything I do."

"I won't tell Papa."

"You promise?"

"I promise."

"All right, I'll tell you! They put me down in the basement. I'm a stamper. I stamp out frames. But I'm thankful, nevertheless—now I am a worker. I got respect! I got dignity! No more spoiling my hands!"

"My mother understands her historic role in society," declared Usher.

I never saw Usher's mother so happy, and I never saw Usher behaving so well. She would go off to work after her husband left, return before he came, have the supper ready, the house cleaned, and Usher's old man was none the wiser. The trouble was, as Usher said, that she began to understand her historic role in society.

One night, they were all at home. Usher's old lady was washing dishes. Usher was doing his homework, and his father was reading the newspaper. From the kitchen I heard Usher's old lady say, "We Jews live in three worlds: The *Yiddisher velt,* the *arbiter velt,* and Roose*velt!*"

A grunt from Usher's father.

"The bosses! The bosses!" she sang as she washed the dishes. "They make us work like horses. They are so mean! They feed us lean! And then, they double-cross us!" Then she turned to face her husband, "You might as well know. Today, I was made a supervisor. I am a supervisor in the stamping department at Meltzer's factory."

"Yes!" she said. "I am a supervisor. The working class can kiss my ass; the supervisor's job I have at last!"

Usher's father rose to his full height. He did not bang his newspaper on the table; no! he took it in his hands, opened it and slowly, ever so slowly, tore it to bits.

"No wonder," he said, "Goldberg met me on the street, and when I tried to speak to him, Goldberg said, 'I'm not talking!' I met Feigenbaum and said, 'Hello, Feigenbaum! What's new?' and he said, 'I'm not listening!' I put my hand out to Needleman and he said, 'Needleman is not shaking!' I thought it was because they were jealous of me. They know, Avrum is always right, that Avrum stands with both feet firmly planted on the ground, and has always taken the correct historical line. And never, never once have they ever been able to dislodge me from my position. Thirty years in the labor movement! Who helped organize the garment workers? The sewing machine operators came to knock at my window and to warn me that the bosses had hired gangsters and were out to get me and smash the union. Whose hand did Alfred E. Smith shake on the steps of City Hall when he came to make a speech? To whom did Mayor Hylan say, 'Hello,' on the boardwalk? A million people were on the beach in Coney Island that day. And to whom did Franklin D. Roosevelt nod, but to yours truly, when Roosevelt drove by in his limousine? And you, you betray me and my thirty years in the labor movement! A snake! I've harbored a snake in my own house! A supervisor, indeed! Don't you know Meltzer's has been on strike for two years, that the workers are fighting for union recognition, that the police have smashed a dozen heads, and that you're a strikebreaker, pure and simple! A supervisor, did you say? Had there been no strike, you would never have been hired even to sweep the floor, let alone sew a button on a crooked seam. No wonder Goldberg is not talking, Feigenbaum is not listening, and Needleman is not shaking. I've sheltered a class enemy in my own house!"

And there stood Usher's mother with her back to the sink and a look of utter amazement on her face.

Then Mr. Yakov came to pay the rent. Usher was doing his homework on the kitchen table.

"Sh!" whispered the old man. "Even if my daughters are not at home, let it be, 'Sh!' Everything is all right, and if everything is not all right, it will straighten itself out in the end. Not a word!" he said, looking over Usher's shoulder. "Do your Hebrew homework. That's right, child! That's how you make an *aleph*! Yes, that's how you make a *beth*! Ah!" he continued. "My heart is breaking. But, 'Sh!'—not a word to anyone. I was coming from *shul* when I saw my Mashie and my Bashie at Meltzer's. And Mashie was on a stepladder, shouting. You promise, you won't say anything?" he pleaded with us. "You promise, it'll be 'Sh!'? On Friday night, she was making a speech on a street corner. How can I even tell my wife—the shame of it would kill her! Go ahead, child! Don't let me interrupt you. Continue with your Hebrew homework! Yes! Yes! That's how you make an *aleph*! That's how you make a *beth*! And my Bashie was shouting, 'Down with Meltzer!' Did you hear? She shouted, 'Down with Meltzer!'—he, who was so good to her; he, who helped bring her to America. 'Death to those rich bloodsuckers, who use your sweat to line their pockets!' she was shouting. 'While we starve, they buy the choicest cuts of meat! While we go on foot, they drive around in big limousines!' "

At that moment, who should walk in, but Mashie and Bashie.

"We saw you," cried Mashie. "We saw you from the stepladder."

"Spying on us!" cried her sister. "That's what you were doing! Oh, I wish we didn't see so much, we'd be better off!"

"Who asked you to bring us to America," screamed Mashie, "to this land of thieves and prostitutes? They're all gangsters here. Even the children are gangsters. They run around the streets with guns, playing cops and robbers—or cowboys and Indians. America is training its children for the coming struggle for power against the first workers' republic. One has to be blind not to see it. We were happy in the Soviet Union; there we were working for the future. What have we here—football, Hollywood bathrooms, and empty heads? Can you imagine a country where the workers are on the side of the capitalists and fancy themselves the bourgeoisie? Strikebreakers, stool pigeons, traitors—that's what they are! When the revolution comes to America, the first ones we'll have to liquidate will be the workers. And who is the biggest traitor of all—you, with your prayer shawl and prayer book and your precious phylacteries? You are the biggest stool pigeon of them all. In all of America, there isn't a stool pigeon as big as you. Why did you bring us backward to capitalism? There is no future here!"

Soon the radio was blaring as they ran into their room, slamming the door behind them. In a second, Bashie opened the door again and stuck her head out. "We are in exile!" she wept, the tears streaming down her face, and shut the door.

Comrades, form your lines on the Pitkin Avenue *Prospekt*! The revolution is on!

Mashie was standing on a stepladder outside Meltzer's factory; Bashie was at her side. The street was black with people; they filled all of Junius Street, up to Blake Avenue. Perhaps it was not only Meltzer's factory they were facing, but the memory of bloody pogroms, the Black Hundreds, and the murderous Cossacks. Would they storm the factory like the Bolsheviks stormed the Winter Palace? Is the cruiser *Aurora* ours; has it come over to the side of the workers? Fine chaps, they've done it! What is the Loew's Premier garrison about; will it join the revolution? Hip! Hip! Hooray! They've turned their guns against the manager and have killed him! And the battleship *Missouri*; will it fire and kill the counterrevolution- aries? Save that child in the baby carriage, rolling down the steps in Odessa! Flushed with victory, the Loew's Premier garrison is coming to the aid of the workers! The sealed train! Mashie and Bashie at the Sutter Avenue Station! Ginsberg the rabbi has come over to our side! Ma, I'm not going to Hebrew school anymore; the revolution has come to Brownsville! A strike that shook the world! Two who made a revolution! Up with the red flag of socialism! Bread and peace! The Interna- tional Soviet prevails! Capitalism has gone under! Comrades, we have just issued a communication: Bourgeois democracy is dead! Stand up, ye wretched of the earth! Promise of a better world! Promise of human dignity! Human redemption! New foundations! We shall attack Meltzer's factory first; and after the factory, the revolution will sweep straight to P.S. 109, that citadel of entrenched reaction, where we will drive out all the rotten Irish teachers who set up Christmas trees for Jewish children—all, except Mrs. Reynolds, she's good to the chil- dren—and we'll free all the children so that they won't have to go to school anymore! Go to it, laddies! That's it, laddies! Hip! Hip! Hooray!

Suddenly the most impossible thing happened. Up the street, past his own factory, came Meltzer's funeral cortège. Through the glass window of the black wagon, looking surprisingly innocent, a pine box was visible. Was there really someone in it? "Meltzer should be glad he died for the revolution!" came a voice from the crowd. "His death was an historic necessity!" "They are burying him with his phylacteries and prayer shawl," said another voice. "A Jew remains a Jew!" said still another voice. And I envisioned an angel with enormous wings and white feathers, leading the cortège and blowing a trumpet. "Make way! Make way!" the angel was saying. "Make way for the first victim of the revolution! Make way for historic necessity!"

"They killed my Meltzer!" came a woman's voice from behind the wagon as everything turned ghastly.

"Death to the capitalists!" Mashie was shouting. "Down with the profit system!"

And as luck would have it, right in front of the factory, one of the wheels of the wagon got caught and was stuck.

'Tis the final conflict! cried Mashie as she turned her back on Mrs. Meltzer.

"Meltzer, take me with you!" screamed his wife as shivers ran down my spine. "Why did you abandon me and your children? I was a good wife to you. What sin have I committed that I should remain alive and you dead? Take me to the grave with you! Allow me the honor of lying down by your side!"

The funeral turned into a nightmare.

"He was standing in the bathroom, taking a shave," wept his wife, "when suddenly he fell over. The Angel of Death came and took him. He died of a heart attack." Then she pointed to Mashie and Bashie and screamed: "But they are the murderers! As sure as I am standing here, they are the killers. Had they held a gun to him and sent a bullet through his heart, they couldn't have done a better job!"

"Workers of the world!" orated Mashie. "As the ruling class goes down, it gets more frantic in its desperation, seeking to pit worker against worker!"

"What worker against worker?" asked Mrs. Meltzer. "It's Jew against Jew! Jews of Brownsville! They killed us in Kishinev! They killed us in Odessa! Where did they not kill us? And they will kill us again, just as they killed my Meltzer! First they kill us as capitalists, then they kill us as counterrevolutionaries. Where is your revolution? There is no revolution!

Where is your factory? There is no factory! Where are your jobs? You have no jobs! You've got nothing because there is no more Meltzer!

"Hear, O Israel!" she cried. "The termites have come up from out of the earth and have climbed to the top of the ladder. They advertise, 'Kosher meat—five cents a pound!' A glass of blood—as cheap as *kvass* in Russia! Eat! Eat! The meat is kosher! Chew! Chew! It must be fully digested! Czar Nicolai, how was the table service? Comrade Stalin, with cabbage soup or without? Reb Trotsky, did they smash your Jewish head in with an ax? I hope the ax was kosher!"

Suddenly the wagon was freed and the cortège was on its way.

"Meltzer, take me with you!" she moaned. "Why did you abandon me and your children? I was a good wife to you! What sin have I committed that I should remain alive and you dead? Take me to the grave with you! Allow me the honor of lying down by your side!"

And the funeral turned into Blake Avenue and was no more.

"Surplus value!" cracked Mashie's voice. "Dialectical materialism!" she went on as the crowd began to thin. "The doom of the capitalist system!" she continued as more drifted away. "The victory of the proletariat! The workers' paradise!"

Soon the street was deserted, but Mashie went right on, "We are approaching the Final Conflict! Let each stand in his place! The International Soviet shall be the Human Race!"

She was speaking to an empty street.

Now if a revolution is not a revolution, but just plain murder, it follows that the Angel of Death is behind it all and is always victorious. Further if the revolution kills you, first as a capitalist, then as a revolutionary, then as a counterrevolutionary, it may be true that it is the Angel of Death who gets you in the end as a Jew. This is not a contradiction! It merely means that the bloodsucking capitalists have enlisted the aid of the Angel of Death on the side of the profit system. The question remains: What happens to that one cent? For if an item costs one dollar and one cent, the one cent is more important than the dollar. The dollar is the cost of production, and the one cent is profit; and the profit can make or break the capitalist. Let Meltzer live, let Meltzer die; let Mashie talk forever to an empty street, let Bashie be the only one to listen, the question remains. And if it is the Angel of Death who has to answer, let him answer!

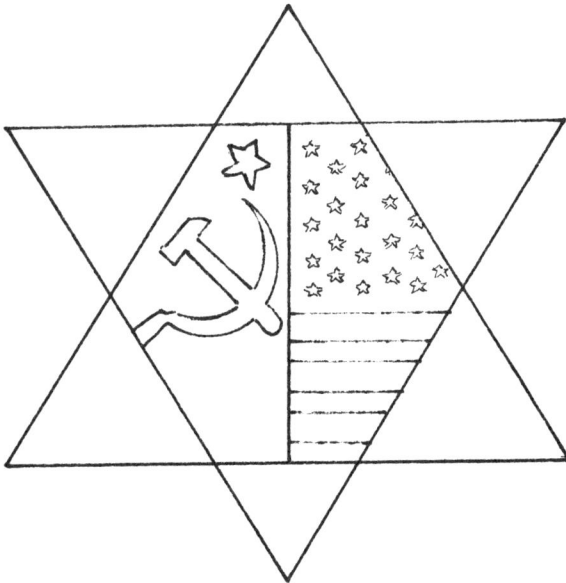

Songs My Mother Taught Me That Are Not in
Hamlet; or, "Come into My House, Horatio!
There Are More Things under the Mattress than
Are Dreamt of in Your Philosophy!"

ANDREW CARNEGIE WAS A SCOTSMAN WHO MADE A
great deal of money. Knowing time was running out, he wanted
to set up a memorial to himself; so, he decided to build libraries. He went to the City of New York, and said, "I'll build the
libraries; you put in the books!" By doubling the number of
libraries before they were built, he succeeded in making a one
hundred per cent profit, even before he went. Not bad!

Thus it was that the First Free Public Library for Children in
the World arose in Brownsville on Stone and Dumont Avenues
between the market where the pushcarts ended and the abattoir
where the sheep were slain. The Tudor-styled brick building
would have been more at home in the English Midlands;
instead, it squatted here, although with great dignity, among a
vast sea of tenements and an endless array of clotheslines.

221

Brownsville did not remain silent in its criticism: morning, noon, and night, the clotheslines squeaked against the ivy-studded walls, the beveled windows, the oak paneling, and even into the enormous fireplace where there was enough room for five children to stand reading with the fire burning and come out unharmed. No matter—the children of Brownsville had a magnificent building where the vaulted vastness of the reading room served as a refuge from the incessant din on the outside—except for the squeaks.

That lady from France may have said, "Let them eat cake!" but in Brownsville, it was, "Eat books!" And truthfully, we did not "eat" books, we devoured them. Here, on the inside, we ate English; there, on the outside, Yiddish. Further, on the inside, we dared not speak—neither English nor outside Yiddish—else we were grabbed by the scruff of our necks and forced right out.

One cold winter night, I was sitting in that library, just before closing time, reading inside English. The room was empty of readers, except for me and a lone shadowy figure, huddled up in a heavy overcoat at the far end of the room.

Suddenly a voice boomed out, "This is Karl Marx speaking. Get your dirty feet off that chair! Think, would Mother Bloor approve of such a thing?"

I froze in my seat at the power of that voice as it boomed across the reading room. Through a glass panel, I could see the startled face of the librarian who was so riveted by the shock that, for once, her bracelets were not ringing.

"Did you put your feet on the chair?" she demanded, as she suddenly loomed larger than life at my side.

"I would never do such a thing!" I answered defiantly.

"The sounds came from here!" she said.

"Why should I advertise my own feet on a chair," I gasped, "when I don't have them there, in the first place?"

In the second she spent looking at me suspiciously, I knew she was deciding whether or not I had killed Christ. The punishment for such a deed was to be booted right out of the library.

As she reluctantly returned to her perch behind the glass panel, I had to admit the sounds appeared to have come from me. Then, as if it were I myself speaking, again it boomed, "Karl Marx is back again—this time with Vladimir Ilyich Ulyanov, otherwise known as Lenin. Don't think we didn't see you dog-ear the corner of that page and spoil the book for good readers who don't do such things. The library belongs to the people. For such a criminal act, you can be prosecuted to the full extent of the law. And while we're at it, who killed Sacco and Vanzetti?"

Now the bracelets really began to ring as the enraged librarian flew across the room and swooped down upon the hooded figure at the other end. Digging her claws into the top of the overcoat, she brought out someone's ear and dragged him clear across the room.

"Let this be my last testament as they lead me to the slaughterhouse," rang out the voice, now from the fireplace. "This is your friend, the cobbler's son, the People's Commissar, Yosif Vissarionovich Dzhugashvili, also known as Stalin, speaking. You are witnessing before you a librarian, a crass hireling of the ruling class, who feeds the children of the workers the opium of fairy tales, when they should be reading Marx, Engels, and Lenin, whose books she has seen fit to lock away in dark closets and throw away the keys. You, who are witnessing this forced eviction of a hero of the working class, if you have any feeling for justice, arise and come to the aid of this hapless victim of capitalist tyranny! Long live a Soviet America! And don't forget the Carnegie Steel strike!"

As the furious librarian dragged the culprit down the aisle, I realized her motive was not all books, but included the destruction of a Soviet America. That was the way it was with the Irish in those days!

Meanwhile, from under the table, the voice came again,

"This is Sigmund Freud—the crazy doctor—talking. An old maid librarian with virtue intact, but ego stunted, who gets her kicks from books—and you know what kind of books— jealous of a youth in the first full flush of his manhood, tears at him with a strange sexual passion. From the right walnut of her brain where she sees a penis, her cathexis crosses the oatmeal to the left walnut into the mnemonic area where she gets it mixed up through improper cross wiring, and it comes out as an ear. So says Sigmund Freud. Down with Jim Crow!"

As the librarian was about to fling the culprit out the door, from the ceiling came, "This is God speaking! Know ye, that things have come to a fine pass if I have to move my old and weary bones and come down from heaven to tell you that—"

Alas! It never came; instead, what came was, "Free Tom Mooney!" for at that moment, the librarian flung open the door and out the culprit went. Just then, the bell, announcing the closing, began to ring; and I swooped out of the library as if the furies were in hot pursuit.

It was cold outside. The wind came down the street, careening wildly around the corners and creating havoc with the tops of garbage cans that banged and rolled as if auguring the arrival of the sheep to the abattoir. From the abattoir itself could be heard the distant bleating of the unfortunate animals; and since the sounds were muffled, I imagined their throats had already been cut.

"She thought she hurt me," came the voice again, this time, weakly, "but I fooled her."

There, huddled in a heap on the library steps, lay the culprit, bright and shining. Now that his head jutted out from the folds of his enormous overcoat, he was like a toy that had jumped up from the box when the lid was lifted. Topped by a crown of flaming red hair, his face with its saucer eyes was shaped like a pumpkin's. His skin was so white, it appeared as if someone had cast flour over it. And when he smiled, and the lines about his eyes and mouth turned into wrinkled parchment, I thought him to be a jackanapes who seemed older than he really was. It was not until he stood up that I realized he was undersized, and his body was wider than it was high, confirming the pumpkin impression. He would have looked very good lit up in a window like a jack-o'-lantern. It was obvious, he was born to trouble.

"You see how I fooled her," he said as from the inside of his coat, he pulled out a thick volume, *How to Conquer the World through Ventriloquism*, and held it up for my inspection. "I'm twelve years of age," he said, "and have too many names: Hi, Hal, Harry, Harold, and Herschel. Since I don't like any of them, you may call me the Ventriloquist."

"Oh!" I exclaimed. "You're a ventriloquist!"

"Practice! Practice! That's all I do is practice!"

Digging in again, he pulled out another volume, *The History of the Communist Party, U.S.S.R.* by Joseph Stalin, and held it up.

"My father hollers at me and says I should be studying Stalinism—my father is a big Stalinist. He says, if I don't, I'll be responsible for the Revolution failing. It's too terrible to think about—that I should be responsible for another Eighteenth of Brumaire, such as Louis Napoleon triggered, because I don't study enough. I'd study Stalinism more; but my father says, Stalin says, ventriloquism is counterrevolutionary. If Stalin says that, then Stalin is counterrevolutionary, and I'm anti-Stalinist!"

Digging into his coat again, he brought up another volume, *The Mysteries of the Cabala.*

"Head of a frog! Tail of a toad!" he began. "Turd of a goat! The Thirty-Second Spirit—knoweth thou who he is?" he shouted, opening his eyes wide. "He is the great King, strong and powerful! He appeareth with three heads; whereof, the first is like a bull; the second like a goat; the third like a ram. Tail of a serpent, mouth of flame, feet toed like a goat's, he sitteth with his fundament on an infernal dragon, and carries a lance with a banner."

"My mother argues with my father," he continued. "She asks

him to explain what happened to the Jews in Russia. 'There are no more Jews in Russia,' he says. 'Not one?' asks my mother. 'I left my mother, father, and sister there; so, there must be, at least, three left!' 'Religion has been abolished!' says my father. 'You mean, the Jews have been abolished!' says my mother. My mother is very religious."

Digging in again, he brought out a Bible, returned it, and dug again. This time, out came *The Ego and the Id* by Sigmund Freud.

"My mother can't sleep at night," he said, "she worries only about my sister. She says, my sister is not getting married because I cause them a lot of trouble by not keeping myself clean. She says, my sister can't bring any boy friends into the house because of me. Meanwhile, the house is always kept ready in a spic and span condition, and my sister practices the piano, so that she'll be ready to play in case a visitor makes an appearance; but nobody comes. Nobody is getting married these days. Conditions are pretty bad."

"You stole all those books?"

"Practice! Practice! That's all it takes is practice! I wiggled out of my overcoat and left it sitting on the chair. Across the floor I crept, to the closed section where the hard books are kept, took them out one by one, and crept right back into my coat."

And here, he began to pull out more books.

"I fooled her," he said as he began to put the books back into his coat, "because with ventriloquism you can do almost anything. And if you think that's all there is, come to my house, Horatio; there are more things under the mattress than are dreamt of in your philosophy."

"Who's Horatio?"

"Never mind," he answered as we began to walk towards Christopher Street.

I should have known that anyone who stole books, especially forbidden books, too difficult to read, would be likely to live in an odd house; and neither he nor his house was to be trusted; but the sweet song of ventriloquism from this Pied Piper lured me on.

Soon I found myself mounting the stairs of a dark, dank hallway as he clutched my arm and banged on the walls, crying, "Head of a frog! Turd of a goat! Obey in the name of Berlensis, Paumachia, Apologia Sedes, and the Bal Shem! I am Alexander the Great! I am Michael Palaeologus! Spirits—avaunt!"

Suddenly I realized I had come out of a world of light into a world of darkness; and that I was suspended on a stairway on Christopher Street between two hells, unable to retreat for fear of the void that reigned below, nor go forward for the ghosts and demons that dwelt above. I was beginning to think I had made a mistake.

He urged me on. At the first landing, he removed a key from under a mat and opened a door. We entered a bright and shining kitchen that was so large it was able to accommodate a dining table with eight chairs. Immediately, he began to bang on the floor. By now, I had grown accustomed to his strange antics and assumed it was his way of placating the spirits. All at once, he sat down at the head of the empty table.

"You shouldn't do that!" I burst out.

"Why not?"

"I'm not going to say anything about people stealing books like the Bible that say, 'Thou shalt not steal!' But I am going to say that this same book also says, 'Honor thy father and thy mother!' You shouldn't be sitting in your father's chair!"

"Oh!" he said. "It's that book which is worrying you. I didn't steal it; I merely borrowed it as a short-term loan. Besides, if you keep your mouth shut, my father won't know about the chair, and God won't know about the book. And what they don't know, won't hurt them."

Throwing imaginary powders into the air, he closed his eyes. "The Cabala says," he began to intone. " 'The Holy One took the two letters of *esh*, 'fire,' added the two letters of His Name,

Yh, the *yad*, to form *ish*, 'man,' and the *heh*, to form *ishah*, 'woman,' and He said, 'If together they follow my ways, My Name abides between them and delivers them from trouble; if not, My Name is removed from them, and they become a consuming fire of passion!'

"Come, Horatio!" he said.

"Who's Horatio?"

"Never mind," came the answer as he led me into the living room and opened the lid of the piano. He waited a moment, and then down came his hands to form a series of crashing chords that began at one end of the keyboard and ended at the other.

"You play the piano?" I asked in amazement.

"No!" he answered. "My sister plays. She gets the lessons. I play by ear. I don't know how to read notes.

"Go ahead!" he urged. "Ask me a question."

"What should I ask?"

"Ask, 'What did Louie do?' "

"O.K.! What did Louie do?"

Then he began. With his left hand, he strummed back and forth, and with his right, he struck a melody as from behind my ear came,

"King Louie pledged his loyalty, but what's a vow to royalty? Since he betrayed his vow, we give no mercy now. Let us united stand, aristocrats are bound to fall—Andrew Carnegie, first of all. Stand firm, if they attack, we'll send them reeling back."

"What's that?"

"That's the dreaded 'Carmagnole'!" he answered. "It's from the French Revolution. You can get arrested if you sing it."

A forbidden song! Prison! I was impressed!

"Go ahead!" he said. "Ask me another question." And before I had a chance to answer, he began, "Queen Antoinette had promised, she would cut the throat of all Paree. But this she could not do. So Antoinette is through. Remember well the 'sans-culottes,' for life and liberty they fought. The patriot defends the land; a million brothers take his hand. And when the cannon sound, with him, we will be found. So dance the 'Carmagnole'!"

I followed him into the bedroom. Again, he began to bang on the floor while I waited patiently for the "spirits" to depart. He removed his coat, and from it he began to draw out his horde of stolen books, lifting the bedspread and shoving the books under the bed.

The area under the bed was packed. I had enough time only to see it included: Thomas Jefferson, Karl Kautsky, Plekhanov, Kropotkin, Feuerbach, Engels, Rosa Luxemburg, Karl Liebknecht, Josephus, Henry George, Plato, Plutarch, Tacitus, and—this I could not believe—five copies of the Bible.

I heard the front door open, the sound of people entering, then the house shaking as they began to bang on the walls, followed by a long ominous silence. I buried my head in my hands for fear of what was coming next.

"I want to talk about chairs!" announced his father, breaking the silence. "Don't I have the right to talk about chairs?"

"You've just elected yourself a conversation," said his mother. "Who can stop you?"

At the sound of the word "chairs," the ventriloquist turned whiter than he was. Frantically, he began to push himself under the bed, but it was so packed with books that he could make no headway. Emma Goldman fell upon Leon Trotsky, Leon Trotsky collapsed on Bukharin, Bukharin sat on Voltaire, and Voltaire and the Pope embraced one another.

"The chair is the symbol of the unity of the working class," shouted the father.

"Some unity!" said his mother. "A pack of thieves, unified by their jealousy of other thieves!"

As the ventriloquist pushed under the bed he began to throw his voice hysterically, emitting a succession of peculiar sounds, as if he were cracking the musical scales. From the walls, he rebounded in a deep bass, seeming to deepen and enlarge the

room. From the pipes, he reflected in a high soprano, constrict-
ing and narrowing the space. Sometimes, he combined two
pitches in a weird dissonance, so that the room opened and
closed like an accordian. And as the books began to speak, he
got them all mixed up: Bukharin became Bakunin. Bakunin
became Bokhara. Christ became a Menshevik. Jesus became a
Bolshevik.

"Lev Davidovich Bronstein," said Emma Goldman. "The
end of all revolutionary social change must establish the sanc-
tity of human life, the dignity of man, the right of every human
being to liberty and well-being."

"To accept the workers' Revolution in the name of high
ideals," answered Trotsky, "means not only to reject it, but to
slander it. You haven't paid any attention to the chair. Go to
the chair and study Marxism; you might learn that the Revolution is strong to the extent to which it is realistic, rational,
strategic, and mathematical."

"It begins at the Cemetery of Père Lachaise where the revo-
lutionaries were cut down," shouted the father, "and ends at
Woodlawn Cemetery where the counterrevolutionaries are
buried. It is to the chair that the questions are directed; it is
from the chair that the answers—always pure Marxism—are
transmitted."

"Before you send Emma Goldman to the chair," interrupted
Karl Marx, "I must tell you, I'm not a Marxist."

"It is obvious," added the father, "that the chair is subject to
counterrevolutionary movements. One must be careful, even in
the kitchen. The chair has been moved."

"We know the chair has been moved," said the daughter,
"but what about the piano lid being lifted?"

"Ha! Ha!" laughed Bukharin. "German and Jew, Marx and
his chair is authoritarian."

"Well," said Chaim from Brownsville, "what do you expect
when Marx's grandfathers both were rabbis?"

"As long as the subject of Jews has come up," interrupted

Voltaire, "we all ought to become Jews, because Jesus was a Jew, lived a Jew, died a Jew, and he said expressly that he was fulfilling the Jewish religion."

"We are all spiritual Semites," laudamused the Pope.

"*Oy! Vey!*" credoed Jesus. "When I hear the anti-Semites say they love the Jews, I know another pogrom is coming."

Then the bedroom door opened to admit the sounds of his sister crying. "How can I play the 'Minuet in G' knowing that someone put his dirty hands on the piano?" And there in the doorway stood his mother.

"It's easier to clean a piano," she said, "with a little soap and water than it is for Stalin to drop dead." Then her eyes fell on the ventriloquist, still attempting to get under the bed. "But," she screamed, "a bedspread is not a laughing matter!"

"Wait! Wait!" cried his father as the ventriloquist and I shot past through the kitchen. "They'll advertise him yet in the *Daily Worker*, shoot him in Coney Island, carry him on the Brighton Line, hold the display in Union Square, and bury him in Woodlawn Cemetery, if he continues to carry on in this way. I had hoped he would grow up to honor me; and instead of reciting the *Kaddish* for me when I died, he would stand on the corner of Pitkin and Hopkinson Avenues and deliver speeches, making the citadel of capitalism tremble. Were he to do so, I would die gladly and rest in my grave. To think that I myself might have to go to the *Daily Worker* to report my own son as a renegade, and to see a caption in the paper the next day, warning party members that he has been expelled, even before the party has admitted him. Believe me, if I have to do it, I will not hesitate! Who would have ever dreamt that he, who at the age of six declared himself an atheist, would end as a Thermidorian reaction?"

Out into the hallway we flew; and I found I was running after the ventriloquist into, of all places, a toilet at the far end of the passageway.

"O Adam Kadmon, from the realm of Sephiroth," he

intoned as he began banging on the walls of the toilet. "First Manifestation inserted between the Beginning and the World. Divine Effluvium, I call upon thee to disperse Belial, whose Prince is Samaël; I call upon thee to overcome the Kingdom of Keliphoth and its many myriad demons, hidden in these walls on Christopher Street! O Archetypal Man, Logos, obey in the name of the Cabalistic Tree and the Pillar of Arrangement!"

As dark and dank as was the hallway, the toilet was even more so. If hell had one end and was hot, this was the other end and cold; for from the windowless opening that faced the street, the wind came as though it were some forgotten adversary that had lain in ambush and now sprang out gleefully to continue its assault.

He unfastened his belt, let fall his trousers, and sat down on the stool; immediately, he began to moan and groan.

"Why do you and your family bang so much?" I asked.

He looked about, raising his eyebrows as if the answer was obvious, and said, matter-of-factly, "It's rats! The place is full of rats!"

All at once, I was aware of the evil things that lurked there: they scampered in the walls, peered out from behind pipes, ran into open holes, as they bore down with their heavy weight and slid away like professional dancers.

Even as I ran, I knew it was not only from the rats, but also from his world of absolute defiance—of fathers, of Stalin, of God. Perhaps this triad was an unlikely amalgam, but I had need to affirm it, so that the world could have a happy ending. I even admitted to myself that, although his noises seemed to emanate from the insidious brouhaha of the abattoir and were frightening, mine seemed like the irate squeaking of the clotheslines and were ineffective.

"Once there was a wicked, wicked king," came his voice as I flew down the stairs. "His sword was sharp, his darts did sting. What was his name?—Stalin. He came to Moscow's holy quarter and shed our blood like water, water. What was his name?

—Stalin. He came and burned the Torah, Torah, put out the Menorah, Menorah. What was his name?—Stalin."

"The Revolution!" maintained his father.

"The piano!" insisted his sister.

"The bedspread!" declared his mother.

"The pogrom!" cried Jesus.

And as I ran into the street, I could still hear him from the stool, "This is Sigmund Freud—the crazy doctor—talking, 'Where the Ego is, the Id stinks!' "

You could not get me into the library for the longest time; and when I finally ventured, I was sure I would be arrested, or the books would begin to speak. But instead of their speaking to me, I argued with them. "Emma Goldman," I asked, "what kind of revolution do you believe in? Your revolution is so perfect, even the capitalists would not be against it. Is that possible?" "Leon Trotsky," I said, "in your revolution, if 2 plus 3 equals 6, you borrow 7 from the air, or some other revolution, add to 6, subtract 8 to form 5, and insist it works because it is mathematical." I argued with Voltaire and the Pope, "If you are Jews, as you claim to be, go into the abattoir and stop that slaughter." But what disturbed me the most was that the ventriloquist was counterrevolutionary against God. Free the Scottsboro boys!

Saturday night at the movies. The swami had been well-advertised: on Powell Street he was shown sawing a woman in half; on Junius Street he was forcing an elephant to kneel; on Stone Avenue he was crossing Niagara Falls. I do not know what he was doing on Christopher Street; I never went by there, anymore.

The screen went blank; the film was over. A boy scout entered from the wings and began to blow taps. It was very sad. Verdun, Ypres, the Marne. Put out the lights; the soldier boys are dying. Bodies piled high. Bodies laid to rest. Crosses row upon row. When taps were finished, the boy scout held a respectful pause, and blew again: Ta-rah! Ta-rah! Happiness! Happiness! The war was over! No more dying! The future was bright.

The swami came on stage in a dhoti and a white turban from which sprang a long, thin feather into the air. From the center of his forehead gleamed an emerald that sent flecks of light into the movie house. His complexion was swarthy—something oriental! His face was a mask—something insidious! His manner was remote—something ubiquitous! In short, a true swami!

Ta-rah! Ta-rah! Out on the stage came a gypsy, all tessellated in her gypsy clothes, with her gypsy navel showing. Her mouth was open—nothing teleological! Her feet, dancing— something mercurial! Her hips, gyrating—the secret of the universe!

"Ladies and gentlemen," she began. "Swami Kwami is Indian swami with three degrees. He also have degree in transportation. Yesterday, he, in India; today, he, in America. Figure that out! Comes here by invitation to raise spirits— dead or alive. Takes them from up, brings them from down, or grabs them from in-between. What you think? He no scratch head. He stand on stage in dead center, wait for customers. Who you wanna raise—dead mother, runaway father, lost sweetheart, live enemy? Who you wanna speak to—George Washington? What you wanna say? Write quick on piece of paper and give to gypsy me."

No one in the audience moved. "What you no believe me?" cried the now-irate gypsy as she turned to the swami. "Swami," she said, "do your stuff!" Quickly, the swami drew out a gun from his dhoti and fired. When the smoke cleared, presto!— there, in front of the swami stood a table with a crystal ball. The audience cheered.

Ta-rah! Ta-rah! Now the theatre was filled with scraps of

paper, passing from hand to hand over the heads of the audience to the gypsy. "Swami Kwami, no fake," said the gypsy. "Other Indian swamis, plenty fake—not Swami Kwami! You ask question and presto!—spirits appear."

Ta-rah! Ta-rah! Opening the first scrap of paper, the gypsy began to read and then stopped. "What kind of crazy question is this?" she asked. "It says, 'This question is addressed to Stalin. Can the swami communicate with Stalin? If so, let Stalin answer the following: What can grow without dew?' "

Suddenly from out of the darkness, a hooded figure, wearing a heavy overcoat, ran down the aisle and took his place at the piano. Down came the now-familiar chords. Everything happened so quickly, the gypsy and the swami never had a chance to close their mouths; so that, as the ventriloquist threw his voice, it appeared as if the gypsy asked, and the swami answered.

"Stalin! Stalin! Tell me true: What can grow without dew? What can burn for years and years? What can cry and shed no tears?" "You silly fellow, you cock-a-doodle, you've no brains in all your noodle: A revolution can grow without dew. A Jew can burn for years and years. But Stalin can cry without tears."

"Stalin! Stalin! Tell me true: Do the Jews have a state? Does the State have the Jews?" "You silly fellow, you cock-a-doodle, you've no brains in all your noodle—your views will be demolished. Yes, the Jews have a state. No, the State has no Jews. The Jews have been abolished. And that's the answer true!"

Again the swami drew his gun and fired. This time, a series of varicolored balloons shot out and floated into the auditorium. Hands reached out to catch them as they burst. With every crack of a balloon, the audience laughed and cheered. But now the ventriloquist had other plans. As he thumped on the piano, he threw his voice into the auditorium.

"I've a bit of news, news. See the Marxists killing Jews. What's so special about such news? After all, Jews are Jews! That a bit of socialism for you!"

"I've a pair of traders, traders. See the traders selling freighters. None but Jews are selling freighters. Kill the Jews and free the freighters! That's an ideology for you! "I've a pair of moneylenders. They are not the bigtime spenders. Christian spenders are not the lenders. Kill the lenders and free the spenders! That's a religion for you!"

The voices, seeming to come from everywhere in the movie house, made it appear as if the moviegoers were in total agreement; it cowed even those who did not agree. The audience became strangely quiet.

Again the swami fired, this time, a host of flags shot out. Still the ventriloquist would not let up. It was now the gypsy's turn to ask and the swami's to answer.

"Siggy! Siggy! Tell me true: What is the Ego; what, the Id? What, the *Goy*; what, the Yid?" "You silly fellow, you cock-a-doodle, you've no brains in all your noodle—here's the answer true: The Ego is the *Goy*; it goes, *oy! oy!* The Id is the Yid; it goes, *vey! vey! Oy! Vey! Oy! Vey!*"

"Id, so strong; Id, so little! Let me ask you a very hard riddle: What is quicker than a Yid? What is stronger than an Id?" "You silly fellow, you cock-a-doodle, you've no brains in all your noodle. An Id is quicker than a Yid! A Yid is stronger than an Id! And that's the answer true!"

Again the swami fired; this time, soap bubbles shot out. Again the ventriloquist turned to the audience as from a far corner of the movie house came, "Freud makes for me a hammer; the hammer, it goes like this: Bang-bang, bang-bang, bang-bang-bang! That is how the hammer goes. He makes for me a coffin; the coffin, it goes like this: Knock-knock, knock-knock, knock-knock-knock! That is how the coffin goes. He makes for me a prayer; the prayer, it goes like this: *Yisgadal veyiskadash shmey rabo*! That is how the prayer goes. Hammer, coffin, prayer! Hooray, I am dead!"

"Hey, Siggy! Do you love me with all your heart, or is it just my pretty head? Like a real black murderer—you have slain me dead. When a murderer slays a man, he slays him with a knife. You have slain me, and not slain me—leaving me half my life."

Then things really got out of hand: the swami fired repeatedly at the ventriloquist; a succession of balloons, flags, and soap bubbles came out of the gun; the gypsy shouted in her true voice, "Hey, Rube! Get that kid! He's trying to break up the act!" The boy scout suddenly appeared and ta-rah! ta-rah'ed! The ventriloquist ran from the piano and bounded up the aisle. "From the looks of things," said one of the moviegoers, "this is not going to bring us any closer to Jerusalem." "What's your rush?" said another moviegoer. "You've waited so long; you can wait a little while longer."

Oh! Oh! Jerusalem is lost! The heroes are falling! Plato, Aristotle, Aristophanes are crashing down on Eastern Parkway from their pedestals on the top of the Brooklyn Museum. The Screw of Archimedes will not work in my mother's sink anymore. Good-by to the Pythagorean Theorem on Herzl Street. Forget about Newton's Law of Gravitation; from here on, everything will fall up, not down. Lost! Lost! Galileo's lodestone will not be sold from the pushcarts on Dumont Avenue. How will Brownsville survive without Euclid's Book II? And how about Leeuwenhoek's lenses, Agamemnon's mask, Ohm's Law, the "Spinning Jenny," the treasures of Troy, and Faraday's ether? Ideology is dead on Pitkin Avenue.

Ay, go! Tell them that I sailed from the library for the deep blue Sea, and that my ship foundered far offshore! By Holy God, I have no more hope! To Holy Cities I can go no more!

How I managed to get out of the movie house, I shall never know; but even when I sensed the cold air against my brow, I still felt besieged. I began to put as much distance as possible between the ventriloquist and me as I ran. But on Dumont Avenue, outside the abattoir, my heart sank as I heard, "This is the Cabala speaking. Look down and see!" and sure enough! I looked down and there lay an open book on the sidewalk. "Listen carefully," said the voice. "Everything will go! Stalin will go! Freud will go! Already, Emma Goldman, Trotsky, Marx, Lenin, Plato, Voltaire never happened! The only thing that will remain is the Cabala! It has no heart, no face, and needs no people!

"Be warned! The Cabala is a dangerous subject. Do you know the story of the four sages? The first entered the garden and was slaughtered. The second entered and lost his reason. The third tried to destroy the garden. Only the fourth went in and experienced ecstasy. He came out another man."

It was then that I understood the most frightening thing of all: He had entered the Cabala, and there was no way back. And as sure as I was standing outside the abattoir, and as sure as I was that the book at my feet was the Cabala itself, I knew that God would send lightning to strike him dead; but because I had listened when it was forbidden, it would be just my luck for the lightning to fall on me.

"So, Horatio!" the voice continued. "They gave us books to eat. That was the way they thought they could silence us. With books, they could slaughter us, just as the sheep in the abattoir were slaughtered. But they did not count on ventriloquism, for ventriloquism can do almost anything. Down with Andrew Carnegie! Down with the First Free Public Library for Children in the World!"

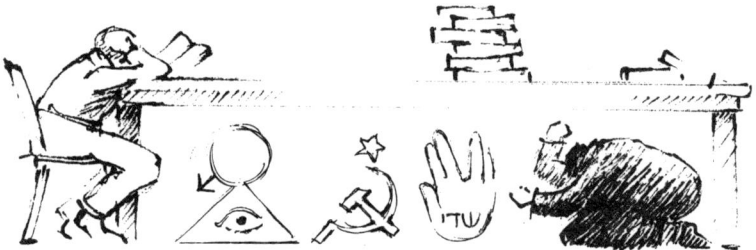

A Fable

I Went to the Market Place to See the World! Oy, Mama, Oy!

THERE ONCE LIVED UNDER THE FLOOR OF A JEW two mice, who fought like cats in private, but were exceedingly well-behaved in public. When the family upstairs went to bed, the mice would make their nocturnal appearance. So well-mannered and refined were they, they would be sure to leave no tracks behind. In fact, they cleaned up after they retreated. If they found the canister of flour open, they would not put their snouts and paws in, but lapped up the delicacy with their tongues as if they were elderly ladies sipping tea. And if God should help and the fish be out on the table, these two mice, as they ate, would be sure to pick out any whiskers that fell in. Further, when the good woman upstairs lit the candles on Friday night and said the prayers, the mice would show their respect and listen attentively—not a peep out of them. As for going upstairs and distracting the lighter of the candles just at this time—never, never, would the mice dream of it. I sincerely believe these mice were a blessing to the household; as clean as the good woman kept the house, the mice saw to it that it was cleaner.

Now it is a law of life that if two mice live together, sooner or later, there are going to be more mice. As well-behaved as the mice were, I can not begin to tell you what went on under the boards of that floor when their five little ones appeared.

"Ma! Ma!" cried the eldest. "Give food! I'm hungry!" "Ma! Ma!" cried the youngest. "Food! I'm dying of starvation!" "Ma! Ma!" cried all five. "Food! Bread! Water! Fish! Buckwheat cakes! Raisins! Almonds! Wine!" "Ma! Ma! The world!" "Ma! *Hamantashin* and the moon!"

Hamantashin! The world! The moon! What kind of monkey-business was this?

"Papa!" cried the mother mouse. "Do something!"

"What do you want me to do?" asked the father mouse. "We can't go upstairs now. The family is saying its prayers."

Bang! Down on her children, the mother mouse brought her tail and said, "I want quiet! Prayers are being said upstairs. Show some respect and listen; maybe you'll learn something! I just gave you enough food to fill your stomachs for a week! There will be no noise! This is a respectable house!"

Then as her children listened (and there was not a sound out of them), the mother mouse turned to her husband and complained, "I don't know how you feel about *your* children, but *my* children are going to grow up to be well-behaved and respect their parents if I have to break every bone in their bodies. Were I to leave it to you, they would end up as hooligans and crawl on street corners. I asked my mother (may she live in a lighted Paradise!), 'Should I marry him?' 'What does he do?' she asked. 'He's a mouse,' I answered. 'If he's a mouse, he'll always walk on all fours!' she said. 'I love him,' I said. 'Love tastes sweet,' said my mother, 'but bread tastes sweeter.' 'He wears a fur coat,' I said. 'Every goose is a swan in the eyes of its beloved,' said my mother. 'I want to marry him,' I said. 'Well,' said my mother, 'it looks as if my mouse finally found its louse. Here's my samovar; guard it well. After the wedding will come the funeral. With him, I promise you, you'll always live in the dark.' Why, oh why! didn't I listen to my mother?" moaned the mother mouse.

I must apologize for the words of the mother mouse. Perhaps if you were without Torah and worried constantly where your bread was coming from, you, too, would act the same way. I firmly believe that her screaming was the way in which she showed her concern for her children. How else do you expect a worried mouse to act?

In any case, that night the father mouse returned with a pot of chicken soup.

The mice were sitting and minding their own business when they suddenly heard an awful banging upstairs on the front door.

"Open up, Jew!" cried a loud and raucous voice. "I've come to take your house away! I go in and you get out!"

Oh, how the mice cringed at what happened next. The front door down! Boots on the floor! Cups and saucers smashed! Tables overturned! People arriving! People departing! A fire outside the windows! Boots on the floor again! A search for gold! Drawers ransacked! Furniture shattered! Mattresses split open! Silence!

"Nu," said the mother mouse.

"Ma! I'm hungry!" cried the youngest mouse.

"Go upstairs and see what's doing," said the mother mouse to the father mouse.

"Right now?" asked the father mouse.

"When then? The children are hungry!"

"It occurs to me," said the father mouse, "that maybe next week would be better."

"Why, next week? What's wrong with now?"

"Next week is not now," protested the father mouse. "Where does it stand written that one must eat every day? The times are bad—and upstairs everything is upside down. In fact, if you ask me, I see no reason why it is necessary to go up even next week—next year would be still better. We got new tenants—or didn't you hear? It isn't nice to barge in on people uninvited. Give them time to settle down."

"Listen to him," said the mother mouse as she turned to her little ones, "that's your father speaking. Some father!"

"You go," urged the father mouse.

"I!" exclaimed the mother mouse. "A mother's place is beside her children! It's a job for a father!"

"I'll go! I want to see the world!" volunteered the eldest.

"I'll give you—the world!" threatened the mother mouse. "You'll go nowhere!"

"Ma! I want *gefilte* fish and horseradish!" demanded the youngest.

"Ma! Raisins and almonds!" cried the eldest.

"Ma! *Hamantashin!*" cried the youngest again. "Ma! The moon!"

No *gefilte* fish and horseradish! No raisins and almonds! What *hamantashin*—not even bread and water!

"Papa," urged the mother mouse. "It's a week and we haven't had a drop of food to eat. Give yourself a shake and go in a one, two, three. For myself I don't care. If I died a thousand times a day, I would not be missed; but think of our children—their stomachs are swelling, they are turning green, and what's worse—they are strangely quiet and listless. As God is my judge, I wish they were screaming like before, even if I were to give it to them with the tail. Let my eldest cry for the world; I swear, I'll deliver it. Let my youngest cry for *hamantashin* in the middle of December; were I to hear his voice again, for me it would be Purim. Let him ask for the moon in midday; I promise, I'll make it shine."

"Ma!" whispered the youngest. "It's getting dark before my eyes."

"I'm going!" said the father mouse as he gave himself a shake.

Lo and behold! He gave himself a shake, shake, shake; was through the hole in a one, two, three; out in the open in a four, five, six; and in the middle of a shambles in a seven, eight, nine.

There on the floor lay a *muzhik*, snoring away: an empty whisky bottle for a cushion, one, two, three; wine bottles for a blanket, four, five, six; and slivowitz at the feet, seven, eight, nine. The cupboards were broken. The chairs were smashed. Clothes were strewn all over the floor. But on the oven was a pot with a piece of meat in it.

Hotch! Potch! The mouse was in the pot. Pish! Potch! The meat was got. Hotch! Potch! The mouse was down the hole. Pish! Potch! The little ones were eating.

"Nu," said the mother mouse, ready to discuss the events of the day.

"The Jews are out," explained the father mouse.

"Terrible! Terrible!" said the mother mouse.

"The *muzhik* is in."

"It's an old story," said the mother mouse.

"What shall we do?" said the father mouse.

"It's cold outside," answered the mother mouse. "The snow is a foot high."

"We ought to find another place."

"We're accustomed to this one."

"We can get accustomed to another."

"Let's be thankful for what we got. What we don't have, we don't know."

"All right! We'll stay!" agreed the father mouse.

It was quiet down below. Only the snores of the drunken *muzhik* came through the floor, only the noise from the children's digestion. They had eaten and were revived; now they were dozing off—good for the night, or so it seemed.

"Ma! I'm dying!" cried *Hamantashin*, who was really the youngest.

"Ma!" cried the eldest. "I'm dying, too! It's my stomach that hurts!"

"You're dying, too?" cried the mother mouse. "Keep on dying this way and you'll wake up the drunken *muzhik* upstairs; and then you'll really know what dying means."

"Ma!" cried the youngest. "It's true! Our stomachs! The food was poisoned."

"Poisoned! The food!" exclaimed the mother mouse. "Some enemy of ours wants to destroy our children!"

Now all the children had their hands over their stomachs and were screaming something awful.

"Papa," cried the frantic mouse as she put on her kerchief, "I'm going to Basha Chivieh the Witch—she's the only one who can help. Some evil spirit is at work here. It's a job for an expert."

"Basha Chivieh! Basha Chivieh!" exclaimed the mother mouse as she burst into the witch's house. "My children are dying. The angels in heaven were jealous of me and my happiness, and sent an evil demon to plague me. Happy moments, I have had few in my life, but this is the worst. Never, never, did I dream that an evil demon would try to get at me through my children. Have pity and cast a spell."

"Good friend, worthy neighbor," answered Basha Chivieh, not moving from her perch, "let me finish drinking tea. What's your hurry—it's snowing outside. Who knows, on a night like this, it might be just our luck to walk out the front door and meet a cat. What do you think—spells are cast so quickly? One has to fortify oneself with a glass of tea and a piece of lemon. A little money also helps to give the shoulders a shake, shake, shake, and move the feet a one, two, three. Children have been known to have had stomach aches before. It comes and goes with them."

"Witch," shouted the distraught mother mouse, "is this the way to talk to a mother of five children? I've come through the snow. In my house the Angel of Death is hovering over us, deciding whom to take with him. In one second, he could pack us all under, and I wouldn't put it past him to include you in the package. And you, you sit there sipping tea. Here's money!"

I don't know what made Basha Chivieh move so fast; perhaps the knowledge that the Angel of Death makes such quick decisions; in any case, you could hear the money jingle in her pocket. Out of the house, over the snow, it jingled; and continued to jingle even as Basha Chivieh's heavy breathing could be heard over the five children, who were, by this time, more dead than alive.

"Nu, Basha Chivieh," asked the mother mouse. "Where's the spell?"

"Pfui," cried Basha Chivieh as she spat out in disgust. "I was sitting peacefully in my own house, bothering nobody. My closets are filled with linens. My two cupboards, with expensive dishes. Blankets, I'm not missing. The samovar is boiling and I am drinking tea. You come in snarling like a cat, upbraid me, drag me through mountains of snow. I'm sure I've caught my death of cold. And here I am."

All at once, Basha Chivieh opened her eyes wide and filled the room with an unearthly glow. "Cats!" she cried, so that even the mother mouse grew frightened. "Cats! It's the cats that are responsible for all our troubles. Do you think I enjoy being a witch? Do you think it's easy? But the cats with their deadly preening ways, which begin as a washing and end as a slaughter, forced me into it. For you, I would invoke the cat demon himself. But don't fool yourself; if you think for one moment that I would be so unguarded as to tell you his name, you're greatly mistaken. A woman so foolish as you is quite capable of conjuring him up and then not know how to get rid of him. I came prepared with twenty-three prayers to bring him out, seventeen to lay him away, and one good curse that never fails to finish him off. For this, you called me?" cried the Witch, as she pointed to the five children, who were now sitting up and listening very attentively. "I came ready with so many spells, it would have knocked a dozen demons into a million pieces and driven them into wild animals. Even the cats would have gone crazy. Can't you see, you foolish woman, it's all your fault. The meat was all wrong."

And with this, Basha Chivieh stormed out of the door.

"What's right is right," admitted the mother mouse. "It's all my fault. I take the sin on my own head. It happened because I'm nervous. The children, with all their screaming, got me further unnerved, and I didn't inspect the meat. Look at my little darlings; they've stopped crying and are living again. The meat was not kosher and I forgot to salt it. Woe is to me that a *muzhik* should be responsible for my troubles."

Salt on the meat! Milk and meat separate! Candles on Friday nights! The children in Hebrew school! Prayers before the meals! Pots scoured! No handling of money on Saturday! Wash your hands! Put on your hat! Take your prayer book! Read Torah! Praise the Lord!

The mice had learned their lesson.

It came to pass while the mother mouse was salting fish, the eldest child packed himself a bundle and made off. Long and loud were the cries and lamentations that filled the house when the mother mouse discovered her son missing. She tore her hair, called on her dead mother for aid, recounted her courtship, and could not be consoled. After three days, a small mouse, more dead than alive, made his appearance on the premises with his tail missing, his eye closed, and his whiskers trimmed, and many other things wrong, too; so much so that better-looking ones were often buried.

"And who is this?" asked the mother mouse.

"This is your son! Don't you know me?" said the son.

"I shouldn't know from any troubles—that's how I know you. Papa! Papa!" called the mother mouse. "There is a mouse here who claims he is our son. One eye is closed and the other, open; one ear, up, the other, down; the lip is torn, but the mouth is still working. Come quick and give me a report. What does it look like to you?"

The father came running in.

"It looks like a mouse," he said, after long speculation.

"That's what I thought," agreed the mother mouse.

"But about it being our son—I'm not so sure."

"I'm not sure either," admitted the mother mouse. Then turning to the new arrival, she said, "Where have you been, you good-for-nothing who claims to be my son? Surely, you must have a mother. What do you mean by going off without saying a word to your mother? Don't you love your mother? About not saying a word to your father, you don't have to answer."

And here, the new arrival burst out crying. Under the boards of this house, he wept; and he, who was so small, seemed even smaller because he had been trimmed down. And he wept so many tears that, I swear, he grew even smaller because of the endless drain that came from him.

"Oy, Mama, oy! Why does it hurt me so? I went to the market place to see the world! Oy, Mama, oy!"

"To the market place, to see the world! Only cats and cut-throats, vagabonds and thieves congregate there—everybody knows that! And what did you do in the market place, my seeker-after-truth? And what did you do, my foolish young man?"

"I looked for *hamantashin* in the bakery shop window! Oy, Mama, oy!"

"*Hamantashin* in December can never occur—everybody knows that! And did you see raisins and almonds, my trouble-maker; sponge cake and strudel, my agitator? What did you see, my foolish young lad?"

"I saw them baking Jews in the bakery shop ovens! Oy, Mama, oy!"

"So what's the surprise? Upstairs, the Jews are used in a steady diet—everybody knows that! And what did you do after the Jews were baked, my traveler in the world? What did you do, my joy and affliction?"

"I went to the butcher shop to see the meat! Oy, Mama, oy!"

"And did you see the meat in the butcher shop window, my troubled philosopher? Did you see the meat, you silly goose?"

"I saw the Jews hanging from hooks in the butcher shop window! Oy, Mama, oy!"

"And what did you do next, my long-lost soul? What did you do next, my monkey-face?"

"I went to the village square to look into the well! Oy, Mama, oy!"

"Why, the square and why, the well? Didn't you have enough of hell?"

"The moon! The moon! To see the moon!"

"And did you see the moon, you upside-down goon?"

"I saw the moon! I saw the moon!"

"And how is the moon, you crazy loon?"

"It is broken!"

"So why are you crying, my *kaddishile*? Everybody knows that!"

"I'm crying," said the child, "because the world is a disappointment. Oy, Mama, oy!"

"Bah!" said the mother mouse, spitting out. "That I could have told you from the start; you didn't have to go upstairs to find out. Papa! Papa! Our child has returned. He has just discovered the world is imperfect and has come back crazy! Oy, Papa, oy!"

"If a child wants the world," said the father mouse, "when it can't be delivered and *hamantashin* when it isn't Purim and the moon when the sun is shining; it isn't that he's crazy, it's just that he doesn't know his Torah, let alone the time of day."

Then the mother mouse gathered together all her children, gave her tail a shake, shake, shake (the same with which she hit them), looped it into a circle in a one, two, three, and said, "You see—the moon! Look how it follows me about the room!" The she went to the cupboard in a four, five, six, and brought out some buckwheat cakes which she had baked, baked, baked. "Here are *hamantashin*! Eat as many as you want—even if it is December!" she said, said, said. "As for the world, I give you the world: Here I am; there is your father (and he's not so bad—I've seen worse!), and there are your brothers, one, two, three, and your sister, four; one head shorter than the other." Then she stopped, looked straight into her son's one eye and said, "What do you say to that, my child? What do you say to that, my dear?"

"I say," said the child. "I say," the child began again. "I say, 'Oy, Mama, oy!' "

A FABLE

With a Herring in One Hand and a Bottle of Schnapps in the Other; Oh! How He Did Dance!

Part I

T HERE ONCE LIVED IN OUR TOWN A SHAMUS, A father of two children, a man of property, a keeper of the Sabbath, a tailor by trade, who had a habit of bringing home from *shul* all sorts of people, especially on Friday nights when the loaves were on the table and the fish alongside them, and sometimes in the middle of the week, too. And in the midst of everything, between the bread and the fish, he liked to take out a whisky and to dance. Oh! How he did dance!

251

His wife took to calling on her dead mother for aid, and found that the only way to keep from going insane was to polish a broken-down samovar that she had inherited; and as a testimony to her despair, the samovar, cracked as it was, gleamed like the sun. Perhaps this good woman would have accepted the situation as it was, but when she found that the knives, the forks, and the plates were missing from the table after the guests left—this was too much. At last, her patience gave out; inarticulate as she had been, suddenly she found a voice and poured forth lightning and fire.

One Sabbath night, the *shamus* entered his house, washed his hands, and sat down at the head of the table.

"For us," intoned the good man, "it is a good Sabbath, and let us thank God for that; but for other Jews all over the world, it may not be so good. Naked and forlorn, they are going about the streets just as we sit here and drink soup."

Immediately, the suspicious woman ran to look for a visitor behind the door.

"Ach," she noted, heaving a sigh of relief when she found no one. "Don't bother the children with such things. They will have plenty of time to worry about it; so, at least, give them the pleasure of drinking soup in peace. Time is long; pleasure, short!" Then turning to the children, she added, "One would think from the way our great provider speaks, our cupboard is larded with gold. He's got nothing in front of him, but what worries him is that others may have less."

And before she could utter another word, the good man was at the door, shouting into the yard, "Reb Shmuel, Reb Shmuel, come in, come in. Everything is all right. Close the door, take off your coat, make yourself comfortable; a piece of bread, a bit of fish, perhaps a glass of whisky."

"You might as well come in," moaned the good woman in despair. "If it won't be Reb Shmuel, it'll be a Reb Feivel; if not Reb Feivel, Reb Beril. So whoever you are, whether Shmuel, Feivel, Beril, or Shmeril, come in, come in. Even a dog shouldn't be out on such a cold night." Then, turning to her husband, she sighed and said, "A fool is an eternal sorrow."

That night, a pot of cooked soup disappeared and Reb Shmuel with it.

Now although this *shamus* didn't know how to read, he out-rabbi-ed the rabbi in the concern for things holy, and was exceedingly suspicious of anyone and anything that came in or happened in our *shul*. Perhaps this was the reason he was so adept at catching thieves who went after our prayer books.

It was a Friday night and snowing when the *shamus* was alone in the *shul*. He had finished sweeping the floor, had emptied the buckets, had bolted the door, and was proceeding to the rear exit when from the front came a thump! thump! and from the Ark, a tinkle!

"Dear God," he cried, terrified. "The bells are ringing from on top of the Torah; its crown is jumping up and down; the breastplate is heaving in and out, and here I am alone in the *shul!*" So from out of his coat came a bottle and into his throat went a whisky. "Who's that?" he shouted. "Who's that thundering at the door?"

Thump! Thump! Tinkle! Tinkle!

"Who's that? Who's that?" he demanded again, rushing back to the bolted door. "Whoever is knocking—they should knock on your head like you knock on the door; you're knocking so loud, you're going to knock the Torah to pieces."

"It's me," squeaked a high-pitched voice from the other side of the door.

"Who's 'me'?" asked the *shamus*.

" 'Me' is Velvelie the Redhead," came the answer.

"Such a fine how-do-you-do!" cried the *shamus*, not very impressed. "Now that we've been introduced, what do you expect me to do—bend and make a toilet?"

"Some squeeze notes and are converted to mortgages," began the voice. "Others work leather and become boots. I search for odds and ends and am a rag—I'm a ragpicker. From the moment I was born, my head was stuffed. If misery is a a hammer, I'm a stone. If life is a saddle, I'm a horse. If water is trouble, I'm sunk. As for learning from teachers—I never went to school. As for learning from books—I can't read. But I got so many troubles that from them I learned plenty. To tell you the truth, I'm a little crazy. But considering the state the world is in today, this is no dishonor. In fact, when I see what the ones do who are not, it is a pleasure to be crazy."

Thump! Thump! The door banged. Tinkle! Tinkle! The Torah rang.

"*Shamus, shamus,*" appealed the voice, "it's snowing outside, and I haven't had a bite to eat nor a place to sleep; have pity and let me in."

"Who's keeping you out?" asked the *shamus* as he opened the door. "Come in, come in; what are you banging on the door for? A member of the *shul* you are not; but in, you can come."

And there fell on the *shamus* in the *shul* not a stone, a horse, nor a drowning man, but a cloak, a hat, a stick, a bundle—in short, somebody's mistake. The shoes didn't match, the stockings were crooked, the pants were green, the jacket was yellow, the hat was brown, the stick was broken; as for the bundle—it was very big. And as if this were not enough, one eye went right and the other left; and on the head, covered with dirt as if it had recently rolled in ashes, burned a fire of flaming red hair, the likes of which you never did see. Even to a *shamus*, who had seen everything, this was too much.

"*Shamus, shamus,*" cried the Redhead as he fell upon the poor man's chest and held on to the lapel, "I've a story to tell; I've seen the devil!"

"The devil!" gasped the frightened *shamus*. "Quick, come in and close the door; and be careful, you're tearing my lapel."

"To hell with your lapel!"

"What!" exclaimed the *shamus*.

"*Shamus, shamus,*" cried the frightened Velvelie as he began to hit himself on the chest, "my soul is pure, my body is clean; I stand before you, an innocent man. But I tell you, I was going to say, 'God bless the *shamus!*' when out came, 'To hell with his lapel!' And this is not all!"

"You mean, there is more?" cried the incredulous *shamus.*

"I want to say, 'Praised be the Jews!' I say, 'To hell with the Jews!' 'Next year in Jerusalem!' becomes, 'Never in Jerusalem!' I kill Jews left and right and let the *goyim* live. Passover becomes Christmas; Christmas, Passover; good becomes bad and bad, good; sweet becomes sour and sour, sweet. The sky lies on the earth and the earth on the sky. Everything is turned upside down and if I'm not already crazy, I'm getting there fast."

"With the devil," sighed the *shamus,* wearily, "it is a tale without an end."

"So you see," wept the unfortunate Velvelie as his eyes went back into place, "with the devil on my back, I have no place to go. He has sat himself down on my shoulders and won't get off. It's bad enough I'm burdened with my own sins, I have to be burdened with a devil. I have come to you, therefore, with a plea. I met Beril carrying four spoons, Feivel with four plates, and Shmuel with a pot of chicken soup. 'Oy Berilie, Feivelie, Shmuelkie, with such wealth, who knows what is possible!' I said. 'What's possible?' asked Beril. 'Anything!' I answered. 'If you have four spoons, and Feivel has four plates, and Shmuel has chicken soup, it is possible we can sit down and drink soup.' So we sat down to drink soup.

" 'The soup is sugar-sweet, the spoons carry their weight, the plates are precious; from whence comes such perfection?' I asked. 'We got it for nothing,' answered Shmuel. 'Who gives for nothing? Tell me where this miracle takes place and I'll stand in line,' I said. 'You don't have to stand in line; one at a time is also all right. You go to the *shamus*'. 'Stop!' interrupted Feivel. 'You're giving the wrong directions. He goes to the *shul* before he comes to the *shamus*.' 'You see,' continued Beril, 'there is this town, and in this town there dwells a Jew, who is as pure as the snow. A softer heart, a nobler spirit, never existed; he is without a gall—goodness itself—this is the one who gives everything away.' "

So pure was the *shamus* that he didn't even know he was the subject in question; instead, he began to split hairs.

"In this town! A Jew! Pure as the snow! Without a gall! Goodness itself! Gives everything away!"

"So *shamus*," continued Velvelie, "I'm ready. Lead me to this Jew. I've got a bundle so big, I promise you I'll clean him out."

"It's not so simple as that," answered the *shamus*. "If we were dealing with another subject, perhaps it could be arranged; but a Jew, pure as the snow, is not a laughing matter.

"Besides," he added, continuing his disputation with the new arrival, "even if such an unheard-of thing were possible as someone giving everything away, I'd be the first in line. You see, I am willing, but my wife is not. Thunder and lightning she pours forth. A good woman she is, a finer, never existed, but when it comes to a good deed, she is not at home."

"To hell with your wife!" said Velvelie the Redhead.

"Who knows where any one of us will end up?" sighed the *shamus*.

The night was cold, the night was dark as the *shamus* and the Redhead began their journey. From the roofs of the houses, the snow slid—plop! plop! From under the feet, their heels clopped! clopped!

"Tee dum!" cried the *shamus* as he stretched out his arms and stamped his feet.

"What did you say?" asked Velvelie.

"Tee dum!" answered the *shamus*. "Tee dee! What a beautiful world!"

And truthfully, the world was oh! so beautiful as once in a

while the lightning lit up the darkness and everything glowed in a silent white with the windows showing lighted candles and families sitting around their tables. And so beautiful was it that there in this lost and forsaken world, the *shamus* had to—he just had to—put first one foot forward and then another; snap one finger and then another; and dance, dance, dance.

Suddenly the *shamus* heard a voice in the distance and came to an abrupt halt. Surrounded as he was by the white and silent snow, it was as if the Redhead and he were the only two people in the world; and here was this intrusion. "Bronislava! Bronislava!" came the intrusion from the distance. Who but a demon could be out on a night like this?

"Here, Bronislava! Bronislava!" sounded the voice again, this time nearer. "Here, Bronislava, my darling, my dear! Where are you? There will be no sleep, no drink, no life for me if I don't find my Bronislavitza. Where are you hiding, my beauty?"

"Oy," said the *shamus*, "it's a living person." Then greatly relieved, he cupped his hands and joined in, "Here, Bronislava! Bronislava!"

Out of the night came a *muzhik*, his face black with rage.

"Why are you calling my Bronislavitza?" he demanded.

"I'm helping out," said the *shamus*, meekly. "I heard you call and I joined forces with you; perhaps between the two of us, we'll find her yet."

"What business is it of yours?" roared the *muzhik*. "Do you know her?"

"I should know from no trouble; that's how much I know from a Bronislavitza," cried the *shamus*, now frightened. "Have a drink!"

"Bronislava is my horse," said the *muzhik*, crossly, as he took a drink from the bottle. "She took it into her head to unhitch herself from her bridle and run off. It's hours since I last saw her. Mary, Mother of God, I bet that son of a bitch of a horse is dead!"

"Oh, a horse!" exclaimed the *shamus*. "And I thought it was a person. Have another drink. Tee dum! Tee dee!"

"Give!" demanded the *muzhik*. Then, taking another swig from the bottle, he turned to the *shamus* and said, "You dirty Jew!" and disappeared into the darkness.

"Tee dum! Tee dee!" sang the *shamus* when it suddenly occurred to him that the Redhead was missing. "Velvelie, where are you?"

"I'm here," came a voice from down below.

"Where is 'here'?" cried the *shamus*.

" 'Here' is the ditch," answered Velvelie.

"And what are you doing in a ditch on a night like this?"

"I'm sitting," answered Velvelie. "And what are you doing?"

"I'm standing," answered the *shamus*.

And sure enough, there was the Redhead sitting in the ditch.

"Oy," said Velvelie as the *shamus* jumped in. "I've been sitting here thinking and thinking. 'This must be you in front of me,' I think. I see a big, black spot. I smell its unholy breath, and I've been saying, 'To hell with me, to hell with your wife, to hell with you, and to hell with everything!' And suddenly you jump down as if from heaven itself."

"No, it was not me you were talking to. Tee dum! Tee dee!" said the *shamus*. "My worthy brother, Velvelie my friend. I'm not a big, black spot, my breath does not smell; and unless I'm mistaken, you've got your face in the posterior of Bronislava. Oy Velvelie, you're really crazy! What a beautiful world! What a beautiful world!"

And there in the ditch, he danced and danced. Oh! How he did dance!

Now all this time the *shamus'* wife had been very busy. She had made the beds, had washed the floor, and had turned the house upside down; and while she was doing all this, she cursed and cursed.

"Ma," asked her youngest, out of melancholy eyes, "whom are you cursing?"

"I'm cursing my mother," she answered as she peppered and salted fish.

"It's forbidden to curse one's parents," noted the child as his hand rose to the fish.

"Don't sprinkle salt on my wounds," cried the good woman. "I'll send my mother wherever I want, and don't tell me what I'm forbidden or what I'm not forbidden to do. It is also forbidden for philosophers to put their hands where they don't belong. This fish is not for you." Then she pushed another bowl in front of the child, "This is the fish for you."

"Ma," continued the intrepid child, "why do you have two different kinds of fish; and in one you put a lot of pepper and salt, and in the other little?"

"Pretend you don't see," she answered. "It's a surprise to blow someone's head off."

Then she proceeded to pepper and salt the first bowl with greater vigor; and when she finished this, she peppered and salted a bottle of whisky. It seemed that in her fury, she would have peppered and salted everything within range; and had the *shamus* been available, she would have covered him, too.

Thump! Thump! The *shamus* banged on the door.

"Come in, come in!" cried the *shamus'* wife without bother-to look up as she continued to pepper and salt. "I know— another guest! What would he like: perhaps the chairs, the table, the forks, the spoons; or maybe he'd like the samovar my mother gave me? He can have anything he wants. If I won't give it away, the *shamus* will, anyway; so instead of having an argument and eating my heart out, he can give whatever he likes now and finish the business. With my fool, we'll be eaten out of the house sooner or later; so why not now?"

"Up with the devil!" announced Velvelie.

"Israel be praised!" she cried as she turned to the apparition. "I don't believe my eyes. *Shamus*, is this what comes from the *shul* nowadays?"

"Enough!" said the angry *shamus*. "I don't want to hear

another word. A guest comes into the house and this is how he is received?"

"Things have come to a fine pass if I can't say a word in my own house," complained the good woman. "This is a guest? A crazy dog greets me with talk of the devil, and I'm supposed to keep my mouth shut."

"What devil, who devil?" asked the *shamus*, trying to look stern. "Serve on the plates, and let there be no noise about devils, shmevils, and other such womanish nonsense. We have a guest, a guest, a guest. Let's have a song, a dance, a piece of bread, a bit of fish, a drop of whisky."

"My dear woman," pleaded Velvelie, "I'll not be a bother to you."

"You don't have to apologize to me," answered the *shamus'* wife. "At you, I'm not angry; it's my mother who makes me grit my teeth. I went to her and asked, 'What do you think of him?' 'Not much,' she answered. 'He drinks,' I told her. 'If he drinks,' she answered, 'consider yourself dead—he'll drown you both.' 'What shall I do?' I continued. 'Do you have any better prospects?' she asked. 'No,' I answered. 'Then here's my samovar and guard it well,' she said, 'after the wedding will come the funeral.' So why shouldn't I be angry at my mother? She didn't take out an ax and chop off my head—that's why I'm angry."

"So," added the good woman, "sit down and eat."

Truthfully, the *shamus'* wife was not really angry at anyone, least of all, her mother; if anything, the good woman began to call on the dead one for aid. "Oh, my dear mother, my departed one, my one and only friend!" she cried. "May you rest in a lighted Paradise! May your bones remain forever undisturbed! I'm standing here in an oven, roasting, and the flames are licking my body. Help me, or I go under."

And really, she was not far from going under. There was the *shamus* about ready to give forth with a dance—only one more drop would do it. There were her two children, all she had in the world, ready to join her, burning in hell. And there was the new visitor, whom she did not dare take her eyes off, sitting with an open bundle in front of him, and deciding already what pieces he was going to take.

"Here," she said as she slapped the food down under their noses, "here's fish, here's raisins, here's almonds, here's wine."

Suddenly her youngest gave forth with a sigh.

"What was that?" cried the frightened woman.

"I thought I heard the bedsprings move," answered the Redhead.

Quickly the good woman ran into the bedroom.

"It's not the bedsprings, and if it were—who cares?" she said as she quickly returned. "We're going under as it is, so what am I fooling myself with bedsprings springing? When they come to take the furniture, I'll say, 'Ha! Ha! Take it, who needs furniture? Ha! Ha! Who needs a roof over our heads, spoons, chairs, a bed, a table? Live, we can live in the open. We can sit on the floor, eat under the sky, sleep on the ground—we'll be buried there soon, anyway.' Drink, my children, drink; we got nothing as it is, so we might as well drink ourselves to death."

Again the child sighed.

"What was that?" cried the *shamus'* wife.

"I thought I heard a mouse stirring in the kitchen," answered the Redhead.

Quickly the good woman ran into the kitchen.

"It's no mouse, and even if it were a rat—let him take whatever he wants. Here, we give away free," said the *shamus'* wife.

Now it was the *shamus'* turn. He got up on the table, put first one foot forward and then another, snapped one finger and then another.

"Sha! Still!" ordered the *shamus'* wife. "Don't make a move! The *shamus* is walking on tables now. It isn't enough that they have shunted us off to a far corner of the world to die; he has to hurry it up for them. Sha! Still! Do not cry! The *shamus* is dancing at our funeral now. And as the *shamus* dances, the walls will dance with him. Let's all clap, clap with the hands; make, make with the sides; stamp, stamp with the feet; hammer with the nails; close down the lid; pack in the earth; sing for the dead; and enter our graves. He's finished us off! Redhead," she cried, turning to Velvelie, "what do you want?"

"What could I want from you?" asked the Redhead, quickly opening his bundle.

"Will you be satisfied with fish?" cried the *shamus'* wife.

"I'll take it!"

"Now," she cried, giving him the fish, "if I give you fish, you've got to have whisky to go with it; so, here's whisky," she shouted as the bottle followed.

"My dear woman," moaned Velvelie with joy, "I don't want anything, but as long as you're giving, what else have you got?"

"My samovar!"

"Ha! Ha! Ha!" cried Velvelie with tears in his eyes. "I'd never dream of taking it!"

"Take it! Take it!"

"Never!"

"Take it! It was only my poor mother's. May she rest in a lighted Paradise! If my poor mother were only to know where her samovar was going, she'd turn over in her grave. Take it! What use do I have for it, anyway? Where I am going, they don't serve tea."

"I'll take it!" said the Redhead as the samovar came flying into his bundle.

Again the child sighed.

"What was that?" asked the *shamus'* wife.

"It sounds like a faucet leaking," answered Velvelie.

"It's not the faucet leaking," cried the good woman as she returned quickly. "It's the child crying."

"The child—crying?" said the astonished Velvelie as he turned to the boy. "Child," asked the Redhead, "why are you crying?"

"I don't know! I don't know!" said the child. "I don't know why, I'm crying!"

"What's this! A child crying, and he doesn't know the reason," said the irritated Velvelie. "What kind of monkey-business is this?"

"I don't know! I don't know what kind of monkey-business this is!" answered the child.

"You've been eating almonds and you've been drinking wine," continued Velvelie. "What reason is there for you to cry?"

"Oh!" sighed the child. "I've been eating almonds and I've been drinking wine; but whenever my father dances, he makes me, he just makes me, want to cry!"

And as if a mouse leaping, or as if a bedspring springing, or from a faucet leaking, first one tear fell and then another, and he cried and cried. Oh! How he did cry!

Boy, did that *shamus* get it! His wife began to jabber—twenty-four hours a day. She accused him of everything under the sun. The moment the Redhead left with the bundle, she began to chop logic and continued for two years straight, without a stop. The *shamus* was taking the bread from her children's mouths. He killed her mother. It was he who gave away the samovar, if not, why didn't he stop her? And when she finished, she began all over again: the bread, her mother, her mother's mother, the samovar, the fate of Israel, the end of the world, a lighted Paradise. Further, she was going out on strike; no more cleaning of the house—they were going to die, anyway; food she'd cook, but nothing else; let him hit his head against a stone wall.

So it fell to the *shamus* to take care of the house. What else could he do?

Part II

It was snowing when the *shamus* came home from *shul*. After the evening meal, his wife departed in a huff to visit a neighbor. The *shamus* had washed the dishes, had swept the floor, had changed the bedsheets, and was proceeding to empty the buckets when from the front came a thump! thump! that thumped with such thumpness that the *shamus* was sure he could hear the Ark in the *shul* give a tinkle! tinkle!

"You don't have to make an announcement that you're here by banging on the door, Velvelie; I know who you are," called out the *shamus*. "I haven't heard from you for two years—so, two minutes you can wait until I empty out the buckets."

"*Shamus, shamus*," cried the Redhead as the *shamus* finally opened the door. "I've got a story to tell that will make your hair stand on end."

"Come in, come in," called the *shamus*. "Close the door, take off your coat, and make yourself comfortable—a piece of bread, a bit of fish, perhaps a drop of whisky."

And there fell upon the *shamus* a fedora hat, a double-breasted suit, a timepiece across the chest, a vest with all its buttons, a coat with a fur collar, a cigar that was blowing smoke—everything special; in short, a new Velvelie.

"*Shamus, shamus*," began Velvelie as he stepped into the room, "that which is crooked can be made straight, out of devils can come angels, from nothing can come something, and a ragpicker can even become rich."

"Oy, Velvelie," exclaimed the *shamus*, "you're still crazy!"

"I'm not crazy," indicated Velvelie. "You remember, when I came here with a twisted tongue in my mouth and a devil on my back. Look at me now! See my fine coat—fur collar! Look at my hat—five dollars! See my cigar—imported! Can't you see, I've got prosperity!"

"To tell you the truth, Velvelie," said the *shamus*, "if I passed you on the street, I wouldn't recognize you—you're so full of improvements. But with me, things are not so good. It's my wife—complains, complains, without a stop. When she had the samovar, it was only her mother she cursed and I went free. Since she gave the kettle away, it is on my head that the curses fall. It's only a wonder that I haven't been cursed into my grave yet. And so I stand here and think and think."

"What do you think?" asked the Redhead.

"I think I should throw you out."

"*Shamus*," continued the Redhead, "from fortune to misfortune is just a span, but from misfortune to fortune is quite a distance. If things keep up this way, I'll have to study French. God forbid that I should say it in Hebrew! And I would say in French, 'If God lived on earth, all his windows would be broken.'

"When I left you with the bundle, my troubles first began. You remember how it was with me. If it had rained dollars from heaven, the coins would have only knocked holes in my head. If I had sold lamps and candles, the sun would have shone all night. Were selling shrouds my business, no man would have ever died! If I had been destined to drown, I'd have drowned in a spoonful of water. I was born with two left feet!

"Oy, how the snow plopped and plopped! How the wind chopped and chopped! It thundered, it lightninged! It burned and burned! I was walking in a cemetery at my own funeral, while Ashmodai and Amalek were giving me a push, and I didn't even know that I should be suspicious. In fact, my bundle—thanks to your wife, that brilliant diamond—was so heavy, it weighed me down, and my only regret was that it was not heavier so that it could crush me.

"I trudged on a road and it became a river. I came to a bridge and it changed into someone's back yard. I thought I saw a house and it turned into a tree. I could have disappeared in that snow up to my neck and appeared ten years later the size of a toothpick, and no one would have been any the wiser. Even when the lightning struck, for me it didn't light up—I saw black.

"All at once, the veil lifted from my eyes. There were no more houses, the road was gone, I knew I was lost and going to my grave. Cemeteries, funerals, coffins—all in my honor—passed before my eyes. I dared not even cry out—I knew I'd say the wrong thing. And if I so much as opened my mouth, what was happening to me then, as terrible as it was, would have become a forgotten pleasure.

"Picture me," continued the Redhead, "in the middle of nowhere, abandoned by God, forsaken by man, a blood-brother to the devil; when, as luck would have it, the earth opened up before me, and I fell into a pit. And to tell you the truth, by this time, Velvelie was not without curiosity about the next world.

"I lay, no longer recognizing anything—neither the snow, the freezing cold, nor even my own troubles. 'Velvelie,' I said, 'at least, there is one thing good about the way you're going out; you won't have to pay for the funeral!'

"And I dared, dared ask of the devil what I never dared of God! I was in a pit, surrounded by mountains of snow, already in my grave, developing a two-way conversation. 'What is the secret?' I cried. 'Tell me, tell me the secret of the universe!' When suddenly the ground, the very earth, trembled under me. *Shamus*, the lightning struck, the wind roared, I saw flames, my hair stood on end, I stopped breathing. Out of the mire can come life! What an animal makes, the world takes! Where the horse was is very slippery! I was lying in the ditch again on Bronislava!

"I was not lazy. I gave a shake with the shoulders and stood up. Into the animal's mouth, I poured the whisky. God bless your wife! A finer woman never existed, too good for this world, meant only for the next! How is her mother, by the way? Then I pushed the fish between the horse's teeth, and what was left over, I finished off myself and fell back, exhausted under the animal's stomach.

"*Shamus, shamus*, I lay under the horse's stomach, when—a twist here, a twist there, a turn here, a turn there, and boom! boom! there came an explosion, but such an explosion! Boom! went Bronislava and Velvelie boomed, too—it was an inside job! The ground shook; I heard railroad trains, whistles, push-cart peddlers, my mother's singing. 'Hello, Bronislava,' I said, 'hello, salutations, greetings! How come you're not dead yet? So as one corpse to another, tell me, tell me the secret!'

"Nuts and bolts, kitchen sinks, old shoes, old clothing, what you throw out, what you take in, and the horse lifted her leg and passed water. Not only was the devil at it, doing his dirty work, but Ashmodai and Amalek were helping out, assisted by Igrath beth Mahalath and her eighteen myriad dangerous demons. So, wet and on all fours, I crawled to the animal's posterior—at least, there it would be warm.

"The next thing I knew, Beril, Feivel, and Shmuel drew up in front of me as pallbearers. And when my sainted father, long since dead, whom I haven't seen in twenty years, appeared and beckoned to me, giving me his address in the next world, I knew from what direction the wind was blowing.

" 'Hello, Beril,' I said, 'hello, salutations, greetings! How come you're not dead yet? Did you hear the latest? They're killing Jews in the market place; they're killing me in Poland! The *shamus* gives me bread to eat; it twists my head, it turns my stomach. How can I eat of bread, bread, bread, when so many Jews are dead, dead, dead; and every piece of bread I eat, sticks in my throat and kills me?'

" 'Hello, Feivel, hello, salutations, greetings! How come you're not dead yet? Did you hear the latest? The Jews are hanging upside down on hooks in the butcher shop windows, hanging upside down in the butcher shop windows! Chop, chop, chop! The *shamus* stands on tables to dance, dance, dance; gives me whisky to drink, drink, drink; and throws me fish to eat, eat, eat. How can I eat of fish, fish, fish, when it rips holes in my stomach and kills me; for the Jews are hanging upside down in the butcher shop windows, hanging upside down in the butcher shop windows, and oy! oy! the meat is kosher!'

" 'Hello, Shmuelkelie, hello, salutations, greetings! How come you're not dead yet? Did you hear the latest? No more Jerusalem—not even ashes! No more Israel—not even bones! There are no Jews left in the world, anymore! They have been chopped up into little pieces! Beat the drums! Ring the bells! Flush the toilet bowls! Happiness! Happiness! The world is *judenfrei*; the demons have devoured them, and the Jews are coming out as farts and belches! Oy, Shmuelkelie, oy! All the problems of the world have been resolved, peace reigns, Paradise is all around us, the angels are blowing *shofar*, and the world stinks from us! Oy, Shmuelkelie, oy!'

"Then I turned to the horse, 'Bronislava! Bronislava!' I pleaded. 'Tell me, tell me the secret; I'm going out like a light!' When, at that moment, she let out with a blast, but such a blast—it could have made off with Rothschild's millions. *Shamus, shamus,* an extra sorrow didn't bother me. If the animal covered me up—I was covered enough as it was; my troubles didn't let her touch me. But what came out was not *hamantashin*!

"Old shoes, old clothes, broken bottles, kitchen sinks; the horse was up and snorting. Torn socks, nuts and bolts, dead Jews, what you throw out, what you take in; I was on the animal's back, and we were off before I had a chance to drop dead. Rotten apples, tarnished silver, stale bread, decayed fish; as I clung to the animal's back, it occurred to me (remember, I was crazy!) that what a horse lets out is no idle gesture. And here I am!"

For a while, it appeared as if the *shamus* had nothing to say. Finally he observed,

"In a world where one asks secrets of the devil and horses become philosophers, you don't have to tell me that, sooner or later, Jews will be killed. In fact, in such a world, they'll pack us away so fast, there won't even be time to give the world the stink it deserves."

"So what are you going to do?" asked Velvelie. "Are you going to invite me in, or are you going to throw me out?"

And here the *shamus*—and he was drunk already—did not even bother to climb to the table; he began right on the floor.

"Promise, me, Velvelie," he cried, "you'll see to it they say *Kaddish* for me when I die. And while they're saying *Kaddish*, if you should decide to throw in an extra herring or two and a bottle of schnapps into my grave when no one is looking, who's going to stop you? Promise me that they'll say *Yishgadal veyishkadash shmey rabo* for me so loud that I'll hear it in the next world. I guarantee you, I have only to hear the *yish* before the *gadal*, and I won't stay long, but come right up. And with a herring in one hand and a bottle of schnapps in the other, I'll dance, dance, dance. I'll make so much noise dancing, I'll knock the grave to pieces. Your old shoes will join me, your old clothes will flap, the broken bottles will fill up, the kitchen sinks will flow; and Bronislava will lie down in the ditch again and not quote from stolen Torahs. And as I dance, if I should manage to spill a little schnapps here and a little schnapps there, as if by accident, until every grave is wet with it and every corpse is drunk, whom is it going to hurt? Oy, Velvelie, can you imagine the dancing that will go on when all the drunken corpses get up and shake? I tell you, Velvelie, I'm dying from laughter already—they kill us left and right, and they can't get rid of us! Broken heads, smashed jaws, fractured skulls, torn prayer books, gold fillings, diamond rings, feathered beds, rivers of blood, dead Jews! Further, if the corpses should decide to leave the cemetery, and each one find his killer and never leave the murderer, under such circumstances, it might be worth dying.

"However, be that as it may, I notice that you have carefully mentioned everything but samovars. So even if we die right now, I must tell you, the samovar, which is the point in question, is still missing; and my wife, who is tireless, is still at it, sawing the air and brewing up storms. Coming right down to particulars, I think I should throw you out."

"You can't throw me out!" insisted the Redhead.

"Why not?"

"I'm rich! Before, when I was a ragpicker, you had a right to throw me out; not now!"

"No?"

"No!"

The *shamus* arose. He raised his arms above his head.

"I can't," wept the *shamus*, lowering his arms. "I can't ever change, so you might as well close the door, take off your coat with the fur collar, remove your hat—prosperity itself—blow out your big cigar, and make yourself comfortable with a piece of bread and a bit of fish and a glass of whiskey."

And with this, he began to dance! Oh! How he did dance!

As for what was happening in the cemeteries, God only knows!